McKINNEY'S GROWTH

Thomas James Taylor

CONTENTS

CHAPTER 1

Life had taught Kevin McKinney many things. It had taught him that one must chase after those things which brought enjoyment and a sense of worth into the equation. It had taught him that, even in choosing a thing, time seemed to have the ability to slip inexorably by at its own speed, heedless to the manner in which it was spent or the importance one attached to it. The years had taught him that unless one's heart was in the doing of a thing, it was nothing more than abatement unless it was done with purpose in mind, used positively until the one, real, meaning-ful something arrived to announce that this is the thing one was look-ing for all along—the special something which will employ to greatest effect one's unique abilities—the one true thing that was uniquely you.

And Kevin viewed life very seriously, studying it from a philo-sophical standpoint with intense curiosity. At forty two years-of-age his life thus far had amounted to very little. He had followed many paths of interest over the years, self-educated in those things which interested him the most, taken employment in jobs demanding physical endurance and strength of will if only to satisfy himself that he understood as many walks of life as he reasonably could before youth had morphed into middle-age. Life for him was something amazing. That the original uni-verse, being comprised of so small an array of elementary particles, had given rise to life, intelligence and who knew what other, future wonders, it fascinated and inspired, and he marvelled at it all. And of mankind—he viewed mankind with a great curiosity along with no small measure of alarm. In all, life was a dizzying array of fact, frenzied activity and circumstance which he felt ever unable to grasp; never enough to bring it near to anything approaching full understanding.

'Not if I were to live for a thousand years,' he murmured to him-self, reclined and waking from his afternoon siesta on a banana lounge, under the verandah at the rear of the house.

Lately it had dawned on him that so much time had been taken to observe life, attempting to define its purpose and meaning, that time had gotten completely away from him, leaving him with only a handful of pithy expressions, a modicum of understanding and an opinion on most things, but lacking the one ingredient in the way of commitment. It was this self-observation which had brought him out here to recline at the rear of the house on this bright summer's day, to laze in deep contemplation, and, perhaps, to arrive at something of a plan for the future. It was time, he had decided, and not for the first time—time to stop thinking about doing, and simply to do!

The problem, he imagined, had been that he had never allowed himself simply to respond to life as others do. By over analysing everything, he had cheated himself out of being able to engage with life on its own terms. This particular observation had been mentioned on occasion by more than one acquaintance, but, of course, he had not taken the time to consider the accuracy of the remark. Now it seemed an exceptionally valid point. Many times he had found himself so overly concerned with the possible ramifications of a thing, all possibility of spontaneity and change had been lost, and so his life had continued on, unaltered, unchanged even in the appearance of possible chance interference, something outside the structure of his so very well ordered existence.

Throughout the remainder of the day this self-observation plagued continually as he attended to cutting the lawns and trimming the edges, while showering and preparing an evening meal. Even while attempting to distract himself with a favourite movie, the thought of breaking from a lifetime habit of living his life as an observer, rather than being a participant and actually playing a role on the great arena of life nettled and goaded without letup.

The condition continued into the following day. It was there when he woke in the morning and he was becoming concerned by its persistence. Never before had a thought goaded for so long a time. It was now beyond a mere annoyance. The thought occurred that this might be a symptom brought on by some physical anomaly; a tumour, perhaps an old sporting injury that had lain dormant for many years only now to erupt into something nasty. No such sporting injury had occurred though. He had never played sport and always avoided watching it whenever possible. He would have to find a means of distraction, he decided, and after digging out his old runners and tracksuit, he embarked on an ameliorative run along the jogging route he had long ago measured out for himself; a seven kilometre distance skirting the neighbourhood and taking him along a scenic track constructed years ago by the city council.

It didn't take long before his stride found its rhythm; his muscles remembering the steady pace which carried him along, allowing his mind to wander wherever it pleased while the blood surged, cardiovascular enjoying an influx of oxygen and the olfactory again tasting the sweet natural scents and aromas of the outdoors.

The route took him around the edge of Apex Park before diverging to connect with what once used to be a railway, the tracks long since torn up. The run was doing just as he had hoped, his mind clearing of the crowding minutia and opening itself up again to the larger world, a sense of piece and order. He was very glad he had decided to do this again, and he thought he might return jogging as a regular fixture to his routine, perhaps to run the circuit at least once a week as he used to.

Carefully making his way down the steep slope alongside the tunnel, allowing pedestrians passage beneath the embankment, he was surprised by what sounded to be a distressed squeal coming from within the deep shadows of the pedestrian tunnel. It caused him to pull up, and he stood, wondering at the sound he had heard, whether to investigate; or had it been a bird cry? It might have been that after all.

The squeal sounded again and more urgently. Now there was no doubt of its meaning. The sound of a woman in distress was not one to be mistaken, but what to do about it?

He instantly recalled his thinking on being a participator and right then he resolved to act. He charged into the darkness calling out, 'What's going on here?'

The light at the end of the tunnel revealed only silhouetted outlines; three figures, he thought he saw, one on the floor of the tunnel and with maybe two standing above.

'Help me!' a female voice called to him as he approached at a run, and increasing his pace he rushed at the assailants.

Lunging, he sent the nearest sprawling across the concrete, and attempting to find balance, he wheeled about in time to receive a crashing blow to the head; something heavy and unyielding. There came a bone crunching sound as colourful stars exploded, and then blackness claimed Kevin's world.

Cognition did not return in a manner usual after being knocked senseless. He had been brained a couple of times before but had never experienced quite as this. As reason strove for dominance, beginning to rise up out of the grey abyss, he found himself in an altogether unusual realm of awareness: a kind of limbo, he observed, and noted in bemusement; the condition persisting, neither allowing him to submerge back into the depths of unconsciousness, nor fully emerge back into the land of the living. If ever asked he would have to say he felt to be encompassed in a warm and comfortable void. The ability to consider this, he reasoned, proved he was not bereft of reason. But why was he not even now opening his eyes in wakefulness? he had to wonder. It was a pertinent question he knew well enough.

The condition remained, and as it was not an altogether uncomfortable state, he allowed himself to entirely relax within the peculiarly peaceful ambience of it while reviewing what had happened: the alarmed female's call for assistance, his decision to render aid; not at all what might have been his usual response, but he had after all, only that morning, resolved to be much more a player in the game of life. And this was the result!

He should have been more wary, he realized, instead of blundering in. At least he could have armed himself with a lump of wood, or whatever was at hand.

On reviewing the incident it occurred that the whole thing might have been a setup. Perhaps a gang of three had lured him in upon seeing him jogging along the top of the embankment. The female had been the bait. The old *damsel in distress routine*. The though was very depressing and made him more than a little angry. The world was full of scoundrels and it only served to strengthen his overall view; the way it was headed. The area had always had its drug addicts, desperates and assortment of malcontents who thought very little about waylaying and assailing a person for the few dollars they might carry upon their person; and that was certainly the perfect location for such a ploy, although, why would anyone expect a jogger to be carrying anything of value—anything worth stealing? No, it was unlikely to be a trap. Then it was indeed as he had first thought. An attack on a female by two men. The thought cheered him; at least he had acted properly. Well, *acted*, anyway. A weapon would have been a wise precaution, but his action had quite likely saved the girl further, perhaps severe injury. This attempt at reentering the world and participating in it had not been a complete failure. The notion pleased him immensely, but why was he still in this half conscious state and unable to wake?

'Kevin? Kevin Theodore McKinney.' The voice emanated from outside of the surrounding envelope of grey murk. Kevin did not respond. The disembodied voice caused him to halt the internal conversation and wait silently, fearful and astonished, too scared to respond, in case the voice came again. 'Be not disquieted. I am the angel, Gabriel, and I bring you great tidings.'

'Oh, God,' he responded, realizing at once that the comment may have been inappropriate.

'Be not alarmed, Kevin,' the unseen speaker continued in a deep, resonant and oddly familial tone. 'For thou art blessed and chosen to do *His* work. Your immortal soul resides in *his* safe keeping. Rest peacefully now and be no longer in doubt. A path of great import lies before you. As one imbued of simplicity and forthrightness, you will be to your kind one to emulate, surmounting the violations of man which have become prevalent. Speak only with veracity. Deny the prevarications, avarice and devious mien become commonplace. Sleep now, Kevin, and when thou does wake, be transformed from the pupae form as a herald creature, graceful and free of guile. Rest—your journey awaits.'

The coma lasted three days. Doctors at the hospital had become increasingly perplexed. Monitoring of Kevin's vitals revealed that they were stable enough, and closer examination revealed no more than a severe concussion, but as the condition continued into the third day, concern began to escalate.

At three in the morning the attached monitoring devices began alerting staff to the fact that Kevin was at last waking. The alert brought the intensive care nurses hurriedly to his bedside and a small penlight was aimed into one eye then the other. While a nurse registered the readings displayed on the machines, another greeted him.

'Hello at last—' Relief evident in her tone.

Kevin did not reply, only gazed at her confusedly.

'My name is Amelia. I'm the ward sister here at St Mary's. What is your name?' She picked up his hand and placed her own hand in his. 'Squeeze,' she instructed.

The nurse attending to the charts paused to observe the response. His brow furrowed as he searched for the answer to the question. In a moment he appeared to give in and abandon the search for his name, instead responding, 'I feel so weak—' and limply he closed his hand around hers. 'I feel. As weak as a kitten. What happened to me?'

'Don't you worry, dear. All will be revealed when the doctor arrives. You had a little accident. He will explain all to you.'

He accepted this without protest, watched as the other nurse replaced his chart on a hook at the end of his bed, moved to pour a measure of water into a plastic cup from the jug on the night stand at his bedside.

'Here you go. Take a sip, darlin'. Your throat must be as parched as a desert.' Her voice betrayed an Irish heritage, unlike her colleague's whose accent suggested a Canadian connection, but he felt too fatigued even to hold the thought.

'I cannot remember my name.'

She took the cup from him after he had emptied it, set it down and began refilling it. 'You will. Don't you go worrying over it. After a knock on the noggin like that I'd have been surprised if you could.'

He raised a hand gingerly toward the top of his head to search for damage, but Amelia, the ward sister reach out, forestalling the action. 'Don't you dare go messing around up there. Not after the fine job Katherine here did bandaging it—' and she smiled in allaying any further concern, lowering his hand to the blanket and giving it a playful slap. Be a good patient and do as we ask, okay?'

'Okay,' Kevin agreed.

The sister departed, citing a patient in the adjoining room in need of attention, leaving Katherine to sit watch over him. She came up to him, gently grasping his wrist, silently counted his pulse while monitoring the second hand on her nurse's watch, fastened to the front of her tunic with a gold safety pin. In a moment she released his wrist and seated herself in the chair nearby. There to occupy herself by flicking through the pages of a pocket notebook, scratching notes here and there with a pencil pulled from her pocket.

Kevin lay, looking up to the ceiling, quietly perturbed and troubled by the fact he could not recall his own name. Three names had emerged in his mind as possible candidates: Jim, Tony and Kevin, though why those three, he did not know. They were nice enough names, in no way disagreeable and they seemed somehow to suit. He realised, also, that he did not know where he lived, if he had any friends in this life who might be concerned for his whereabouts, or what at all his life was about. What did he do? What was his manner of survival?

Apparently he was not the excitable type. Many, he assumed, would be terribly shaken to be in such a position as this. Yet here he was, lying quietly in a hospital bed, having suffered, he reasoned, a serious concussion which had brought about total loss of memory. *Amnesia:* Yes, he remembered well enough the word applied to the condition. He also found that he knew roughly where he was. This would be the Newton Memorial Hospital. Newton was the next town over from Erin Vale, his home town. But when he attempted to narrow down exactly to where he lived. . . . This was the weirdest thing!

He had lived in many places in and around the area, and he ticked them off the mental list. The odd thing was that, even though he recalled the places well enough, the order in which he had dwelt in each would not come to him. There were short period rentals up and down the coastline he had lived in during the hot summer months, and there were the longer term. He remembered living at the family home; using it somewhat as a base when he was much younger—as somewhere safe to retreat whenever independent survival became too much a handful and he had returned to the comfort of family. *Parents!*

The awful memory hit him. *Mum and dad are dead. They died a few years ago.* He recalled now the funeral services. First his father, and a few short years afterwards, his mother. It was a blow, and the loss hit him afresh.

A good while later, just as sleep was about to overtake him, the doctor strode purposefully into the room. Fifty-*ish*, a short, stocky man with thick, grey hair, heavy set, the ubiquitous white gown, black rimmed spectacles, stethoscope draped about the neck, and with piercingly clear, blue eyes.

He strode directly up beside Kevin and at once commenced the procedure with the torch in the eyes, adding the follow-the-finger routine and inspecting the head for he knew not what: Bleeding? Swelling? Head shape?

'The chart, please, Katherine,' he pronounced crisply to the attending nurse, who had been so startled by his rapid and unannounced entrance that she had almost over balanced and fallen across the bed as she had shot quickly to her feet.

'I am Doctor Kelly,' he announced to Kevin, peering keenly at him while receiving the patient chart from nurse Katherine.

'Hmmm—' He flicked, leaf by leaf, though the pages attached to the clipboard, taking hold of his chin in cogitation of the graphs, readings and notes contained in them. At last he held the charts out in an extended hand for Katherine to return to the clip at the foot of the bed, addressing Kevin as he did so.

'Someone tried to brain you. How did that come about?'

He made an effort to review his memory, only to find the nothing which had been there since awakening.'I don't know—' and he shook his head, slowly, finding that the motion caused his vision to swim.

'Careful now,' the doctor cautioned, noticing the way Kevin's eyes roamed about. 'Dizzy?'

'Quite,' he responded, being sure not to nod. 'How long am I going to be couped up here?'

Dr Kelly grinned amusedly to both girls. 'I don't know. We give people a bed, free meals, the best service we can manage, and all they can say is, *How soon can I leave?* Anybody would think a hospital is an unpleasant place to be.'

His face then became sterner as he regarded Kevin once again. 'You have received a serious concussion, Mr McKinney. You understand *serious*, don't you? You have been in a coma and only surfaced a short while ago. If all is well I will review you again in twenty-four hours. If things are going exceptionally well, I might let you go home soon after that. Do you have someone to watch over you at home?'

'I don't know,' Kevin replied lugubriously.

'Perhaps we can attend to that,' he responded. 'We have a home care facility. If you're so keen to get out of here, maybe we can find someone to look in on you from time to time. Until then—' and he turned then to include nurse Katherine in the conversation '—total bed-rest. You are not to rise from that spot until I see you again this time tomorrow. And plenty of fluids. Hot flushes, chills, inexplicable weariness, sick in the stomach, blurred vision. . . You know the drill, nurse. . . and I want to know about it. You *are* on the mend, lad, so let's just be sure it continues.' He scratched a note on the patient file, signed off and bid Kevin goodbye before resuming his rounds.

Tiredness overwhelmed him now. A hospital meal was only minutes away, but hungry he was not. Just tired, and the rest of the day he decided he would spend sleeping. Perhaps he would feel a little better when he woke, he considered, exhausted, and so deciding, willingly gave way to it, allowing the balm of sleep to sweep irresistibly over him, erasing all troubles and consideration from the mind, to be taken up again at some far future juncture if he had anything to do with it.

Again came the oddness contained within his dreams. Crowds of people, protesting, it seemed. Chanting. . . Some were angry, waving placards. Some shouted fiercely at the lines of police in front of barricades. Barbed wire, ferocious police K9's, armoured vehicles and helicopters poised overhead with video cameras being aimed downward on what now was clearly to be seen as an increasingly impatient mob. The dream took on an episodic quality as the entire scene became obscured by a thickening grey smoke, and the screaming grew more distant. Now there was a mass public assembly, a man dressed all in white at a high dais, speaking, his voice amplified and filling the great arena filled with tens of thousands of people. Every word he spoke was being absorbed by all with faces upturned and full of admiration.

Worldwide news networks intently focussed on the scene, and on this man, broadcasting every word he uttered. The man all in white; a powerful figure. Who was this man and what was he saying to capture the rapt attention of the host who had gathered in such numbers to listen? The face. . . elusively it would not come into focus. The face of this charismatic, powerful, enigmatic figure, so infuriatingly obscured and just beyond recognition.

CHAPTER 2

On the morning of Kevin McKinney's discharge from hospital, Doctor Kelly had given him a thorough once over and declared him fit to resume his life. Sister Amelia, the chief ward nurse, came to him with the hospital discharge papers and to wish him well. Dressed and ready to venture out once more into the world, the sister had accompanied him to the main doors at the front of the hospital, watched as he climbed into the taxi she had summoned to deliver him back home, and he breathed a tremendous sigh of relief that the episode was over with as he opened his front door and entered his quiet, two bedroom suburban home on the outskirts of town.

The afternoon found him lazing in the hammock which he had strung up between a sturdy spruce tree in back of his yard and the back corner of his shed. The shed he had hand built and used both as shelter for his restoration project on an early model Rage Rover that his father had partnered him in before his death. The rest of the shed he used as a workshop for sundry projects in metal or timber. He lay ruminating over the attack he had suffered; what possible reason might have lain behind it, the mentality of those involved? It was not a train of thought he might usually pursue, he was well aware. Being accosted and robbed by strangers would have, in the past, certainly given rise to great resentment and a need to punish those who had perpetrated the vicious attack. Now, though, he found himself questioning the alignment of circumstances needed to precipitate such an event in the fist place.

This had been an act of desperation, he considered; a feigned attack to lure in the hapless victim, and then the violence willingly enacted to relieve him of whatever cash he carried, which, fortunately for him, had been zero. Why then had they not considered the odds against a jogger carrying cash and valuables? He chuckled at the thought of them realizing their stupidity in hindsight. These were stupid people.

Just then came a male voice. It called out his name from behind the gate on the narrow pathway leading along the side of the property, hidden from sight by the rear corner of the house.

'Are you home, Mr McKinney?' the voice came again. 'Yes' he called out in response. 'You'll find the gate unlocked,

whoever you are. Just give it a shove.'

In a moment a tall, middle-aged man rounded the corner. He smiled upon catching sight of Kevin reclined in the hammock at the far end of the yard.

'Glad to see you taking it easy after your recent experience.' The man had an easy grace in his movement as he strode across the intervening distance. His face was clean shaven, lightly reddened as if he had lately caught a little too much sun. The somewhat worn, grey, casual suit and fedora perched slightly forward on his head told Kevin as much as he needed to know for the moment.

'I am Detective Inspector Klein. Tony Klein, from Newton Serious Crimes Unit. How are you today, mister McKinney?' he added congenially.

Kevin made to rise in greeting but was dissuaded from doing so. 'Don't trouble yourself,' Klein assuaged. He nodded to the weathered wooden chair parked against the shed. 'May I?'

'Of course. What can I do for you, detective?'

'I didn't like trouble you while you were laid up in hospital. Truth be told, the staff were very protective and made a fuss, so I've waited until now to hear what happened to you. An official police report,' he clarified, placing the battered chair alongside the hammock and seating himself with a muted sigh.

'I really am sorry to trouble you on this fine day. No escaping it, I'm afraid.'

Kevin considered the notion without comment.

'Are you recovering well?' Klein asked, reaching into the breast pocket of his jacket and withdrawing a small notebook with pen attached.

'Well enough,' he answered, brushing the question aside. 'There's actually not a lot to tell you about the attack. I thought I had come across a woman being assaulted. Possibly being robbed, and I tried to assist, copping a bruising for my trouble.' 'That's a modest description, Kevin.

May I call you Kevin?' 'Sure. It's my name. Although it took me a while to remember it. Amnesia. . . it's the weirdest thing.'

'I'm sure it is,' Detective Klein agreed, nodding. 'I hope that doesn't mean you remember nothing of the attack?'

'I remember everything. That's odd, isn't it? I didn't think about it until now. It was my long-term memory that was affected. No problem with recent events.'

'That *is* curious,' the detective agreed. 'Why don't you tell me what happened?'

I was running my usual route, although I hadn't been for a run in some time, when I heard what sounded like a woman in distress. The sound came from within the tunnel under the old railway embankment, adjoining the Apex park at the East of town.'

'I know it,' Klein nodded, making a note.

'I was running North along the top of the embankment. I had just come down the narrow track onto the mown grass beside the tunnel. At the disturbing sound I investigated, saw what looked to be an attack, and realized I had to intervene.'

'And what happened then?'

Kevin's brow creased in trying to recollect. 'I'm not entirely sure, now I have to give an account. I guess I challenged the men. Yes, two men. One standing over the woman. She was crouched down against the side of the tunnel, defensive like, with him standing threateningly over her. I charged him. I guess the other one clobbered me, and that's as much as I can tell you.'

Klein asked while he wrote in his notepad, 'What can you tell me of their appearance? Two males and a woman. Tell me about the woman.'

Kevin thought about it for a while. 'Wow. This is harder than imagined.'

'What about the men?'

'About my size.' In a moment he shook his head in frustration. 'The tunnel was dark, with daylight coming from the end of it. Everyone was in silhouette.' He raised his palms in shrugging. 'If I had to swear to it, I couldn't even promise there were two men. It's just what I thought I was seeing. I feel a little foolish, now. I'm sorry, but all I can tell you is what I thought I was witnessing. There was so little light in there.'

Detective Tony Klein finished making a note and looked up. 'It's okay. It's the way it was and if that's what happened, and if the light conditions were poor, you've given me what you can. Did any one of them speak?'

'I don't think so. No, there was just the woman. She called for help. *Help me,* she said.' And the thought suddenly occurred to him. 'Was the attack ever reported?'

Klein shook his head in responding.

By the time detective Klein departed, Kevin was left feeling quite foolish. It was pointless to expect anything would come of the investigation, given there was absolutely nothing to go on. But then an important memory suddenly emerged. As he had thrown himself at the woman's assailant he recalled the scent of aftershave. He hadn't even thought of it at the time. It had not registered—not properly—but the aftershave was decidedly familiar. He had once used the scent himself. It had been a Christmas present from his mother. He disliked it immensely, although he had worn it on occasion just to please her. The stuff had been called. . . *champ? Champion? Champaign!* Yes, *Champaign,* and it was some cheap, awful stuff, he recalled.

Klein had told him not to give up hope. Although there was little to go on, the fact that there were three acting as a team was important, and he was not without his hunches. Like Kevin, he was of the opinion that the culprits were drug users, and not without *form.* Meaning, they almost certainly were already known to police. He would talk to some of the local cops, beat the bushes and see what broke cover.

In the remaining hours of the afternoon he took to further reviewing his life, remembering that just prior to the incident he had decided it was about time for a change. But what exactly that change might involve right now, he had no idea.

Perhaps it was time to get a little cash behind him and put it to use; a small business maybe. He could finish the vehicle restoration project in the shed. That would provide a useful sum for starters.

'Anybody about?' a female voice called.

Again, someone at the back yard gate, and he really wasn't in the mood. Instead of responding, he remained silent, hoping the intruder would go away, but then he heard the sound of the gate being pushed open, and footsteps approaching.

'*Yoo-hoo!* Is anybody at home?'

He squinted his eyes just enough to appear as if he were dozing in the warm sunshine while, between narrowed lids, he spied a young woman step out from behind the corner of the house. Well dressed, wearing a contour hugging, navy blue dress, high heels, sunglasses pushed up to the top of her head, and with a black leather bag slung across her shoulder.

She stepped onto the lawn, having caught sight of him in the hammock at the far end of the yard, and stood, considering her next action.

'Mister McKinney,' she called loudly. '*There* you are. I tried the front door, but there was no answer. I thought maybe you would be out here enjoying the sunshine, and I was right. What a glorious day, too.'

Playing possum was obviously not working. The woman was persistent, determined to further upset his afternoon, and now she was walking towards him affecting a broad smile as if it was of no matter to be barging into his personal domain in this manner. Who did she think she was?

'Hello,' she intoned sweetly, and coming closer still. 'You must be Kevin? Kevin McKinney, who was recently attacked?' She extended a hand in greeting. 'Laura Maggs. I'm with the *Tribune*.'

He found himself extending his own hand in reciprocation. 'Miss Maggs. I was just–'

'Relaxing wonderfully,' she enthused. 'An ideal day for it. Your ordeal,' she continued without pause. Are you quite recovered? My editor has sent me to find out how you are, and to let our readers know all about what happened. A dreadful thing to have happened, but you were so heroic to do what you did. Five days in intensive care, was it?'

At last she had paused, but she was no longer looking at him.

Instead she had whipped out a microphone attached to a recorder carried within the smart-looking leather shoulder bag. The microphone was thrust toward him, and she waited.

'Five days, was it?'

Kevin remained silent. She had entered like a mini tornado, unsettling what remained of his afternoon when all he had wanted to do was to recline peacefully in his hammock, soaking up the quiet atmosphere of the surroundings, and, hopefully, make a little headway in making some small plan for himself, for the future.

Her hair was the colour of bright copper and cut to shoulder length. Her eyes were the colour of blue emerald, clear and bright, and she was looking at him now, completely intent on anything he might say. An attractive girl, he considered at that moment, but. . . *Wow, what an attitude.*

For her brash intrusion he considered demanding that she leave, or maybe he would simply climb out of the hammock and go indoors without a word. Although, maybe there was another course of action.

'I don't know what the fuss is about,' he told her. 'Hardly newsworthy, I would have thought, miss. . .'

'Maggs,' she reminded him. 'Laura Maggs, but call me Laura, please. And as for being newsworthy, I assure you it is, very much so.'

He twisted himself around in the hammock to better take stock of the young woman, his arms folded across his chest. 'How long have you been a reporter for *The Tribune*, Laura?'

She hesitated a moment before replying. 'A year.' Her arm appeared to be getting heavy as she kept it outstretched, holding the microphone.

'How long is your internship?'

She lowered the microphone to rest the arm. This wasn't going quite as she had planned. 'My internship finished last week.' Kevin watched as she answered, as she struggled to maintain her aplomb. 'This wouldn't be your first assignment, would it?'

'No-o-o. I've written lots of columns—' her voice rising almost a full octave. 'You'll see my name on plenty of stories if you check the back issues.'

Kevin found himself regretting having taken this line. She couldn't be much over twenty years-old and here he was taking her to task over her credentials. He considered the likelihood of her having written *'lots of columns'* at the *Tribune* and found himself doubting the claim, unless the boss had allowed her to write a short feature on the local, annual CWA fund-raiser. A seasoned reported she was not, and even now she was looking decidedly uncomfortable under his gaze.

'I'm sorry, miss Maggs. . . Laura,' he corrected, and offered a smile. 'I've only been home a short while and I have already had the police here, asking questions about the incident. I'm not usually so impolite. Allow me to start again, won't you?'—and he heaved himself out of the hammock. 'I was about to make coffee. Would you care to join me?'

The ambitious young reporter from the *Tribune* offered a wan and disarming smile. 'This is my first *on location* report,' she confessed. I usually write from my desk, but June was sick today and the chief editor gave me my first crack at the real thing. Did I come on a bit strong?'

'Just a tiny bit,' he told her, resulting in laughter from them both.

Kevin brought the coffees out to the table on the verandah, complemented by a plate of chocolate biscuits. Laura had discarded the bagged recorder in favour of a pencil and notepad and they relaxed for a moment, until Kevin took up the conversation.

He described, in detail, and as best he could remember, what he referred to as *the big drama*.

'I've had ample time to think the whole thing over. I was simply in the wrong place at the wrong time. You can't slide through life without bumping into trouble of one sort or another, and this was such a minor thing, really. If this is the most exciting or dangerous thing that ever happens to me in this life, I can only say I've led a very sheltered life. Some people find themselves up against much worse. Being conscripted, for instance. An automobile accident which maims or kills, and that's just two possibilities. No, this was small potatoes.' He took a last sip of coffee, returned the mug to the table before lighting a cigarette.

Laura looked up from jotting her notes. 'I would have been terrified. Such a vicious attack. Who were these people, do you have any clue?'

'I'd put my money on them being drug addicts.' 'Why's that?'

'It was such a stupid and desperate act. Who on Earth decides to mug a jogger? I find myself feeling sorry for them.'

She glanced up from writing. 'Really—?' holding his gaze in soliciting further clarification.

'Well, yeah. My injury aside, what do you suppose it takes to push anyone into such an act of desperation? I've had time to think about it and there's no doubt in my mind. This was no more than an ill conceived, hastily contrived act, committed by drug addicts. I'm sure of it.'

The look on the reporter's face briefly betrayed scepticism before she scratched further notes on her pad. The look did not go unnoticed.

'Have you ever been down to that park, Laura. . . seen the tunnel?'

'I can't say I have.'

'Well if you had, you would notice how secluded it is, and you would have noticed, too, the type of people who now linger around there. It was once a pleasant enough place where people walked the dog, sat with their partner or simply strolled about in the fresh air for the enjoyment of it. But nowadays people avoid the park. The stream and nearby nooks and crannies are lately littered with disposable syringes, and it has become a meeting place for drug dealers and their patrons. In fact, if I had stopped for a moment to consider what I already knew of that place, I would have chosen a different route for my run. Maybe your readers should know that?'

'You sound as if you're blaming yourself, Kevin. Are you?' 'Not at all, but I guess what I'm really saying is, maybe it is a perfect opportunity to look at the less obvious component of this *story*?'—and he pronounced the word with emphasis.

'What exactly are you getting at?' she asked, somewhat taken aback. 'You were the victim of a violent crime. That's the story.' Kevin took a deep breath before replying. 'That's the problem I'm finding in all this. Look, I am not being critical. Not personally so, at least. I have a problem with the way this incident will be portrayed. Correct me if I'm wrong, but the angle will be, what? *Innocent jogger waylaid by dangerous drug fiends?* Something along those lines?'

Laura merely remained attentive, allowing him to continue. 'It makes a good headline I suppose, and I understand that headlines are what sell papers. But in approaching it that way the real issue is being ignored when this event presents a perfect opportunity to scrutinize it.'

'The *real* issues,' she repeated, and he caught the scepticism in the tone.

'Never mind.' —thinking he would let it drop. He would let her do it her own way. *Man mugged by drug fiends. Park a danger to innocents.*

'Okay. Go on,' she prompted, managing to sound sincere. 'What do you see as being the real issues, other than citizens minding their own business being under threat of attack while enjoying taxpayer funded recreation parks?'

'Is that honestly all that you see?' he quizzed. 'Try looking at the scenario from a slightly wider viewpoint, why don't you? As a reporter it would serve you well, always, to look a little deeper into the issues surrounding an event. The instance of cause and effect, particularly.'

The *Tribune* reporter was again having trouble. A look of doubt momentarily upset the practiced look of interest she had been affecting up to now.

Kevin noticed this with some amusement as she looked at her watch, displaying, it seemed to him, the first signs of disconsolation since she had arrived. He needed to be careful, he realised. The young reporter was on her first real-world assignment and already the cracks were beginning to appear. But, *damn it*, he though. He may never have such an opportunity again, to speak of things he regarded as important in any meaningful way, and to reach a good number of people, possibly even to make them think about it. Perhaps to change people's minds about the things they never really paid any attention to in the first place. Important things—things which *should* be paid attention to.

'What occurred in that park,' he began afresh, 'was no more than a small symptom of the sickness society is suffering and has been suffering in recent decades.' He looked closely at Laura Maggs' face, searching for any sign that she had lost all interest. Detecting nothing of the sort, he pressed on.

'I've noticed how the recent generations have become increasingly disparaged, searching for fulfillment in their lives which they just seem unable to find. Society has become so much more pressurised. Competition for jobs has soared, even in unskilled positions. A good education is fast falling beyond reach of many family's ability to afford. Investments are dropping in value. Businesses are failing and banks are tightening the purse strings. The number of employed young people is ever plummeting while society's expectations of them ever increases. The laws of the country are becoming more numerous and tightening around us so that we are now becoming afraid to speak what we regard as the truth for fear of being regarded a racist, as bigots, anti-feminists or god knows what else. Political correctness has frightened many into keeping from voicing their thoughts for fear of possible repercussions. The whole tone of society has changed noticeably in recent years and it's absolutely unhealthy. Amid all these things and others besides, the kids have had to find a path, a means of becoming independent, and while all this is going on, how can they ever experience the kind of freedom and joy of existence earlier generations still brag about to this day.'

'That's all very well,' Laura replied, 'but what's your point?' 'No jobs, very little freedom, a crazy, increasingly complex society obsessed with political correctness, poor education, mounting pressure, lack of true freedom outside of this inordinately controlling system, anxiety for their future and you want to know *What's my point?'*

He became embarrassed. 'I'm sorry,' he told her in a quieter voice. 'I'm not sure where that came from. 'I didn't realised how strongly I felt about these things. But do you see what I'm saying?'

'Not really,' she answered, looking somewhat perplexed. 'Is there a connection between all this and what we were talking about?'

He looked thoughtful for a moment, wondering how best to illustrate the notion which, even now, was only just beginning to come to focus within his own mind.

'My generation was the last generation who remembers what true freedom is. . . or was. When I was young I was able to travel this country unfettered and without a care. I could just pick up and head to some far destination, knowing I could survive by picking up a few days' work here and there. Settle wherever and whenever I wanted to, being quite sure of finding good employment and being able to build a decent future for myself. It was a relaxed existence, without social pressures, fear of pandemics or persecution for speaking my mind, and there was an altogether much lighter feeling to life in general. But today? I would hate to be young in this day and age. There are those in existence today who will never know such freedom. For them, they do not get to hear of or be influenced by the notion of free thought, the right to hold an opinion. *Real* freedom, I'm talking about. Everything is so intense and competitive and micro managed by a controlling system.

'What I am getting at is this. Young people are turning in on themselves because something vital is being denied in their lives. Risk taking, unnatural behaviour, even crime and drug addiction are on the rise because their natural appetites and tendencies are denied them by a society which has become ever more deformed as time goes on, promoted by self-serving governments, politicians, industry and multinational business who use people as pawns and the population as no more than raw material for their control and grasp for power and ever more wealth. Maybe these kids see it. Maybe they don't, but they feel it, and it surrounds and binds them more every day of their lives. It's a disturbing part of their psyche and they probably have no idea what is causing them so much angst and frustration. Is anyone really surprised by the rate of drug abuse, disassociation and so called aberrant behaviour which is rife among the population today? If this model of society is allowed to continue, what kind of a world will this be?'

CHAPTER 3

Laura Maggs returned to her desk at the *Tribune*; a new desk she had been provided with as reward for her achievement in successfully finishing her internship. Being on the ground floor of the two-story building, it afforded a pleasant view onto a well tended garden where employees occasionally sat at lunchtime, if the day was a pleasant one or if the notion took them, to sit in the sunshine discussing one project or another. She pulled her notebook from her bag and placed it on the desk.

The interview had not gone quite as expected. The plan had been simply to gather the facts of an assault, to report on his condition and to probe how the event may have impacted him; the sort of thing readers of a local newspaper would be interested in. Her editor had told her he would allow a couple of hundred words at on page five of the issue, where human interest stories were generally placed. She lifted the receiver of her telephone and connected to the editor's office upstairs.

Chief Editor, Bill Brier, a tall, heavyset man of fifty seven years lifted the receiver, flicked a switch which allowed him to talk hands free while he lifted a half smoked cigar from the ashtray and applied a flame to it's tip, puffing it into life while he responded.

'Laura. How did the interview go?"

'Fine, Bill. Fine, but I was just wondering. . . This guy, Mr McKinney, he's an interesting type. I got what I needed and, frankly, it isn't the most interesting story. I mean, a mugging really is hardly news any more, is it?'

'You want to scrap it?' Brier asked. The edition goes to press tomorrow. I hope you have something as a backup.'

'No, it's not that. Just, I think there's more in this than was immediately obvious. I mean the attack, the fact that it occurred at one of our public parks in broad daylight is a story, I suppose, but this guy raised some interesting points while I was talking to him.

He's over the attack already, which is pretty amazing in itself, seeing as he received serious and even life threatening injuries, but he tells me that he holds society accountable. He presented an angle I hadn't considered and I'm thinking I could write a much more insightful piece if I had the time.'

Brier leaned back in his chair, blew smoke at the ceiling. 'Your first day as a fledged reported and you want to write a feature?' he asked, chuckling.'

'I do have a backup piece, Bill. The old couple who are being evicted to make room for the burger joint at the edge of town, remember? I can type it up right now and have it in by the end of the day.'

The editor gave it a moment's thought, leaned forward to tap the white ash from his cigar. 'I remember. That's a good public interest story. Alright, submit the burger takeaway iniquity, but I don't want you burning up too much time on this other business. If fact, I want to see what you have in mind. A sketch of what you're planning before you end up chasing rainbows. I'll take a look and give the go ahead if I think it's suitable. Bring it up tomorrow afternoon. Will one o'clock give you the time you need?'

'Sure. Thanks, *boss*,' she expressed wryly.

She replaced the receiver, smiling to herself. Her first day as a solo reporter and already she had partial approval to write a story she had sniffed out on her own. Of course she still had to convince the chief editor it was worthy of inclusion. She became suddenly nervous.

'Come on, girl,' she encouraged herself. 'There's a good story here. But first, *The Takeaway Iniquity*.' Actually, that wasn't a half bad headline, she considered, and set about the task.

———

Two days had passed. Kevin was out and about. He took himself into town, parked his car in the large car-park beside the hotel and strolled from there into the heart of town where he might find a men's apparel store. His mood lately had lifted appreciably. The weather was warming nicely and it had occurred to him that morning while rummaging for something suitable to wear that he had not updated his wardrobe in far too long.

The spate of clement weather had brought out a good many towns-folk. Perhaps they also had decided today was a good day to replenish whatever was needed or purchase those things in need of replacement. It had been quite some time since he had come into town on a Saturday morning and he had forgotten how lively the place could be, with the foot traffic crowding the pavement, kids dashing about and cars tooting as pedestrians made dangerous course changes at the edge of the pavement.

During these past few days he realized that his energy level had risen considerably, and that he had discovered a new zest for life, or perhaps re-discovered some of the old vigour which had without notice slipped away during the winter months when he wasn't paying attention. His mind, too, he knew, had picked up its pace, and although it wasn't unusual during wintertime to become somewhat sluggish, it was more than that. His mind had been picking up on things with much more interest. His world seemed to have expanded somehow. It was all quite odd. He was enjoying the increased energy, taking renewed interest in everything around him instead of being the usual, passive observer. A roll he had played for far too long.

At a men's store he selected an assortment of shirts, trousers, summer shorts and footwear, favouring anything with a little flair. Balinese print designs appealed. Polynesian too: all comfortable and casual. A good assortment and variety with which to replace everything which had for so long been taking up much needed cupboard space without being worn; even a hat. He had never previously worn a hat, but why not? As he stood inspecting the affect in the store's full length mirror, he thought the white panama suited him very well, so added the item to his list of purchases.

In the park at the centre of town he set down the parcels to sit with a sandwich and soda to relax a while before returning home. In the quiet hiatus he again found himself reflecting on life, and he felt for some reason that a change was taking place, as though, somehow, he were on the cusp of a transformation, and although he had no idea of why this was so, he liked it very much. He knew that things were beginning to change and he had no intention of dissecting and studying the condition out of existence as he was usually wont to do. Change was good. Change was natural. He would ride along with it for once in his way too careful existence; do as everyone else did and extract a little joy and excitement out of life.

'Excuse me.'

An elderly woman had approach while he was inattentive and lost in his thoughts. She stood beside him now, at the park table, flourishing a newspaper in one hand.

'This is you, isn't it?' she asked, pointing to the photograph on page five of the *Tribune*. 'Kevin McKinney?'

Kevin focused and stared, astonished to see his image looking back at him from the printed page.

'It is,' he answered in surprise.

'I just wanted to tell you,' the woman continued, 'I agree with you. And there will be many who do. And I'm glad you have recovered from that awful attack. It's about time things changed and the government started paying attention. Keep up the good work, young man,' she told him, and promptly departed.

Kevin watched, still stunned, as the old lady made her way across the park, back towards the main street.

'How did my photo end up in the newspaper?' he wondered aloud. He remembered the photo now, from five years prior. A group photo from where he had worked for a short period, at Finlay's timber yard.

'How did she get the snap?'

The initial shock of finding his likeness isolated from a group photo, blown up and printed in the newspaper, wore off after a moment. He searched out and bought a copy at the newsagent. He would read exactly what had been printed when he arrived home.

He scanned the article while reclining in his hammock in the late afternoon sun. It provided a brief description of the attack, as he remembered it, and as he had described to the detective. She must have gone to the police station to interview Klein, he realised at once. The bulk of the article dealt with his critical commentary on the way he saw society going, his view regarding an abdication of responsibility, and his *"Christian-like attitude"* toward the perpetrators of the offence.

Not bad, he thought, putting the paper aside and considering further. Miss Maggs had described his position well enough. He had been quoted accurately, although he did not much appreciate the *"Christian-like attitude"* Laura Maggs had seen fit to relate.

But it was fine—and, he supposed, that was that.

At around nine in the evening, as he dozed peacefully on the couch, clad in pajamas and dressing gown and with the television talking to itself, there came a harsh banging sound—a very annoying knock at the front door.

He would have ignored it if he could, but it was doubtful he could successfully convince whoever it was that there was nobody home, not with the main light being visible through the window.

'Half a minute,' he called, irritated, managing slowly to rouse himself, but when he pulled open the door there was nobody there.

He stepped out onto the verandah, peering about. Nobody in the yard and nobody in the street, but glancing downward the cause of the disturbance was discovered. Half a brick. Someone had thrown it from some distance away to crash against his door.

In anger he moved quickly toward the street, hoping to catch sight of whoever was responsible. At that moment a car approached rapidly, the headlights dazzling him as it pulled up at the curb. He shielded his eyes with one hand while waiting for recognition to strike. He had not seen the vehicle before and could only wait for the driver to emerge. In a moment detective Tony Klein's lanky form climbed from the vehicle.

'Where are you off to dressed like that?' he expressed with humour.'

Not until now did Kevin realize he had walked out onto the street in his dressing gown and slippers. 'Some mongrel tossed a brick at my door.'

'Any idea why?' Klein asked, drawing near.

Kevin shook his head. 'None. What brings you by at this time of day, inspector?'

'I thought you might like to know that we have some suspects for you to take a look at.'

'My muggers?'

'Could be,' Klein told him. 'They were arrested late this afternoon, hanging around that same area where you were attacked. One of them tried to surreptitiously drop half a dozen packets of narcotic into the bushes as the officer approached. They were pulled in for questioning and the one was charged with possession with intent. Two males and a female. We had nothing on the others and so had to let 'em go. The male we arrested will no doubt be bailed in the morning, but we have a make on them now. Prime suspects, all three.'

'And you couldn't phone me and tell me this?'

Klein shrugged. 'Thought I might drop by, see how you're doing.'

It was a dubious response, Kevin thought. Since when did police detectives start just dropping by to see how one was doing? He let it pass.

'I'm fine, detective.'

'I brought the files with me. Mug shots. They're in the car. Do you have a moment?'

'I *did* tell you I didn't make out a real lot in that dark tunnel.' 'Well, you never know.' Klein countered.

It seemed churlish to refuse and so he grudgingly agreed, bidding the detective to follow him back inside. At the kitchen table Klein opened the folder retrieved from the car, spreading the contents across the table-top. Three photos: two male, one female, all looking to be in their mid to late twenties, all pale, under nourished; somewhat unhealthy looking individuals who had seen better times.

Klein studied Kevin as Kevin in turn studied the photos. He peered at them closely, one at a time and then grouped together, at last turning back to the inspector.

'No,' he said at last, 'it's just impossible to say. But, hey, I did remember something after you left the other day. A scent. An after-shave I recognised on one of them. It's called *Champaign*, I'm sure of it. Horrible stuff.'

Klein left soon after, thanking him for his indulgence, wishing Kevin a good evening and telling him there was possibly an even chance of convicting the criminals who had put him in hospital. 'Still, perhaps best not to hold your breath,' he had advised. 'Streetwise kids who know how to play the system. We would do better with a victim's ID.'

As he lay waiting for sleep to come, Kevin held the faces in the three photographs clearly in mind. The faces unsettled him. They might very well have been those who had lain in wait, lured him in and attacked him, but it didn't matter anymore. Even if he knew for a fact that these were the ones who had done it, there was not enough anger or need for evening the score left in him to warrant fingering them for the police. The faces for him bespoke a life of hardship and loss. That such characteristics were so plain to see on these young faces, it seemed one of life's injustices and he did not want to be a part of sending any one of them to prison. For him the matter was over. He would let the consequences of that decision play out however they may. To repay a negative act with the further negative of dispensing cold, codified punishment, thus compounding the suffering, the notion of doing so somehow presented as exactly the opposite of a solution. The notion of crime deserving punishment suddenly ceased to make sense any more, despite all the years he had held exactly that view. Such acts were committed as a result of surrounding circumstances. Most always unhappy ones. Kevin's thinking had changed, he was well aware. Even though the logic seemed counterintuitive, he felt compelled to hold to it for no other than because something inside him, a kind of intuitiveness, *a hunch*, compelled him to.

Over the following days he attempted to fall back into his usual routine, though without success. He contacted the detective to tell him he no longer wished to pursue the matter, to which Klein responded incredulously, telling him that it was a police matter in any case, and that the investigation would proceed with or without his assistance. He knew the case would collapse; without Kevin's collaboration the police had nothing, and that would be an end to it, he hoped.

Laura Maggs contacted Kevin a few days later, via a phone call. She asked if he had been following events reported of late in the *Tribune*, which he had not. She had become interested enough in his story to follow it through. Initially a public interest story with limited newsworthiness, she had planned to let it go until she heard that he had ceased being interested in having the perpetrators brought to justice. She had spoken to detective Klein and she had written a short follow up column further reporting the attack and discussing the broader subject of crime, its apparent rise in the community and highlighting Kevin's own views as he had related them to her during the interview on the day of his release from hospital.

The column had inspired readers to voice their own comment, with dozens writing letters of contrasting views. The sudden and unexpected interest had prompted her boss to keep the Laura on the story for as long as readers continued responding to it. There had been a recent rise in the paper's sales figures. Whether or not the story was in anyway connected the chief editor could not be sure. It was too early to tell. It might have been nothing more than anomaly, but they would run with it and see what happened. Over the phone Laura had asked Kevin if she could come by the house for a second interview. Although he was not initially very keen on the idea, he eventually gave in to her pressing him on the idea of shining a light on the subject of social discontentment and its possible relationship to crime figures. He agreed to allow her to visit again and discuss the notion, but he could not promise that he had anything further of interest to say. He had made it clear, and exactly why he had agreed to the second interview he had trouble explaining to himself. Being in the spotlight was something which had always made him uncomfortable, although a small town newspaper wasn't such a big deal, he had to admit. And the meeting seemed to fit with his new take on life. For once he felt as if he actually had something important to say—something important to *him* anyway. What he had witnessed occurring over the years caused him definite and considerable discontent, and it was not going away. It only increased over the years. He might be able to rid himself of the disquiet which always seemed to nettle whenever he found himself focusing on these things. Drawing others' attention to them might prove positive. If nothing else, it should prove to be an interesting exercise and so he had agreed.

Laura Maggs was due to arrive at two in the afternoon. That morning he had donned his jogging attire and ran the same route which had caused all the drama. The remaining hours he spent working around the garden, trimming here and there, weeding, re-potting a few plants, all of which allowed him the quietude and clarity of thought which recently he found himself seeking more and more.

His health and sense of well-being, he noted with satisfaction, was improving enormously. For a man of middle years he felt as good as he had ever felt in his life, and as he had taken pause to appreciate from time to time, mental clarity and function seemed also to be much improved. He could not remember ever feeling as well and as happy in his life or about life generally.

At one o'clock he showered, prepared a snack of crackers and cheese, gherkins and store bought oatmeal cookies to place on the table; a repast over which the interview could take place in the shade of the back verandah. This done he went into the lounge room, switched on the television to provide an intervening distraction as he relaxed on the couch, awaiting Miss Maggs' arrival, and he may have nodded off in those few minutes but for a news item which suddenly seized his attention. *'Kevin McKinney, the man who was hospitalized after being attacked while jogging alone in the park has withdrawn from assisting the police investigation, a reliable source has reported to channel eight news today. The source told us, ...*

At this inopportune moment there came a knock at the front door. Annoyed by the interruption he stood, but hesitated beside the couch as he continued listening to the news account.

. . . said that an arrest was close, but with Mr McKinney's reluctance to pursue the matter further . . .

Now the doorbell chimed loudly, and further knocking. 'Mr McKinney! Are you home? It's me, Laura Maggs.'

He moved quickly to the door to usher the reporter through, motioning toward the television as he did so, and quickly returned to the television news report.

. . . gained substantial interest, raising public awareness and interest in the apparent lack of State Government support for a problem some say has risen to epidemic proportion. The mayor's office has declined to comment on the situation.

In further news today. . .

'Wow,' Laura Maggs expressed, standing beside him with briefcase in hand. 'You appear to have made quite a splash, Kevin. Impressive.'

'I'm not trying to impress anybody,' he answered, switching off the set and turning to her. 'Actually, I was just trying to make it go away. I don't want this inquiry thing to go on any longer, but the police don't seem pleased.'

'You've stirred up something of a hornet's nest.' 'Eh? How's that?'

Laura looked around. 'We have quite a bit to talk about. Where are we going to do this?'

'Oh, yeah. . . This way.'

He led her out to the verandah where she seated herself at the cane table while Kevin brought out the nibbles and poured coffee for them both. When they had settled, Laura picked up the thread of the conversation.

'Your little incident seems to have hit a nerve. The situation with the rate of rising crime in the state has quietly been fermenting for a long time, and those within the system whose job it is to solve these problems have been caught napping. Not a pretty situation for them. They were likely hoping like hell that nobody would draw attention. But *now—?*' she raised her eyebrows and gave a little shrug. 'You've kinda let the cat out of the bag.'

Kevin chuckled nervously. 'Yeah. Well they should have been doing more. Giving more bang for the taxpayer buck. Serve them right. This is exactly the sort of thing that bothers me. Why the hell do they think they hold these positions? It's what we pay them for. To find solutions. And I mean solutions beyond ordering a police blitz and grinding working class people under the heel. It achieves very little and only causes resentment'

As Laura reached for her notepad Kevin recanted hurriedly. 'Hang on. Please, don't write that down.' His face had flushed slightly. 'I can get a little excited on the topic. About how quick we are to judge and dish out punishment. Especially when society is so poor at setting anything like a good example.'

Laura looked pleased as she crossed through her previous note and directed her attention to him. 'That's just what I'm looking for,' she told him. 'Do go on.'

Kevin reached for his coffee and took a sip. Laura put down her pencil and did likewise. 'This is what I want to hear,' she encouraged. 'What your views are on how we do things. And more concerning law and order.'

'What's most important is how we see it,' he replied. 'We *do* plenty, which in my opinion is totally wrong. We ought to reconsider how we view the big picture. I say we have to start again, from scratch. View crime for what it actually is.'

'And what is it?'

'In its beginnings. . . at its absolute core? Discontentment. Perhaps even *injustice*.'

'The justice system is based on injustice?' she expressed quizzically. 'Really?'

Kevin shook his head as if disappointed that he should have to explain. 'If people would just think about it like with any problem that needs solving. Why is it so difficult to see?' But Laura merely sat waiting for clarification.

'That's exactly the problem, I suppose.' he continued. 'Nobody does. Nobody, that is, who has ever been on the wrong side of the law, because then you have to face it. Being judged, I mean. Anyone who has *never* had a brush with the law ever really thinks on it. They get to just continue on with their sweet, comfortable, orderly lives, without ever knowing what it's like.'

'I really am not following, Kevin.' Laura sat with pencil poised, but she was not scribbling the shorthand he was totally unable to decipher.

He lit a cigarette while pondering how he might explain to this well educated, middle class, straight laced, female reporter with so little life experience. 'Maybe I came at it from the wrong direction,' he mused quietly.

'Okay,' he began afresh. 'Imagine you're growing up in a poor neighbourhood. Your parents are struggling to keep their heads above water, paying the bills, the rent. Kids growing up with that see their parents arguing and constantly bickering over debt and the constant lack of money. The schools they attend, they are poorly staffed, with second rate teachers, more often that not, and often the teachers can be abusive. Certainly they're not inspiring mentors able to cultivate a love of learning or an upbeat prospective for the future. I know that much from personal experience. The whole education experience is often oppressive in poor and lower middle-class neighborhoods. Time outside of school hours and away from tense, unhappy home life is the only time these kids get to blow off steam and decompress. Hanging out with their friends on the streets and nowhere much of interest to go? It's a perfect place for our youth to become disaffected with society, I assure you. Some will find gainful activities, and if they're lucky, scrape through to adulthood with half a chance of making a bearable existence for themselves. For the majority? Not so much.'

He looked to Laura as he stubbed out the remainder of his cigarette to see that she was attentive, and continued. 'I don't need to tell *you* what prospects are for kids who don't do well in the education system, and the education system is a whole other story. Even those with all the qualifications necessary to enter the job market, pitted against the thousands of others, and for only the limited amount of jobs available. . . you know yourself how tough *that* can be. Surely.

'The kids I'm talking about grow up learning how they were behind the eight-ball from day one, and how they never had a chance, while being told *ad nauseam* how damned lucky they were to be living in a first world country. These kids may not be so well educated, but they as hell aren't that stupid, and I'm telling you, they can soon spot a fraud, work out they have been lied to and short changed throughout their short existence.' Again he regarded Laura who was busy scratching her notes. 'That's where it starts,' he told her emphatically. 'Right there!'

'Where what starts?'

'The distrust. They become aware they've been lied to and never again will they ever accept what they are being asked to swallow. And who could lame them? They are suddenly confronted with the truth. That the whole world is dog-eat-dog and everything they thought was real is a pack of lies and cons. The smarter, the better educated, the stronger, or the more cunning, they're the ones who do the best in this world the way it is, and all the while they were being deceived, being told that honesty is the best policy, that hard work will get you where you want to go. And all the rest of the *fairy tales* they're fed, and which only obscure the truth, makes them easy victims unless they join in the game of deceit, because it's the only game in town. But the most important thing, I'm telling you, is that so many youngsters learn they cannot trust what society is asking them to believe. In fact, it's being crammed down their throats. And what do you suppose it translates to? What do you think is the lowest, common denominator linking the generations of kids emerging from this wonderful system?'

Laura only shrugged, wanting for the answer to come from the interviewee. 'Why don't you tell me,' she countered.

'Resentment, Miss Maggs. *Resentment!* And from resentment comes what?'

Again she waited for his to tell her.

'*Hatred,*' he pronounced sharply, 'and *rebellion*. A rejection of all the preaching they have been expected to absorb from the very first day they walked through the school gates, and everything the culture in general stands for. Its advertising. Its mock concern for humanity in general. *The whole kit and caboodle!* And it doesn't take a genius to see where that leads to. The crime rate is climbing because of the disaffected thousands who emerge from the system discovering they have been sold a colossal lie. And those who are not expressing their anger outwardly, are directing it inwardly.

'Rising alcoholism, drug addiction, risky behaviour and all the rest of it. It all eventually translates into crime and yet further discontent. *We* are the reason for the endless rise in crime and the rapidly escalating social unrest. Not they themselves! *We* are the ones allowing a bad system to perpetuate itself. We are even attempting to pass it off as perfectly honky dory. That, or as usual, burying our heads in the sand and hoping everything will work out in time. God, no wonder our future hangs in the balance. It's so easy if you *really* look at it.'

CHAPTER 4

Laura left the interview with way more to think about than she had bargained for. She returned to her desk at the *Tribune* with the notes she had taken, intending to hastily type up the column and go home. Instead, she found herself sitting, watching time tick by, measured by the wall mounted clock in the office as she saw the story growing in her mind, into something much more complex and deep rooted than she had ever imagined. Because of public interest, the *Tribune* had recently released the latest State crime statistics showing a further rise of over twenty per cent above the previous twelve months, and a large number of readers had been writing to the editor, stridently deploring the situation and demanding that the government act.

Crime was suddenly taking centre stage and the feedback she was getting down the line was that officials, the Premier included, was not terribly happy with the *ink* newspapers were lending the subject. The chief editor had even received thinly veiled threats suggesting that funding of the paper might suffer for the unnecessary coverage, accusing the paper of bias. Printed news had been suffering badly during this time of blogging and rapid rise of online reporting. Already her own paper relied to some extent on a government subsidy to keep the presses rolling, but her immediate problem lay in what Kevin had said. Damned if it didn't make perfect sense, and as a reporter she felt bound to follow this story wherever it led. Even if in doing so she incurred the wrath of her editor, and he in turn, the wrath of those he answered to. They, in this particular case, were the shareholders and their accountants.

Laura Maggs departed the office without having written a word. She had until Friday before the story, in whatever form it took by that time, was sent to the presses for the weekend edition special supplement.

As a single young woman Laura occupied a modern, self-contained unit in a quiet section of town which overlooked a tight curve in the Skate River known as Saddler's Bend, where the tranquil landscape had been fashioned as a picturesque park for townsfolk to use for recreational purposes. Her neighbours consisted predominantly of the elderly; retirees who were generally funded sufficiently well to afford living in the particularly upmarket end of town, and who enjoyed the council maintained green expanse and nearby woodland along the riverside. Perfect for a quiet stroll and the kind of moderate exercise doctors often prescribed for those of later years.

That Laura lived here among the senors attracted little attention. It was a community of elderly singles and couples; civil minded individuals who cared little to delve into or involve themselves with the matters of others. She was recognised simply as the pretty young lady whose father had designed and built the complex, and so lived there quietly because of that fact, at number fourteen on the second storey, and paying rent like everybody else.

It was not her habit to take work home with her, but as she sat on the balcony nibbling at the spicy pizza she had picked up on her way home, watching people paddling their rented canoes back to the shore as the sun dipped low in the clear summer sky, she found it difficult to restrain her thoughts from wandering back to the issues Kevin McKinney had raised on his take of modern society; the way he had focused blame away from the perpetrator, attributing culpability to the much antiquated and inflexible system so long overdue for review and ripe for restructuring into a model much more consistent with what civilization had learned over the past two hundred years. The interview had lasted longer than she had intended and it had developed as much more a discussion than interview. The whole notion had been radical, and she should know. Political science and early civilizations of man had been pet subjects taken during her university education. Her changing track and taking courses in modern media and journalism had been nothing more than a sudden and even whimsical event, late into her education. She was well enough versed in the subject to recognise the validity within much of what McKinney had addressed during their discussion. Yet even if he was right—even if everything Kevin had said about the outmoded mores of modern, civilized society had been correct—what in the world could possibly be done to change things? It was and could never be anything more than simply a topic for interesting discussion. Surely.

Already the assignment was beginning to take on proportions way beyond what she had imagined, and she didn't like it. Perhaps she could find some method of dampening the readers' interest and enthusiasm so that she might get off it and onto a new and less complicated story?

'If only,' she said aloud, tossing the remnant pizza crust back into the box. She was faced with a challenge, and Laura Maggs was someone who never backed down from a challenge. In that she knew, only too well, she was her father's daughter.

After a long and restless night of tossing and turning she rose from a sheet tangled bed and made for the shower, in hope to restore vitality. Apart from everything occupying her mind, a thick, blanketing cloud cover had drifted in during the evening, trapping atmospheric heat and making for a breathless, sweaty and most uncomfortable night. Even as she towelled herself off and slipped into a lightweight cotton dress, she knew the effect of the procedure would be short-lived. Looking out through the sliding doors to the balcony, the low, moisture laden cloud still hung oppressively in the sky. The heat was going to persist and there was more than plenty to be done today.

The first problem presented itself the moment she slid her handbag under her desk and sat down to commence work. Rodney, the beanpole of a lad with a tuft of blond hair, who took care of all menial tasks on the first floor, approached pushing a mail trolley along the aisle. Pulling up alongside Laura's desk he rooted out a parcel, read the label and, seeing he was in error, returned it to the trolley.

In a dull, disinterested voice he said, 'Brier says he wants to see you in his office when you come in. In the conference room, I think he said.'

She fell back listlessly into her chair with a sigh. 'Did he mention what it was about, Rodney?'

'Nah. Didn't say.' he replied, and ambled off along the row. She tapped lightly on the glass panel of the conference room door before entering. As she did so she found four people gathered at the end of the table: her boss, Bill Brier at the head, a sharply dressed elderly woman seated to his right, and two be-suited men to his left, all of whom turned to watch as she entered the room and made her way towards them.

'Ah, Laura. Thank-you for attending. We have some guests. Mrs Cora McCartney, our legal advisor whom I think you have met before.' He indicated the lady at his right hand. 'And these gentlemen represent the Citizens's Advisory Bureau. Mr John Knox and Ben Harrison.

'May I present our newest team reporter, Miss Laura Maggs,' he announced in introduction.

Everybody nodded in greeting as she occupied the chair left of the legal counsel, Cora McCartney.

'Good. Now that we're all present. . .' Bill Brier turned to Laura. 'The citizen's advisory bureau are representing the shareholders, Laura. There are some small concerns over the profitability of our paper.'

'Actually,' interrupted the one called Knox, a dour faced little man, 'that isn't quite it.' He turned slightly to address Laura. 'Of course, profitability is a component, but it is the direction we see the journalism within the *Tribune* taking in recent times.'

'Quite,' Bill expressed in stopping the man there.

Laura looked puzzled. 'I don't get it. You have a problem with the direction of our journalism?'

'Yes,' the second gentleman—elderly, rotund, wire rimmed glasses and a poorly camouflaged toupee—affirmed.

Her reaction was to laugh, outright.

Bill Brier attempted to salvage the moment. 'As, *um*. .' he searched for the appropriate word. . . 'watchdogs appointed by the public trustee, Miss Maggs, these gentlemen have a responsibility to keep an eye on the public investment. They had some questions and I thought it might be best to invite them here for a free and frank discussion.'

'It is public money, after all,' the dour faced Knox stressed.

Laura remained quiet as Bill took up the proceedings.

'We were discussing the issue of *Free Speech* when you arrived. Mr Harrison was interested in your currently running story involving Kevin McKinney. His notions regarding law and order.'

Harrison took up the conversation. 'The man's views could be seen as disturbing,' he pointed out. 'I see no reason to criticize the way society deals with its misfits and malcontents. I was saying to your editor here, Mr Brier, how easily the public, young people especially, how easily they can be misled into foolish notions by the kind of sophistry such as you and your mister McKinney are prone to disseminate.'

'Is that so?' she replied, looking askance at her boss. 'And our position on that, Bill?'—but it was the newspaper's legal advisor, Cora McCartney, who responded.

'There is no legal restraint as regards reporting of a person's truthfully held opinions and beliefs. Certainly not in expressing that opinion as a victim of a crime.'

'That is not in dispute,' Ben Harrison pointed out, as he adjusted the glasses on the bridge of his nose. 'It's just. . . Well, to accuse the government, or what's worse, society itself, of creating these monsters. . . It's outlandish. The man has obviously lost all reason and I—' he paused, glanced at his colleague—'and *we* consider his rants to be dangerous and inflammatory statements which would be better left unexpressed within the public domain.'

'Unexpressed within the public domain?' Laura scoffed. 'Go ahead and say it, why don't you? What you're talking about here is *censorship*.'

'That's a little strong, Miss Maggs,' Harris protested, 'and not at all what I am saying. You know yourself, surely, as a well educated young lady, that a great number of the population are easily led when it comes to news media. I am simply concerned that people are being fed false and misleading information. The last thing we need is for issues such as this to become inflamed because of one man's ridiculous views.'

'I don't think you are *simply* anything,' Laura uttered under her breath.

'I beg your pardon?' Harris responded. 'What was that?'

Bill Brier was about to intervene when Laura waved him off, replying, 'I do not see that you are concerned for anything except silencing someone's legitimate point of view regarding society today. *I* think your agenda is to stop anyone rocking the boat, Mr Harris. And I find myself wondering who it is you two are trying to protect by silencing a very important discussion within the free press. I happen to think Kevin is right on the money with his commentary on the way things are today.'

'You are accusing me of having a political agenda, young lady? You should be careful, miss. And by Kevin, I assume that you refer to your Mr McKinney? In what manner, exactly, are the two of you affiliated?'

'I'm sure Miss Maggs did not mean to accuse,' her editor interjected. 'A poor choice of words, is all.'

'I think Miss Maggs understands the language well enough, and has made her position clear,' Knox replied.

'Well at least I don't come here as a wolf in sheep's clothing,' she responded angrily.

'That's enough,' her boss demanded, closed the file folder he had been scanning and tugging on his waistcoat. 'Laura, please leave us. We'll talk later.'

'With pleasure,' she announced standing, and with a final, withering look aimed at the two guests, commented, 'Citizen's Advisory Bureau, *my arse!*' And with that, casually departed.

The meeting continued for a further forty minutes, during which time she worked purposefully on her assignment, fired up by what had taken place. It was her best guess that these grey men were sent, perhaps at the behest of the premier's office, as an attempt to force the paper off her story. Too often she had heard accounts of people in influential positions attempting to swing their weight around in attempting to evade criticism, but this was the first time she had ever witnessed the behaviour, and it did nothing other than to strengthen her resolve in finishing what she had set out to do.

There was no need to consult her notes. Contempt and disgust fueled her furious fingering at the keyboard, knowing precisely what was at play. Her readers were about to receive the wake-up call that was so long overdue.

When it was done she filed the story ready for final edit by the chief editor, Bill Brier. From there it would pass through to the printers, on this occasion circumventing the usual protocol. She also uploaded her rendering directly to the *Tribune's* web server, from which the on-line readership would gain immediate access to the unexpurgated version.

For this she imagined she could likely lose her job. Somewhat ironic, she mused, seeing as how she had only just graduated and become fully accredited. Being an uncompromising pragmatist at heart she was entirely willing to risk it all for the sake of what she knew to be right and true. She had to remind herself that the very reason she had sought to become a journalist was to expose corruption wherever it was lurking, and of exactly the variety taking place here; and to champion intelligent, well informed debate on the most important issues. For her, this was as grievous as it got.

'To hell with them,' she whispered vehemently, straightened her back determinedly and jabbed at the key sending the story directly to the Tribune's on-line platform.

I have my journalist ticket now, she told herself, affecting a sardonic smile. There are plenty of newspapers in this country. And anyway, why would I want to work any place willing to accede to administrative coercion? This is exactly what's wrong with the system these days. Bastards.

She glanced up from sending the story on its way in time to see Bill approach along the aisle. Halting at her desk he leaned over to ask, 'You want to get out of here? Let's go somewhere the air-conditioning actually works.' He smiled. 'Don't, worry,' he said in response to the worried look on her face. 'No drama. You're still employed here.

'Come on. It's close enough to lunch-time. It's damned hot in here. More cash out of the kitty to get the thing fixed again, I suppose.'

Crossing the street they made their way to the Ambassador Hotel where many of the staff gathered, Friday nights, at the end of the long working week, for drinks and a little socializing before making their way home to family, friends or their dull, lonely dwellings.

Ordering lunch at the counter they located and seated themselves at a vacant corner table overlooking the street. Beyond, in the park, office workers already had begun gathering at wooden benches with their lunchtime takeaways.

'I'm sorry I had to ask you to leave the meeting,' Bill began. 'It was all somewhat of a dog and pony act, I'm afraid. Those two pricks. Do you believe those guys?'

'I didn't hear you taking them to task,' Laura offered. 'Politics, Laura. Surely you know that. I hate it but what the hell am I supposed to do? We're in enough of a financial hole as it is. Christ. Trying to run a newspaper in this climate? It's near impossible. Papers like ours are going under weekly.'

'Fair enough,' Lara replied, relenting a little. 'I've never sat in on something like that before. I'm shocked, really. The blatant manipulation.'

'*Attempted* manipulation,' he corrected.

Laura leaned back in her chair. 'You don't know how relieved I am to hear that.'

He looked hurt by that. 'Really? You thought I would be intimidated by the likes of them, just because the paper is in debt up to its eyeballs and our only chance of keeping our jobs is if the politicians and bureaucrats continue to support us?'

She laughed at that, and because of the silly look on his face. 'If I had an ounce of survival instinct in me I would have agreed to their ridiculous, not to mention *corrupt* demands.' 'What happened in there after you sent me packing?' 'Nothing good,' he replied, leaning back to make room as the waitress arrived with their meals.

When they both had sampled the chicken salad, he wiped his mouth with a serviette and returned to her question. 'I'm afraid the paper is shutting down, Laura.'

'No,' she gasped. 'Seriously?'

He nodded. 'The writing's on the wall. Best to get out now, while the getting's good. Before the debts become so big it will be impossible to crawl out from under. The newsprint media is feeling the pinch from the new wave of online media. All the big money is going there. I predict we'll lose maybe our local papers in the next say, twelve, eighteen months, while the industry readjusts and settles itself. The big boys are already beginning to close their smaller holdings. The small urban and country concerns like ours are destined to be a thing of the past as the trend continues. The way of the future, I'm afraid.'

'I can't believe it,' she said, and fell silent.

'Yeah. It's a kick in the guts, ain't it? I've been holding off saying anything to anyone until I was sure there were no options left open. And after today? We've as good as lost the big government subsidy, and that was our one lifeline. Investors should about break even if I announce the closure soon. At least there's that.

'But you have passed your certification exam. You've worked damned hard and you're turning out to be a first class journalist, Laura. This thing with Mc Kinney. I think you're right to pursue it. There seems to be something in it. Follow your reporters' nose with it and I think you might have a real story there.'

'It *is* interesting, isn't it?' she responded, brightening. 'Not just the public interest angle either. I mean, I think there is the kernel of something. A much bigger, more important concern. I really think he raises a topic which for too long has been ignored. People have stopped questioning our leaders and the policy makers on the big issues. And it doesn't get much bigger than what direction society is heading.'

His eyebrows arched in mild surprise. 'You see it like that? Reviewing the question of law and order is one thing. . .' He paused, thoughtful for a moment. 'Perhaps you're right.'

'*I am,*' she demanded. 'Haven't you been reading my copy?'

He offered an embarrassed expression. 'Sorry. Not all. I've had kind of a lot on my plate lately.'

'Yes, of course,' she demurred. 'This guy is something, Bill. Insight, maybe. And he has that *average Joe* persona which, I think, lends credibility. There's *something* about him. Most of all, his story has managed to draw attention to a problem which never stopped growing while we, all of us, were distracted by the pollies old slight of hand trick, and stopped looking at what was right there in front of us. It's actually quite impressive to talk to him.'

Bill smiled broadly. 'Well, if you're impressed, he *must* be something special.'

'Oh, come off it. You know what I mean. This could be a big story.'

'For your sake, I hope it is. But you will have to freelance it, I'm afraid. You have time for a last column. If it sparks the interest you're hoping for, maybe one of the city papers will take it on.'

'Maybe they will,' she expressed, mildly disappointed. 'Stick to it,' he encouraged. 'Here's a tip from an old news hound. A good newspaper man believes in and follows their instinct. *The nose,*' he said, secretively, tapping his nose with extended index finger and finishing with a wink.

'I'll remember that,' Laura told him, laughing. 'I'm going to miss working with you, Bill Brier. Really I am.'

CHAPTER 5

K evin left the doctor's surgery feeling much better. He had been seeing him for years now, whenever a sore throat persisted or a cut required stitches. On this occasion it was the recent spate of headaches which he had been experiencing lately that troubled. The headaches had forced him to take to his bed in the middle of the afternoon on a couple of occasions during the last several days, but the doctor had simply explained that this was not so unusual. The changeability of the weather such as they had lately been experiencing, often caused people headaches. 'The rapid increase in barometric pressure as the humidity rises often causes the phenomenon,' the doctor explained. 'Nothing to worry about. It will pass soon enough.'

It was a relief. He had been wondering if it may have been related to the head injury he had received during the attack a couple of months back. Such things were certainly not unknown. He had heard stories regarding head injuries flaring up into major concerns, and it had played on his mind terribly. The doctor offered to send Kevin for a scan as a precaution, but he saw no outward sign of there being anything seriously untoward going on. The concern alleviated, he slid behind the wheel of his pickup and drove home feeling much relieved.

The telephone trilled on the kitchen wall as he entered from the yard. There had lately been numerous calls from people he didn't know, wanting to congratulate him for his stance on the need for social reform; although, he had never claimed to be taking a stance, merely making observations. It was the manner in which the growing number of interested people were viewing his comments in the newspaper, as reported by miss Maggs. Folk were apparently blogging, discussing the subject on-line, raising awareness, or so he had heard. Whatever blogging was; he had not much of an idea, apart from the fact that it was what people did these days with their social media accounts; again, whatever that was.

He walked over to the telephone and lifted the receiver. 'Hello?'

'Hello Kevin. It's Laura. How have you been?'

'Ah, Miss Maggs. I'm well, thanks. It's funny, I was just thinking about you.'

'I'm flattered,' she said, laughing. 'Or should I not be?'

It was his turn to laugh. 'Oh, nothing too disparaging. What can I do for you?'

'You could start by calling me Laura. I've been meaning to catch up with you again well before now, but I've been rather pressed for time. Just out of interest, have you been following my column?'

'I have as a matter of fact. Well, up until the paper folded over a month ago. What happened?'

'Maybe we can discuss it face to face. Would you mind?' He stalled for a brief moment, unsure. 'I guess so. When were you thinking?'

'What about this afternoon?' she suggested.

She sounded eager, but right now he wasn't at all in the mood for an eager young reporter asking questions. Then again, he had to take into account his desire to continue cultivating public interest. 'What about this evening?'

'Splendid. I will be arriving off the flight from Sydney in around three hours time. I'll grab a taxi home and unpack, decompress for a while. Shall we say about eight o'clock?'

'Eight o'clock will be fine.' Then as an afterthought, 'Perhaps you would care to join me for dinner? It would give me an excuse to cook a real meal. It's something I've not been doing much of lately.'

'Me too, I'm afraid,' she confessed. 'That would be terrific, Kevin.'

'Then how about six o'clock? Do you remember the address?'

Why he had invited her he was not entirely sure. He was pleased she was coming. It had been some time since they had talked face to face. There had been the occasional telephone chat, but they had ceased some weeks back. It was how she had kept her column on the boil, right up until the final publication, all the while calling, asking for comment and opinion on this or that point of argument.

Living alone he had no problem with. In fact Kevin very much enjoyed the freedom of having no one around with whom to butt heads, not to mention all the other drawbacks one usually encountered when sharing space with another human beings. After so long a period of isolation the thought of having someone over, if only for a meal, especially an intelligent, attractive young lady; well, it had been some time since even entertaining such a prospect. The opportunity of sharing an evening meal with Laura brought with it an air of excitement as he realised the implications. Suddenly there was the unexpected thrill of expectation.

'Wine.' he blurted out. I must purchase a bottle of wine.' But what type, and what meal to prepare? He would have to go out again for suitable provisions, he realised with annoyance.

~

By almost six o'clock everything was sorted and under control, even to the point of having tidied the house and attending to personal grooming. In a hurried, last minute decision he had quickly shaved, showered and donned some of the items purchased in his attempt to upgrade his wardrobe, settling on slacks, printed cotton shirt and lightweight summer jacket, the affect of which he felt well satisfied with while inspecting the finished product in the full-length bedroom mirror, and not a moment too soon. The doorbell sounded announcing Laura's arrival. Right on time, too, he noted.

'Hi,' she greeted as the door opened. 'I thought I should grab some wine on my way over—' revealing a bottle from behind her back. 'I hope white is appropriate?'

'It'll do perfectly. Come on in. Make yourself comfortable. I hope you brought your appetite with you'

'Ooh that aroma, Kevin. I certainly did. I haven't eaten a real meal for days on end.' She dropped her handbag onto a lounge chair and followed him through to the kitchen.

'It smells divine. Glasses?' she prompted, holding aloft the bottle.

Wine glasses retrieved and cork popped, they seated themselves on the verandah beyond the kitchen screen door, and for a moment a relaxed silence prevailed while they looked out over the garden.

'So. . . Sydney. What was in Sydney?'

'Two things,' she replied. 'I hadn't seen my mother in far too long, and a potential job. I went to the city to chase up an employment opportunity and in the bargain I got to catch up with mum. I hadn't seen her since my father's funeral. That was almost two years ago.'

'Sorry to hear it,' he responded. 'It's not easy, losing one's parents. Mine are gone, and it's a funny thing. I've never felt closer to them, or more appreciative, than after their passing.'

'Yes, that's true,' she said, reflective for the moment. 'My father was as huge influence in my life. Still is, oddly enough. I always strove to at least equal his achievements.'

'I'm sure it's no mean feat to grow up in the shadow of a parent who is highly successful in life.'

'You're right about that,' she replied, turning to face him. 'What were your parents like?'

'Oh, I don't know. They struggled, like most, but they were happy enough, and good, loving parents. But I'm interested to hear about this job prospect. Losing the *Tribune* must have been a blow.'

'That's what I was wanting to talk to you about, Kevin.' 'Me? What has it to do with me?'

'Let me ask you something before I answer that. Are you still as fired up about things as you were? Your concern over the direction society is travelling?'

'Fired up?' he replied, giving it some thought. 'I probably wouldn't call it that, although I guess it was fair to say that of me a couple of months ago. During the time following the attack, yes, I was fired up. I have to tell you, I was never a terribly community minded sort before it happened. I never payed a whole lot of attention to the world around me, if you know what I mean. I just played my small role and didn't have an interest in the bigger picture. Humanity, society, systems of government, the amount of control governments wield, moral code, where it was all leading. I don't know why but suddenly everything seemed to snap into view. The big picture, I mean, and I found what I saw to be completely unacceptable. Fired up? No, I'm not as fired up. Since I began seeing things as they are and being initially angered by it, wanting to strike out at it, I've become a little more thoughtful and analytical about it all. I mean we are talking about a culture which has developed over thousands of years, and has become so ingrained that it is completely accepted as the norm. The thought of attempting to make any sort of impression on the status quo, to my mind looks about as easy as toppling Everest, or perhaps Olympus Mons. Still, it has to be moved, doesn't it? Someone has to point out that the king is wearing no clothes.'

Laura was grinning broadly. 'I'm so glad to hear you say that.' 'That grin of yours is unnerving,' he told her. 'What are you up to?'

'The reason I was in Sydney, Kevin. When the paper went under I was left with just two things: my newly acquired journalism diploma and a small town story. One which had captured more than its fair share of public interest. I have to thank you for that. Without it I would be right out of prospects. The story has tremendous potential.'

'What have you done?' he asked, affecting a wary expression. She responded with a look of mock superiority. 'I've solved both of our problems in one strategically brilliant move. Would you like to hear about it?'

'I would,' he replied, topping up their glasses.

'My ex boss, Bill Brier, a real sweetheart, set me up with a couple of connections before we shut down. He faxed forward the columns I had written on your story, suggesting to them that it still had considerable mileage left in it. That it had sufficient potential for a feature. An *exposé*. Of course, if they wanted the story they needed to hire me. I'm afraid I took the liberty of telling them you refused to work with another columnist,' she admitted, looking embarrassed now.

'No problem,' he acknowledged. 'I figure that's been our unspoken arrangement. So what happened. . . did you get a bite?'

'I did,' she responded, beaming. 'Ross Henderson at *The Clarion*. He agreed it was a story with merit and hired me to continue to write it for them.'

'Good for you. A toast then. Here's to your continued success in the world of print media.'

They drained their glasses which Laura topped again up while Kevin disappeared into the kitchen, to pull the roast pork leg from the oven.

'We're about done here,' he called, meaning that the meal was ready to serve.

Laura carried the drinks to the dining room table while Kevin carved, filled the plates with meat and vegetables, all liberally covered with gravy.

Conversation became sporadic as consumption of food took precedence. Laura's bottle of white wine was followed by the claret Kevin had purchased to accompany the roast. As the pace began to slow, he once again returned up the subject at hand.

'Does that mean you will you be moving to Sydney now?' At last pushing her plate aside and making use of the paper serviettes at the centre of the table: 'No. That's the really great thing. I can work from home. A perfect arrangement. Boy, that was some great meal. Thanks, I needed that.'

'My pleasure,' he replied. 'If you're done, we can resume the conversation outside, or would you prefer to make yourself comfortable over there on the couch?'

'The couch looks good.'

'Okay. Why don't you go and make yourself comfortable? Take the bottle over and I'll join you after I've cleared up a bit.'

'Let me help,' she volunteered. 'It's the least I can do.' 'Don't be silly. You've had a long day, no doubt. Go and sit, take a load off. This won't take but a minute.'

He cleared away the dishes, washed and racked them, the task taking only a few minutes. By the time he returned to the lounge room he found Laura with her feet tucked up under her on the sofa, sound asleep. He could only smile sympathetically.

'Laura?' he called softly, attempting to judge the depth of her slumber, but she did not stir.

Now he was locked in indecision. Should he wake her, send her home to rest? It really wasn't safe to do so. As tired as she was, and with several glasses of wine consumed, it was unwise to allow her to get behind the wheel. The only thing he could think of to do was to cover her with the spare duvet from the cupboard, ensuring she would sleep soundly. As a precaution he left the hallway light on, affording sufficient illumination to spill into the room, allowing her to orientate herself in the event of her waking during the night, wondering where she was. That done, he quietly wished her sweet dreams before taking himself to bed.

Sleep did not come easily though. It was clear that his life was about to take a new direction. Thus far, working with Laura to fuel discussion in a small town publication had been nothing more than to indulge his newfound desire to publicly highlight the moral problems associated with the status quo. Now though, he was about to allow Laura to step it up a gear, disseminating his practically antisocial point of view via the mainstream media. He lay awake f o r a long while in the realization he had arrived at a crossroad. Should he continue with this there was no way of knowing where it might lead. Public interest was a fickle animal. In a week or so the conversation may cease to be of interest, leaving Laura again in danger of joining the ranks of the unemployed, and himself exactly nowhere: which is pretty much where I am at the moment, he mused glumly. Upon further thought he was forced to admit to himself that this was simply a matter of courage. His world view, to his own mind at least, was reasonable and sound. Many years of observation had identified endless examples within human society which were, if left unchecked by logic and forethought, bound to lead the world of man into a future of absolute turmoil and irredeemable deformation. The fact remained, however, that for someone who had lived their life in quiet anonymity, and for the most part having little interest in the outside world, this was no small undertaking as well as being a considerable departure from the norm. Perhaps it wasn't quite true to say he had harboured little interest in the outside world. On reflection he remembered himself at a young age and soon recalled several incidents during his developmental years where he had come up against troubling discoveries about the world he lived in. There were a good many instances where he had witnessed glaring anomalies in the purported fair and just society he was being asked to abide and accept. It had been blindingly obvious to him that, right throughout his educational years and beyond, his questions focusing on these anomalies had never been adequately nor even reasonably answered. Even the obvious questions asked by children, such as *Why must there be wars?* were never suitably answered.

Kevin suddenly remembered, and he understood instantly, why he had embarked on this path in the first place. For all of his childhood he had been filled with misgivings about the world he had grown up in, and the—*to him*—nonsensical responses always offered. Everyone had always appeared to accept the way things were without really looking at the actual problems surrounding them. Everyone was aware that politicians often succumb to the system they work under, losing sight of their ideals and the very reason they became politicians in the first place. Everyone knew wars were bad and that they should be avoided at all cost, and yet wars erupted, raging throughout every generation and often flaring up under the most bizarre pretexts and conditions.

His mind began to fill with the absurdities; the continuing counts of megalomaniac, demagogic lawmaking, the ever increasing systems of control, segregation, greed and exploitation, religious fanaticism and mutual mistrust. Examples of mankind's lack of direction and logic, it's deceitfulness, it's genocidal trend in the face of want for equanimity, sustainability and simple forward thinking. These incongruities filled his mind, impressing on him a scene depicting i n sanity, wantonness, all ultimately amounting to sense of absolute futility—the same sense of futility he remembered as a child—a child astonished and bewildered to discover himself living in a chaotic world so manifestly twisted and disfigured by the overabundance of madness.

These recollections came to Kevin as a hammer blow out of a pit of darkness. Why had he blocked out all of those childhood fears and anxieties experienced all those years ago? What had caused him to bottle it up and to bury it as if it never existed? The questions held him locked in deepest thought until one notion arose.

Of course the mind of a child would revile any such world he found himself in. And more than that, so too would the culture as a whole. It was a most common action of the mind to turn away from a terrible thing when it deemed that thing impossible to resolve. The thought came as a revelation. It seemed clearly and indisputably to answer the question of why all this madness had been permitted to continue in the world, and this was the simplest, most glaringly obvious explanation. The moment of realization weighed suddenly very heavily on his mind. He had for himself adequately resolved the problem which had for so very long lain unasked and uncontested, yet had plagued him for the most of his life and tonight kept him lying awake, deep into the small hours. Only now did he yield to fatigue, allowing sleep to overtake and envelope like a balm to soothe and dissolve, for the while at least, all care, worry and human concern.

CHAPTER 6

Laura had awoken with the sunrise as it streamed in through the rear windows of the house, immediately realizing that she must have succumb to weariness in the middle of the visit. She smiled to herself, touched by the way Kevin had sought to make her comfortable before retiring without any fuss. He was obviously still lying in and she would not disturb him. He would rise when he was fully rested. On the back seat of the car, she remembered, her overnight bag, still there after arriving home on the flight from Sydney. A shower and a change of clothes were foremost on her mind, and retrieving the bag she made her way to the bathroom to freshen up and to slip into the jeans and sweater she had packed.

By the time Kevin entered the kitchen he discovered her standing at the cooker, frying bacon and eggs, with a fresh brew of coffee percolating on the bench.

'Morning, sleepyhead' she greeted. 'You don't mind, do you? I decided I should cook us breakfast. The most important meal of the day, my father always said.'

'Knock yourself out. Although I don't often cat a cooked breakfast. I'm more your toast and coffee kind of guy, but your father was probably right about that.'

'Your timing is perfect. Sit down and I'll play mother.'

The comment brought a smile to his face. 'I have to admit, I would never have taken you for a domesticated girl if I hadn't seen this for myself.'

'I have my talents. Oh, and by the way. . . Thank-you for being such a sweetheart and tucking me in last night. I really must apologise. I don't usually crash out on peoples couches in the middle of a conversation.'

'My scintillating social skills. Though I've never actually put someone to sleep before. That was a first.'

Breakfast was served—bacon, eggs and coffee—which they sat eating while making small talk between each mouthful.

'Are you well set up at home, work-wise?' he asked.'

'Not particularly, but I'll manage somehow. At the moment I have my pc set up at my dining table. Plugs and leads running everywhere to accommodate printers, storage units and the like. It's a mess and I really should get around to working out a better solution.'

'I could give you a hand with that, if you like?'

'I may just take you up on that.'

'Anytime,' he answered, closing the subject.

At that moment Laura's mobile was heard chirping from her handbag, where she left it upon arrival, on the armchair in the lounge room. She returned to the kitchen while talking to the caller, saying, 'Hold on a second, would you? I'll ask him. He's here with me now.' She covered the microphone end of the mobile while speaking to Kevin.

'It's Ross Henderson. The guy I told you about at the *Clarion*. He's asking if I've made a decision.'

'I told you my decision last night.' 'Are you sure? Really sure?'

Kevin noticed the look on her face, a look denoting suppressed excitement mixed with a measure of anxiety, and realised there was no going back. Fate had somehow conspired to cast him in the roll of public commentator, and regardless of the moderate misgivings he had always felt at being placed in this position, the die was now cast. Besides, seeing her current state, there was no way he was going to disappoint her.

'I'm sure,' he said, attempting to sound just that.

A stifled squeal of delight escaped as she almost jumped for joy, and taking a deep breath she raised the phone to her face.

'Ross? Mister McKinney has agreed to collaborate.

Kevin watched intently as she listened equally as intently to whatever was being said to her. In a moment she lowered the phone again, asking, 'He wants to draw up a contract.'

'What the hell for? My word isn't good enough?'he replied, his voice gaining volume.

Her expression changed as the voice on the phone began talking again. 'He feels his word should be good enough,' she answered in response. 'The man has integrity. Uncommon integrity, perhaps, but I know him. His word *is* his bond, Ross.' She nodded while listening, and what began as a grimace began slowly to transform into a broad smile, which she now turned in Kevin's direction while beginning to bounce joyfully on her toes.

'Yes. Yes, of course, Ross. That's a given. Yes. Okay, thank-you. Me too. Bye.'

When the call was finished she placed the phone carefully down on the table while gazing at Kevin; a look of astonishment and joy. 'I can't believe it,' she whispered.

'What's the verdict? Are we in?'

'We are!' —sitting sat back down at the table. 'I thought we had lost it when he overheard you. But I think he was impressed by it. No contract. A guaranteed two columns, and we'll see where it takes us, he said. God. I'm a columnist at the *Clarion*.' She fumbled nervously through her handbag, located her cigarettes and rapidly lit one up.

'I didn't know you smoked,' he mentioned conversationally. 'I keep a pack for emergencies.' 'Is this an emergency?'

She gave a short laugh, offered a wry smile. 'Do you realise what we have just done?'

For Kevin the next several weeks became a crash course introduction to world of news media. His observations, imparted to readers via Laura's weekly column, sparked moderate interest in the first issue. After the second column was printed came a torrent of phone calls: newspapers, periodical magazines, radio talk-back and even television news programs had seized on his commentary, wanting interviews in person or conducted over the telephone.

Laura pushed him to take every interview request, and had, herself, begun brokering cash deals wherever she could. Kevin generated a great deal of public debate and soon almost all were willing to pay a fee for his time.

'We are going to have to hire a secretary,' Laura told him during a quiet moment on Kevin's verandah. 'I cannot keep up any longer. Holding down a job at the *Clarion* and being your full-time dogsbody. . . I cannot continue.'

'Makes sense,' he said. 'How does one get a secretary?' 'Ever heard of an employment bureau?'

'Okay. Can you handle it? You're much better at things like that than I am.'

'Really? Must I do everything?'she replied, scowling.

'I was joking. Of course I can do that. An employment bureau, you say. Where does one find one of those?'

She almost responded angrily, until realising he had done it again. 'You sod. You nearly had me.'

'What do you mean, *nearly?* He chuckled mirthfully. 'For a hard-bitten newspaper woman, you sure are easy pickens.'

A secretary had been engaged; a third year science student needing a job to finance her tertiary education fees, by the name of Rhonda Goodings. One whole side of Kevin's house was given over to the endeavour of managing engagements, with a new computer being installed, filing cabinets and a separate phone line with a separate number in order to keep work and social activities apart.

When Ross Henderson deemed Laura's exposé to have run its course, her employment, without anything resembling gratitude, had been terminated, leaving her with no choice but to let Rhonda go. The lack of gratitude for her work left her feeling angry and resentful for a time, but Kevin proved adept at alleviating the condition by constantly making sure she knew how grateful he was for her effort.

It was only the two of them again. Local interest had suddenly dropped of; the telephone had fallen silent, although written mail continued to pile up from the still increasing members of the population who felt strongly about their world, but paid engagements had dwindled almost to nothing. Barring two booked interviews remaining on the calendar, there were no other paid engagements ahead of them.

'Well, we gave it a try,' Laura intoned wearily. 'I guess that's and end to it.' Kevin only responded with a look of surprise and a trace of enmity, though he did not say a word. Instead, he stood, walked silently to the rear of the yard to climb into the hammock, there to review the impasse.

Something unusual had come over him, she knew. In the time they had gotten to know one another they had grown very close. It was a relationship of mutual admiration, of reliance for emotional support and even, she had to admit, one of something akin to a spiritual association. It was difficult for her to define.

She had never before met someone who attached so much importance to the future of mankind. Most people struggled through life applying their effort to building a successful career, meeting the right person with whom to raise a family and assure a comfortable future for themselves. Kevin didn't seem to give a damn about such things. For him, if what he had related to her was true, and why would it not be? he had recently come to value, above all, that which he saw human society could overcome. It was a notion which had not occurred to him until later in life, he had related to her late one night, but when the concept had struck, it had struck with impetus, and he now saw it as the most important thing in the world. For that she admired him greatly. It was a noble cause, in her eyes. One he had attempted to champion, if somewhat naively. Especially in the face of how the real world was put together, and how the vast majority viewed things; but, he was not deterred by her observation, replying only that nothing and no one is beyond redemption, especially humanity.

She suddenly felt very guilty for having made the disparaging remark. She knew how strongly he felt about this and she had spoken out of turn. The recent run of events had, for the moment, left her feeling tired and defeated. Kevin was a good man who cared about the direction in which he had chosen to travel. She should have known better than to suggest defeat.

He lay in the hammock, taking an interest in the small birds chirping and fluttering between the upper branches of the tree. He had not noticed Laura's approach until she came up beside him.

'Mister McKinney. *There* you are. I tried the front door and there was no answer. I thought maybe you would be out here enjoying the sunshine, and I was right.'

The smile on his face told her he had recognised the words at once.

'That's amazing. Do you know I was laying here remembering that first time I met you. The eager young reporter, so keen to nail her first assignment.'

'*An annoyingly eager young* reporter.' She smiled affectionately. 'And *you*, pretending to be asleep so I would go away and stop bothering you. I knew what you were doing, but I wasn't going to be put off quite so easily.'

They both laughed, remembering the moment with fondness. Before the silence lengthened overly much, Laura placed her hand on his. 'I'm sorry, Kevin. I guess I was disheartened. I didn't really mean what I said. I'm not giving up.'

He responded by drawing her hand to his chest. 'We're both a little ragged. It's not been easy and has been taking a toll on us both, and I think maybe I'm the one to be apologizing. Right now I honestly don't remember why I started this. It suddenly seems quite stupid. Why the blazes would I want to take this on?'

'I don't want to hear it,' she rebuked, becoming suddenly serious. 'Since I've met you, I've changed, maybe grown up. I see the world more clearly. More as a whole than just my little portion of it. If only everybody else could see it the way you do. It's like having the blinders taken off, seeing it unfiltered and through perfectly clear eyes. It's just as you say, Kevin. It's astonishing. Mankind really has lost its way. We're not giving up. We're finding a way through this.'

'We are?'

She nodded. 'But first, there's something I have to do. It's been on my mind for a too long, and it won't go away.'

His interest was piqued as he studied her, curious. 'Really? Then maybe you had better attend to it. What's so urgent?'

'This,' she said, and she bent herself to him, tenderly planting a kiss of great tenderness on his lips.

He responded without hesitation, as nature dictated, becoming fully immersed as both surrendered to the primal force that had always existed between them, but which neither had been willing, until now, to act upon.

For the following few days they allowed themselves to not worry about anything. Laura only once returned home, in order to grab a few personal effects plus some items of extra clothing. The two of them spent all their time together, strengthening their relationship and resolve, enjoying one another's company and discussing all manner of topics; this mostly undertaken as they lazed atop Kevin's queen sized beg, with food and drink placed strategically at hand so that nothing need distract.

When the weekend came around a trip to the wildlife zoo at Gundiggy seemed an appropriate idea, to coax them back into the world. The ninety mile round trip took them down, out of the surrounding hills onto the Corrawah plains and on to the Murnyup lion park, where not only lions but all manner of native Australian animals, including Tasmanian devils, emus, goannas, crocodiles and wedge tail eagles could be seen and explained by guides who offered to impart as much knowledge about the animals as could be given.

Beside the luncheon bar they found a quiet spot out of the sun, beneath a shady gum tree where sandwiches and cool drink were consumed while sitting on the grass or at one of the benches provided. They stayed on for an extra half hour in order to watch the crocodiles being fed; an exhibition which made Laura squeal, shocked by the speed and ferocity of the huge reptiles, as their keepers displayed almost cool detachment in performing risky moves to entertain onlookers.

The afternoon shadows were already drawing long, and with another fifty miles to travel on their return journey, the sight of an historical roadside inn gave them the idea of staying overnight, to resume the remainder of the journey home the following morning. Both were instantly besotted by the charm and elegance of the establishment, with well appointed, clean and comfortable rooms, and downstairs there was a very good restaurant serving good, wholesome tucker.

Adjoining the restaurant through a single swinging door, the front bar was gained entry to, and from it, as time passed, a general hubbub was heard to increase. The locals—mostly farmers, shopkeepers and general rural types—were gathered, ready for the Saturday night social gathering, with beer, music, conversation, pool and darts being the main attractions.

Laura commented to Kevin, after their ample meal of roast beef and vegetables, how she had never been inside a barroom in her life.

'Your kidding me,' he replied. 'What, never?'

She shook her head. 'Not ever, and I have always wondered what the big attraction is for men, to drink beyond their tolerance, wasting the money they worked so hard for during the week.'

'Oh, I'm afraid you don't understand the working class man at all, do you? I know that you and your colleagues from the *Clarion* often went for drinks and a social get-together at the end of the working week. Why would this be any different? Or have you been watching too many television movies? Perhaps you expect drunken brutes swearing and fighting?'

'Maybe,' she replied. 'I'm embarrassed to say I've lived quite a sheltered existence.'

'You want me to take you through, to see for yourself?' She appeared apprehensive, shrugging noncommittally. Paying for the meal, he escorted her through to the front bar. It was crowded, noisy, with the sound of loud conversation, laughter, eightballs colliding, and to it came the addition of loud rock music as someone started the jukebox playing.

They stood in the entrance surveying the commotion. At the far end of the barroom there were musicians setting up equipment, apparently preparing to play later in the evening.

'Let's get a drink and find somewhere to sit, shall we?' Getting a glass of beer was relatively easy, but finding somewhere to sit was not. Eventually a spot on a bench seat along the wall became available, which they quickly took advantage of, and they sat watching the movement of people, picking up on snatches of conversation here and there.

The jukebox fell silent after the current song played out, and one of the barmen came from his position to switch it off at the wall socket.

'Thank goodness,' Laura expressed, relieved. 'I couldn't hear myself think.'

Kevin smiled broadly. 'All a part of the charm of a front bar.' As they sipped their beers and chatted, the crowd quickly thinned, and while they watched amusedly through the wide front windows, the young men and women climbed excitedly into their cars to depart with wheels throwing up the dust and gravel from the forecourt, and with motors roaring they sped off into the night amid much yahooing and unrestrained vociferous delight.

Laura began to laugh with great amusement while the sounds continued to recede. 'Wow,' she said. 'That was some departure. My ears are actually ringing.'

'Yes, quite a display,' Kevin replied, and intending to be facetious: 'I'm sure we were never behaved that way when we were their age. Come on, lets find an empty table.'

'Well, *I* was never like that when *I* was young,' she said, taking a seat. 'Were you?'

'Sure. All noise and action, with very little substance. Being in with the in crowd and like that. The mating ritual of the young, rural, white, middle class. Some deviation from the urban variety, but essentially the same.'

'I definitely was never like that,' Laura confirmed. 'Not a bit.' 'Of course not. Let me guess.' Kevin regarded her for a moment. 'Miss Laura Maggs, aged eighteen, on a Saturday night. . . I can see you wearing a dressing gown and with your hair in rollers, sitting at your study desk in your bedroom at the family home. You're studying economics. No, wait, that's just the cover of the text book, inside of which you have a copy of *Teen Magazine*, cleverly disguised in case daddy comes in unannounced.'

It had meant to be a joke. He had expected perhaps a punch on the arm, and laughter, but that's not what occurred. Her face had reddened despite obvious effort to keep her composure, and for the moment she seemed lost for how to respond. Somehow he saw that he had touched a raw nerve but he wasn't sure what it was. Without explanation she stood to make her way quickly towards the ladies room, leaving him alone and trying to reason what had just happened.

While he waited a stranger came up to him in a tentative manner; a man of some forty years, tall, clean shaven, quite well dressed and well tanned, presumably from toiling in the sun. A rural air about him, Kevin judged.

'Hello,' he said, smiling amiably. 'Forgive the intrusion, but are you the guy I read about in the local paper? Are you Kevin McKinney?'

'That's me. Guilty as charged. What can I do for you, sir?' 'I thought it was you. My name is Don Davies. I, and a lot of people I know have been very interested in what you have been saying. A breath of fresh air it's been, to hear someone demanding an explanation for the mess we're in. Common sense. I just thought you should know we appreciate somebody pointing out that its all so unnecessary. I know there's little enough we can do about it. We all know the pollies are all too weak-kneed even to speak the truth, but it's been a long time since anyone has called it as it is.'

'That's very kind, Don. To tell you the truth, I was wondering if I wasn't banging my head against a brick wall.'

The man patted Kevin on the shoulder with a large, heavily calloused hand. 'Keep on banging, fellah,' he said with a chuckle. 'Keep on banging. Maybe the wall will crumble before your head does,' he joked before ambling back toward the bar.

'Who was that?' Laura asked, returning to her seat.

'That was Don Davies. He was just telling me what I needed to hear.'

'Oh, and what was that exactly?'

'How about I tell you back in the room? Are you ready to call it a day?'

CHAPTER 7

A great deal happened over the following few weeks. The brief encounter with the man named Don Davies had reminded Kevin of the reasons he had agreed to make a stand in the first place. The desire to act on his newfound cause would not be denied; and as is sometimes the case when enough energy is expended in many directions at once, a flurry of e m a i l responses suddenly arrived at once, from the many inquiries and the process of reaching out which Laura had initiated on Kevin's behalf. While some were merely interested parties, curious and wanting further information, several were proposed speaking engagements. A few were within driving distance while others necessitated the purchase airline tickets. The cost of travelling and accommodation was born by those who had extended the invitations, including the Freemasons and a group called The Society of Man, as well as intellectual groups excited by the prospect of exploring alternative methods society might adopt into the future.

Intellectual groups, it appeared, were not uncommon, being scattered throughout the more sparsely populated interior in addition to the capital cities. He was surprised by his own enthusiasm. In spite of the fact that speaking engagements scared him to death, there was the overwhelming desire to present his vision to anyone interested in listening; those concerned with developing alternatives to the ubiquitous systems of control currently in place.

Laura observed him as he gazed out from the back verandah, lost within his thoughts. His eyes scanned the greenery, rose to catch sight of a bird which had begun to emit a melodious trill in the upper branches of a nearby poplar.

'A penny for them,' she asked.

He smiled at being caught deep in reverie. 'I was, just then, drawn back to my childhood. The pastures and streams. Orchards, vineyards and so many varieties of domesticated animals and wildlife. Have you ever experienced that type of thing?'

'Not quite so agrarian, but we did have a country house where we used to take holidays when I was a child.'

'It never leaves you, you know,' he told her. 'You grow up surrounded by nature and it imbues one with something incredibly valuable. A deep, indescribable peace. It's the most wonderful thing. It's a shame everyone can't grow up with such an experience. I think it would solve a lot of the problems this world suffers. People striving for this and that. It's quite childish and petulant, the way some feel compelled to own and control so much. It certainly isn't natural and I don't understand what impels people to behave the way they do. Do you?'

She pondered the question awhile. 'Maybe it's good old fashioned greed?'

'It's inbred whatever it is. And it's a question worth solving, I think. My take on it is, people are so surrounded by the phenomenon that it has become imprinted. Popular culture, so called. All those television shows that seem to regard aspirations for *more-of-everything* as being laudable, and regarding the behaviour worthy of imitation. I've always found it a repugnant trait, this culture of incessantly one-upping one another in the race to accumulate and dominate. It's so meaningless, and ultimately wasteful. Exactly the kind of behaviour we ought to be correcting. This throwaway, disposable culture.'

Laura simply watched and listed, allowed him to continue. 'The entire culture of humanity needs to be reset, but even to consider how that might be done, it's a vastly daunting dilemma. Somewhere far back in our history we wandered onto the wrong path entirely. I wonder if anyone back then ever saw this coming, tried to warn against it?'

'You've not heard of Jesus Christ?' she responded.

'Yes. Yes, of course. One forgets that he was a social commentator.'

'But the Romans crushed him,' Laura added, 'and he was only remembered in the way of a religion, not for the obvious truths he revealed.'

Kevin nodded in agreement. 'If only everyone had focussed on what he was really trying to say. Recorded his comments about living in harmony and focussing on the important things of daily life. I vaguely remember a few of the stories from Sunday school. . . and, *Yes*, my mother took us,' he replied in response to Laura's amusement at the revelation.

'And you remember this stuff, from. . . What were you? Ten years old?'

'Nine,' he informed her. 'And, yes, I actually remember, quite well, the stories I heard at Sunday school. I enjoyed them a great deal. We weren't preached and so I didn't mind at all.'

'What else do you remember of it?'

'I remember thinking, I like this guy a great deal.' 'You mean Jesus Christ?'

'Yeah, he was a gutsy guy, don't you think?'

Laura nodded. 'Go on. What, as a nine year-old, impressed you about Jesus Christ?'

'He had morals. But more than that, he had morals based on completely sensible grounds. A behavioural code, you know? And he was egalitarian. He didn't much like people lording over everyone else. He actually gave a damn. . . about people's lives! All up I guess I liked him, or at least what was said of him in those classes, because he demonstrated a peaceful existence, respect for others, and he disliked empire building. He was a good guy and absolutely had the courage of his convictions.'

'Like you,' she added conversationally.

Kevin shook his head. 'I doubt it. But we're off the point. I was saying that we set our feet on the wrong path somewhere back in antiquity. Imagine if somewhere along the line we had adopted an existence way more in line with maintaining a balance and a respect for our surroundings. If we had even thought about the possible damage we might wreak by continuing just to plough ahead without regard for possible ramifications. Don't you think our present state of affairs was predictable had anyone bothered to really think about it?'

'I do. But you're not allowing for human nature.'

'Ooh, human nature,' he replied, nodding and making a derisive expression.

'Are you mocking me?' she objected, thumping his arm, hard. 'Ow! Easy up, girl'—rubbing at the sore spot. 'That's some punch you have there. I was meaning, *human nature*. Like, you know, how stupid we humans can be.'

'Oh,' she said, realizing her mistake. 'In that case I withdraw the punch. And point conceded. Yes, human nature. I honestly can say I don't understand it. What about you?'

'Culture,' he replied. 'But before culture comes the example and eventual acceptance into established mores. Mind you, we're talking about a culture thousands of generations ago, but it worked, then, the same way as it does now.'

'You mean like a kind of behaviour that was copied?' 'Exactly like. Accepted because it gained results that were desirable. Desirable to the one initiating the behaviour. Like, *Might is right*. Like that. Perhaps something a little more subtle. I suspect this aberrant behaviour must date back to the year dot.' 'Hang on. I get where you're going, but what about the first kings and queens. Or the Egyptian Pharos? How did people gain so much control in prehistory? Say, when troglodytes existed. Because we're going back to the beginnings with this proposition, aren't we?'

'I don't know. You tell me,' Kevin replied, wanting to turn things around for a moment.

'Okay,' she accepted, obviously enjoying the conversation. 'How about one of the tribe is sitting beside the campfire one night, gnawing on his brontosaurus bone, and he thinks, *Tomorrow I don't want to go on the hunt. I'd rather sleep in.* He says to the guy next to him, 'I want you to take my place in the hunt tomorrow. In fact, you can take my place every day because I'm sleeping in from now on, but I expect my share of the meat at the end of the day."

'Why would the other guy do it?' Kevin asked.

'Because the big guy threatens to club him if he doesn't?' 'Why would the rest of the tribe allow it?'

'Simple,' she responded. 'Because he's a big, threatening guy. A bully.'

'But there's many of them and they don't have to put up with his shenanigans.'

'True,' she admitted, 'but this is where human nature comes in. Perhaps they're not so interested in the plight of the little guy. Simple apathy. If it doesn't impact them directly, why should they be bothered?'

'That's reasonable,' he conceded.

'I say he's a bad tempered brute and they're not bothered and or scared to get involved in the dispute?' she confirmed.

'It could begin as easily as that,' Kevin agreed, 'and became a common event, eventually. They observed a means of skiving off from the effort of the hunt and followed suit. Human nature.' 'Perhaps it's all about disposition,' she suggested. 'That and apathy, which is actually disposition too. So, yeah. . .

Disposition. Give a damn or not, depending on one's mood. It's definitely a human trait.'

'What about in the case of the group taking exception to the brute taking advantage and bullying the little guy?' Kevin mused. 'Maybe they tell him, *'Pull your weight or go without. And by the way, pick on someone your own size."*

'It could go either way,' she admitted.' Nothing startlingly new about that.'

'No, I guess not. *Human nature*, he repeated one more time in mulling it over. 'It's true, I think. Until something affects us directly, we're not much interested.'

He look across to Laura in all seriousness. 'That's how this whole mess got going. And now look at where we are. *The system*. That great intricate lump of a thing we thought we were so clever in constructing. The thing we devised to take care of us and make life oh so much more comfortable and controlled. Now we're controlled by *it*. And have you noticed? The ever so small alterations—the incremental changes over time that we are hardly aware of—slowly drawing the net in, tighter and tighter. Until, one day, we wake up and say, *'Where did all our freedoms go?"*

'Is it so bad?' Laura quizzed. 'Really? Because most people call it progress, and it does allow us to–'

'Control?' Kevin interrupted.

'So what? You going to tell me control isn't necessary? 'The need for control,' Kevin pointed out, 'is a symptom of a larger problem. Yes, we need a system of control when we have deviated so far from the natural order that chaos is likely to break out if we don't keep a strangle hold on things. The thing is, all these structures and complicated systems of control would be entirely unnecessary if we had but followed a less complicated and far superior way of existing.'

'And that is?' She was looking at him now, challenging him to come up with the answer, but before he did, her eyes sprang wide. 'You're going to say, *religion*, aren't you.'

'No-*o-o* ,' he expressed, grinning, and sounding as if it may very well have been what he would have answered, if only for comic effect.

'Not religion. . . A common school of thought. A creed. A devoutly held principal and faith in intelligence and problem solving and not giving up until the correct solution for a problem is found.'

'Science then?' she offered.

'I think a common belief for the future. One that is sustainable and will do no harm, no matter how long the principal is employed. Something which will see us reach our full potential without compromising Nature's delicate balance, and what we know and understand to be sound ideals.'

'As simple as that?' she remarked.

'Why is it difficult?' he countered. 'We all understand the principal of right and wrong, good and bad, fair and unfair. We learn and understand such things from a very early age. I just think some people are willing to compromise basic tenets like those for the most banal of reasons.'

'Personal gain,' Laura obliged. 'The most perennial and base of human motivations. Some people would do almost anything, depending on what the prize is, in order to get to it.'

'It's what I truly despise about our kind. It's a basic animal instinct, and with all of our intellect, our ability to see and understand the baseness of an act, some will still choose to commit the most heinous of acts, especially in the attainment of money. Even when they are sufficiently well off to live comfortable. I truly find it difficult to comprehend, and why the hell do we not strive to become better?'

'Are you expecting me to answer that?' Lara asked, surprised. 'No. I guess I've already given the question some thought. I already have an answer that seems to make sense.' 'So what's the answer?'

He leaned back in his chair, emitting a small sigh. 'A combination of two things, I suspect. First, people can resist a temptation even while the urge is there, or just the notion that a choice is there. But, secondly, if they see others making the decision to take advantage of a situation, and profiting by it without a penalty being applied.'

'Yes, I see,' Laura answered. 'A lack of moral fibre, and I guess the excuse always exists that they saw others doing it without consequences being applied merely and followed suit. So pathetic,' she pronounced.'

'Isn't it though? This world slips further into degradation daily. Maybe it has always been that way, only I notice it so much more lately.

That one distinguishing feature. If we could stop being so selfish, so greedy and small minded. That one thing alone removed would make a huge difference to the world we create for ourselves.'

Laura nodded in agreement. 'Perhaps if we didn't have a system based on money?'

'I've been trying to think along those lines myself. A self discipline instead of monetary gain.'

'How do you mean?' she asked.

'Imagine a world where everyone followed their talent. Worked at whatever they were talented at, maybe to pass the trade down from father to son, mother to daughter. We all understand that there's satisfaction, even joy in doing what one does well. Scientists, potters, mechanics, technicians of all descriptions. Every trade and activity which serves for the greater good. There's worth and there's satisfaction in doing for the good of all. What need for payment if everything needed was provided by a workforce which did not require monetary reward? I'm sure we could set up a system where labour was provided without need for payment, especially if the workforce was rostered allowing for long periods of downtime in which a person could follow their individual desires, fee of the work schedule. Everyone could share of the wealth of human endeavour without having to acquire way more than they need to be happy and contented. If fact, I think we would achieve so much more. I imagine progress at an incredible rate, and in such a system there is, maybe, the seed of such prosperity so that, one day, human conflict can become relegated to the past.'

The pair sat silently, ruminating the idea. After a minute or two Laura looked at Kevin.

'I can't fault it.'

Kevin continued thinking, looking for flaws. In a while he raised his head, saying, 'Do you imagine those on top of the heap will level the playing field? Essentially, they would be lowering what they see as their standard. They could even be rendering their existence superfluous.'

'Let them widen their outlook,' she replied, laughing.

'It would make for an interesting world, though, wouldn't it?'

CHAPTER 8

The itinerary was planned. Seven speaking engagements in ten days was a tough assignment but Kevin felt up to the challenge, hoping to fend off the dose of jitters he felt and to get into the swing of things, simply by throwing himself into the challenge at the deep end, with what he called a *sink-or-swim* attitude.

The following Saturday they drove a rental the three hundred miles to the town of Carrington, signing into their hotel room immediately upon arrival, late in the afternoon. The engagement was scheduled for nine in the evening, leaving just five hours to rest and prepare, partake of a meal and to freshen up as best they could before he addressed the Midlands Prosperity League in the local town hall.

Their contact, a Mrs Emily Bell, spokesperson for the League knocked on their door as they unpacked, introduced herself and outlined the procedure for the night. She stayed only long enough to bid them welcome, answer any concerns Kevin may have had, and then politely took her leave, allowing them to settle in and prepare.

From seven thirty Laura and Kevin watched from the cover of the café across the street, observing attendees as they began to gather out front of the meeting hall.

With some humour, Laura remarked, 'I would hazzard that these women haven't seen the inside of a beauty parlour in their lives.'

'Beauty parlour?' Kevin looked bemused. 'This is the bush, girl. A woman is more likely to attract a mate out here by the strength of her back rather than how pretty she looks in a dress. These people actually work for a living.'

Laura took the information onboard with a nod.

'And there's been a ten year drought. This town is doing it tough, and still they find the time, and the interest, to come out on a Saturday night to listen to some dill from the city waffle on about an idea for future society.'

'It's impressive,' she commented. 'I count about fifty. Not bad for an isolated country community but but for the advent of the internet.'

'Well, Kevin sighed, 'best go and meet with our host. She's probably becoming nervous, thinking I've done a runner.'

Laura laughed, straightened his hair for him as he stood to pay the price of their meal. 'Your maiden address. You'll knock 'em dead. Do you feel good?'

'Ask me that afterwards,' he replied. 'You don't want to hear how I feel right now.'

Emily Bell, a hawkish woman of indefinable age, slender and deeply tanned, greeted them as they entered from the rear of the community hall.

'There you are!'—smiling brightly and with some relief, Kevin imagined. 'We have a few minutes. Is there anything I can get you before we start, dears?'

'My mouth is kind of dry right now,' Kevin admitted, his voice slightly impaired because of the fact.

'I've put a jug of water and tumblers out on the table. Follow me through and get yourself a drink while the curtains are closed, why don't you? You can sit at the table provided until I introduce you. Laura, dear. Can I get you anything?' 'I'm just fine, thank-you Mrs Bell.'

'I've saved you a seat right by the stage, if you like. Or would you rather watch on from the wings, back here?' She indicated a chair which had been placed, stage left, where Laura could watch out of sight of the audience.

At exactly nine o'clock the burgundy curtains were drawn, revealing Kevin seated at the table provided and with Emily Bell standing mid-stage. Emily began to quieten the gathering, comprised of townsfolk and of those who had travelled from outlying properties.

'We are pleased to welcome among us this evening, Mr Kevin McKinney. The Midland Prosperity League became aware of Mr McKinney's ideas some time ago when his views were being discussed on the radio and reported in several news publications. I hope you all find his observations as refreshing and uplifting as we found them to be.

Please welcome —' turning and presenting Kevin, who now rose from his chair—'Kevin McKinney.'

Polite applause accompanied his walk up to the microphone stand. He tapped the ancient looking microphone, causing the sound of it to resound within the now hushed space.

'Good evening all,' he began, and was rewarded by several of the audience responding with a *"Hello Kevin"* in return.

'Hi. Thank-you. Thank-you for the invite to your lovely town.' He turned from the microphone and cleared his throat before preceding. 'I must assume by your being here, that you all have a concern for the future, or at least, some small interest in it. To be fair, I guess that is not to say that those not attending do not have an interest.'

He felt suddenly lost. What had he just said? he wondered, and did it make any sense? He glanced to where Laura sat, attentive, offstage to his right. She smiled, nodded, silently mouthed the words: *Go on. It's fine.*

'Let me thank you for extending your kind invitation for me to be here tonight. The Prosperity League. I like the name. It has a happy feeling about it, doesn't it? What better thing could there be? What better might we strive for than prosperity?

'The future,' he said, attempting to pick up the thread, paused, again uncertain, and took to looking out at the four dozen people seated before him.

'Look at us,' he said, 'gathered here on a Saturday night. My companion, Laura, and I droved all day to come. You guys, likely working all day in the heat, showering, dressing, eating a hurried meal in order to make it here in time for the nine o'clock gathering. And we are, each of us, here because we share a desire for something better than how it is at present. Not necessarily for ourselves, but for our children. For mankind as a whole.

'And while we come here in hope of finding something better for the world, to talk of it and maybe find how we might forge a path toward that goal, much of the world is plotting and working towards the opposite. The worst of it is, most will not even know that they are doing it. They are just following the blueprint which was laid down endless generations ago, before them. All of their days doing what they have to in order to keep the machine running. Working, being schooled, meeting and conversing with friends, watching television and all the usual things we do as ordinary people, just trying to live our lives as best we know how.

'The rhythm of life. All that energy generated and flowing. It is my heartfelt opinion, the blueprint we follow is of a poor design. We forge ahead, nose to the grindstone, shoulder to the wheel, expending all of our energies toward little except more of the very same, as we have ever been doing because mankind, in our ignorance, knows no better way to continue.

'I think there is a better world ahead of us, somewhere. A better existence where all that we can do and be might fully be liberated, and allowed to blossom. From those of us who live comfortably and already consider that we have it as good as it gets, to those who live on a gruelling subsistence level, and those living subjugated lives, under threat of the elements or political persecution, or whatever conditions presently exist to challenge our continuance as beings of unlimited potential and capacity for great joy. That better world already exists. It exists within us and in our minds. It lies dormant now, within our imagination.

'That perfect world where everybody is bound to be treated fairly, is respected and unbridled, allowed every chance at happiness and fulfillment regardless of the circumstances they are born into. But more than that. Not just the apparent inequity, it's the vision as a whole. To me, it's such an old vision. Perhaps it was somebody's idea of nirvana long, long ago, but we have changed and become far bigger dreamers in recent generations. I say we can dream a vision of a more perfect world, and whatever we can dream, we have proved a thousand times over already, we can make it real.

'We have come to accept the way our world is and have somehow lost the idea that we should continue to change and evolve in favour of our ability to modify and reinvent ourselves for the prosperity of all, the most basic concepts on which our society was modelled. Why have we stopped daring to dream big? And with only ourselves who can possibly stand in the way, why are we not hearing a multitude of voices shouting out around the world, to stop the destruction, the waste, the want and constant conflict and warring which seem to consume so much of our precious time and energy? I say that if we can dream it, we can make it so.'

As he spoke, Kevin's sense of himself began to diminish; any sense of time and place commenced to fade so that everything became akin to illusion, having a dreamlike aspect which cast everything in a strange, unnatural light. For a moment he was afraid that maybe he was about to faint, but pressing on for the sake of the audience he discovered the feeling to be uplifting, and without needing to think about the words coming from his lips he found himself speaking of the things which for years had lain dormant, almost without form or coherence but certainly without voice. In astonishment and delight he found himself expressing, in far greater detail and clarity, the idea of a path on which mankind could set it's feet, including the abolishment of the ubiquitous, rigid systems of control currently operating either through force or by the ebb and flow of currency; a new journey to a richness of life and of spirit, an age of fulfillment leading to such a future as the old school of thought's speculation could never imagine for it's lack of faith in mankind's ability to heal old wounds, reconcile ancient, longstanding arguments, erasing physical and idealistic borders which for too long had served only to alienate and perpetuate a stagnation of the culture.

For a moment his senses rebelled at the overwhelming nature of the extraordinary experience. He felt as though transported from his body, viewing the entire scene as from above. As his sense of self gradually returned he discovered his host, Mrs Bell, standing beside him, smiling broadly while directing the spirited acknowledgment of the small audience, now on their feet and applauding for all they were worth.

Kevin responded as he felt was appropriate, still shaken by the experience he managed a self-conscious, perhaps silly looking smile which felt most unnaturally stuck to his face. The spokesperson of the Midland Prosperity League grasped him by the wrist, raising his arm in triumph, as is done at the conclusion of a boxing match, and turned facing him with obvious great appreciation.

'Thank-you,' she expressed loudly, in order to be heard clearly.

The applause died off and she repeated:

'Thank-you so much, Mr McKinney. That was wonderfully inspiring, and I'm sure you have given us all a lot more to think about than we had ever imagined.'

The aftermath included tea, coffee and cake, while chatting with the townsfolk, but Kevin felt oddly exhausted by the experience of his first public engagement, confiding to Laura a need to retire to their room. With as much aplomb as could be mustered in the moment, they withdrew amid expressions of gratitude and promises to them both: an undertaking to disseminate the ideas and the passion with which they had been spoken, among the broader community.

CHAPTER 9

'It was better than good,' Laura told him enthusiastically, as he pushed open the door and they entered their room. 'Where did it come from? I've never heard anything like it before.'

Kevin fell backwards onto the bed in an exaggerated exhibition of showing just how exhausted he felt, began laughing. 'I don't know, but, boy, I've never been so tired. Are we calling it a night?'

'Are we ever,' she giggled, throwing herself on top of him and smothering him with kisses.

'I hope you're not expecting too much from me,' —laughing again, while she slipped off his tie and began unfastening the buttons of his shirt.

'You wanton woman,' he chuckled. 'Really?'

'You're *that* tired?' She studied him carefully. You are worn out, aren't you. Okay, I'll take pity on you this time. There's always the morning.'

She lay beside him, the both of them now looking up at the lilac painted ceiling. After a while she rolled over to look at him, while propped on one elbow with her hand supporting her head.

'Your presentation really was wonderful, you know. The vision of this world, how it could be. You had everyone enthralled. *Spellbound!* A world where everyone contributes according to their want and abilities. A world without competition, everyone working toward a common dream, without the need for financial wealth. It's incredible.'

'Maybe it is,' he replied, sounding a little despondent now. 'No, hey. Don't say that. Why couldn't it be? You said it yourself, tonight. Remember? You told us, *A dream is like a seed*. It only needs the willingness of good, honest people for it to germinate, and the fertile ground of a common goal to nourish it into something tall and strong. We all felt as if we could move mountains.'

'I don't actually remember everything I said, to tell the truth.' 'You have an extraordinary gift, Kevin,' she said earnestly.

Then realising what he had just said: 'What do you mean, you don't remember?'

'I don't remember much of it.' He shifted his gaze from the ceiling to regard the lovely features of her face. 'Sometime after I began talking to everyone, I had a. . . a kind of out-of -body experience. You know? The weirdest thing I've ever felt in my uneventful life.

'How long did I speak for?' he asked, suddenly realising he had no idea of that either.

'Ha,' she expressed in amusement. 'An hour and a half. Perhaps more. And *you* were worried you wouldn't last twenty minutes.'

'Are you kidding? Ninety minutes?'

'Probably closer to two hours, and we could have listened all night. You were amazing.' She wondered at his consternation. 'What?'

'I don't know. Just. . . when I tell you I don't know what I said, I'm not being self-effacing or making light. I really don't know where it all came from. Not how, why or in what manner it was said. It was like being separated from myself and the words just tumbled out, without reckoning or composing any of it. You understand?

'They *were* my own thoughts, alright. Everything I ever thought about over the last twenty years or more was concentrated in what came out tonight. The truth of how I see and feel about things, but then I. . .' He had stopped in mid sentence, looking as though he was attempting to piece the whole thing together.

'But what?'she prompted—made a little uncomfortable by the lost expression on his face.

He shook his head, willing himself back to the now. 'Maybe that's how it goes with this public speaking thing. I *was* pretty nervous. Still, once I got warmed up. . . Like falling off a log,' he told her, breaking into a broad smile. 'Come on. Let's get some sleep. Tomorrow is another busy day.'

What transpired during the following week was a series of near identical days: travelling, unpacking, speaking, waking early the next morning before having to re-pack and move on again, and on to the next engagement. After completing only the second booking, he already began feeling much as though he had been doing it for too long a time.

As far as the gatherings were concerned, the exhilarating thing about it was that, every time, the same irresistible, almost transcendent feeling of being separated, mind from body, had occurred. While preparing for departure to the third engagement, he thought to stop into an electronics store where he purchased a compact audio recorder, a means by which he might be able to review each night's discourse, which now included the addition of a period given over to audience question time. He found the interactive sessions at the end of the address to be most engaging and beneficial. Everyone present became totally involved, allowing for a wider, more general discussion, providing a free and energetic flow of ideas, bringing a warmth and even intimacy to the assemblage, which had been a missing element in earlier engagements.

Confidence began to grow steadily; all the initial self-doubt, which he feared would soon be well founded, had simply evaporated. He now welcomed every question without fear of being caught without an informed answer or explanation. Even the occasional attempts of baiting Kevin, poking holes in his burgeoning design and the "*One planet, One future*" refrain, which had become the banner under which the meetings were now being conducted, he found no trouble in managing to answer all sufficiently well and turn aside occasional reproachful comments by those attempting to instill doubt.

Preparations for the final engagement saw Laura and Kevin abandon their rental car in favour of a flight from a country airstrip out of Broken Hill to the city of Mount Ambgier, South Australia; a sizable community of just under one million people, which had been included on the itinerary for two reasons. The first, Laura wanted to see Kevin face a larger, culturally broader based audience in preparation for what might conceivably lie ahead. The second reason being, she had a couple of contacts here; fellow journalists who had been friends during their college days, and with whom she had kept a loose, semiprofessional attachment, the three of them often sharing newsworthy tidbits, or perhaps some small item of background information about people regarded as being of interest, for the purpose of public consumption.

Kevin began increasingly to keep to himself, often revising the notes he had taken to jotting down in an exercise book bought for the purpose. Whenever the opportunity presented itself he took to reclining comfortably, *'Meditating,'* he said, a means of dealing with moderate bouts of anxiety and the occasional headache. As well, he used these solitary periods to further formulate a broader vision, designated '*the unification of the species,*' which had of late become much more a focus of contemplation: An Earth integrated, egalitarian, culturally all-inclusive humanity, far extending the right to and the purpose of existence, pursuing the development and protection of, not only man, but, to every living creature, these being concepts recently arising during the course of his disparate journey for the acquisition of knowledge and the ultimate attainment of wisdom, the attainment of which had come to be among his most highly motivated goals.

Laura saw Kevin's energy appearing ever to increase. Not only in the physical sense of showing capacity for a greater output of energy, but also from within somehow. His eyes shone, clear and bright in containment of humour and enthusiasm. Every waking moment seemed to be taken up in the pursuit of information, through whatever means their current location provided, and as much as was required to quench his insatiable desire to know. For Laura it had become exciting to watch— exciting to be in the presence of a man so enthusiastic about life, so aspirant and energetic that she had recently been quoted by a local reporter at a small town gathering, revealing: 'I am, upon occasion, astonished by Kevin's insight. . . . his understanding. He has such a love of people, and such a wonderful vision for the future. It sometimes makes me want to cry. I don't know why.'

With Kevin's biggest public engagement only hours away, he and Laura made their way to their small hotel room on the second floor, having left instructions at the desk, asking that no one disturb them for the next five hours; long enough, it was hoped, to enjoy a much needed afternoon nap, after negotiating the too long and far too uncomfortable flight out of the red centre, here, to Mount Ambgier, on the mainland's south coast.

With the heavy curtains drawn and the room steeped in a penumbral darkness they slumbered deeply, while beyond the walls the muted and distant sounding drone of traffic persisted; a kind of white noise; soft, lulling and blanketing everything as the oblivion of sleep entered to soothe the restless mind and near exhausted body.

Kevin found himself transported, back to a place already long forgotten, where half images, soft pastels and tangled shapes twisted and writhed in effort to combine as a uniform, recognisable whole for the mind to decipher.

Again came the emerging vision: a vast, milling crowd; an expectant host of devotees come together to listen and rejoice in the words spoken of hope; coherence, long overdue, and the utterance of reason, the promise to bind all together, to heal and to steer the world away from its continuing, headlong advance toward chaos and rising uncertainty. And again, the appearance on the dias of the single, diminutive figure. He who comes to disperse a looming and inevitable disaster.

Laura awoke with a start amid Kevin's convulsing and the panicked, incomprehensible mutterings, to sit up beside him, not knowing whether to wake him or allow him to settle. A glance at the nearby travel alarm clock indicated that it was set to sound in a short time, and so she moved to rouse him, squeezing his shoulder and soothingly calling his name.

'Kevin dear. Kevin? It's time to wake up, sweetheart. Wake up now.'

He quietened, and in a moment his eyes flickered open, looking around as if unsure of the surroundings.

'The hotel room,' she told him. 'Mount Ambgier. Are you back now?'

'Mount Ambgier?' He repeated the words questioningly, as if they were of an alien tongue and meaningless to him.

'Yes, dear. Mount Ambgier. Population of one million, remember? The Apex community hall where you're booked for tonight?'

'Oh,' he replied, sitting up and making an amusing face with eyes crossed. 'Who are you and what are you doing here? My wife will be back soon. We had better be quick.'

Laura squealed as he grabbed her and pulled her down playfully.

'Stop it,' she giggled. 'There's no time for that, mister.' She dragged the pillow out from under his head and beat him with it. When things had settled she asked him, soberly: 'You were restless in your sleep. What were you dreaming about?'

'It's gone,' he replied, but she new better.

'It upset you. What was it?' She held his gaze now, and he knew she wasn't about to be fobbed off.

'Just a dream,' he told her. 'I think I've had it before, but really, it's an illusive bugger. A phantasm. It has slipped completely away now, really. But it was familiar, you know? I feel sure that I've had it before, possibly several times over.' He mused pensively, trying hard to summon receding images which would not comply, and he finally gave it up with a shrug.

'Gone,' he told her, truthfully, and she allowed the matter drop for the time being, offering a warm and appeasing smile. She knew Kevin far too well after being so long in his company. He would have evaded and cajoled, even resorted to white lies if he thought a truthful response might upset her. Whatever it was that had frightened him in his sleep, it had slipped the bonds of memory, as dreams were wont to do, leaving only the pale and formless ghost of a memory, and soon even that would be gone too.

'Come on then,' she said, breaking the oddly sullen mood. 'Naptime is over. Lets shower and get ready, shall we? Then, if you're a good boy, I'll let you buy my a meal.'

Showered and refreshed, they left their room in the early evening. Laura checked at the desk on their way out and found that her journalist friends from her college days had left a note. She returned with the note to Kevin, where he stood, waiting for her in the centre of the lobby.

'We have a note,' she explained, waving it before her as she approached, 'from a couple of journalist college buddies of mine, who want to catch up.'

She unfolded the paper and read aloud. 'Found you and Kevin registered in the same hotel as us. Rather than disturb, would you two care to join us for dinner at a local restaurant, at around seven?'

She turned to Kevin, looking for his response. 'There's a mobile number.'

'Who are these friends of yours?' he wanted to know. 'I've not ever heard you mention them before.'

'Sure you have. You just weren't paying attention,' she replied coyly. 'You haven't ever heard me mention Jerry Bishop and Christine Ghetti?'

He regarded in amusement. 'Okay. What's going on, girl? These old reporter school chums of yours. They just happen to be here in town when we are?'

She began brushing his jacket free of lint and straightened his shirt collar. 'It's my job, honey. So there's no need to thank me. It's a great opportunity and I get to see my old friends again. What could be more perfect? You can explain what you're all about without them looking for an angle or undermine you. You can trust them, I promise.' She pulled her cell phone from her purse. 'Shall I call and accept, or do we miss the best offer of press coverage you're ever likely to have handed to you on a platter?'

He knew there was no point in even trying, and simply smiled in adjusting her arm as he proceeded to escort her toward the main exit.

'So gracious in defeat, baby.' She leaned her head against his shoulder. 'I've always loved that about you,' she said, chuckling delightedly.

Her phone call to Jerry and Christine provided the name of and directions to the Metropolitan restaurant, only a short walk along the street from their hotel. Laura found her friends tucked away in a far corner, providing some distance between them and the bulk of the customers, numbering a dozen or so.

Christine Ghetti, a tall, slim woman with dark hair and pale complexion, rose and began waving when she caught sight of them entering the restaurant. Jerry, a short, bearded, rotund man with hair tied back in a ponytail, waited until they reached the table before standing, as he did so, upsetting a full glass of water and spilling it across the table-top.

'Oh goodness!' he cried out, but managing to ignore the spill long enough to offer a handshake to Kevin and a warm hug to Laura. 'Jerry Bishop,' he offered. Please to meet you Kevin. Very pleased indeed.'

Laura and Christine embraced, greeting one another excitedly. Releasing their embrace Christine turned to Kevin. 'Hello Kevin,' and in a sudden move embraced him in a hug also. 'Lovely to meet you at last.'

Likewise,' Kevin returned, and regarded Laura with a roguish expression. 'Laura has told me almost nothing about either of you.'

The remark elicited a burst of laughter from everyone as all found their seats. Laura suggest they order immediately, to be sure there was ample time to relax before the public gathering was enjoined.

While Jerry sopped up the spill with all the paper serviettes he could find, Christine engaged Kevin by reminiscing about college, how she and Laura had become fast friends from day one, having both signed on primarily because of the inequity in numbers of women in the profession of news media.

'But not only that,' she continued. 'The boys club was such a bunch of inept, forelock tugging, toe-the-line hypocrites, who never showed a jot of courage in the face of the establishment. And it was an absolute disgrace. Apart from the few, standout male reporters back then, there was not anything like real journalism going on. It took a few good women to call them out before those gutless politicians realized the rules of the game were about to change irrevocably and forever.'

Laura was watching Christine with a broadening grin. 'What's up with you, sitting there, grinning like a Cheshire cat?' Christine demanded humorously.

'You, Christine. You haven't changed a bit.'

Christine responded by doubling down. 'Well, can you tell me it isn't true? Those limp-wristed cowards would report any damn thing those bastards wanted to tell the punters, without so much as a fact check.'

She maintained the outrage for a moment longer before allowing herself to break with a self-effacing smile. 'Perhaps a change of subject?'

Laura turned to Kevin. 'This girl was hell on wheels when politics became the issue. She was once ejected from the House of Representatives for calling the PM a *dickless fascist.*'

'It was, in fact, *"A fucking dickless fascist who wouldn't know the truth if he sat on it,"*' Christine corrected.

Laura was unable to contain her amusement and gave way to laughter. Kevin sat, bemused by it all, while Jerry continued the story.

'Christine's the only person I know, let alone *journalist*, to be charged with assault in the Australian parliament. She plead not guilty, on grounds of it being common knowledge and beyond dispute. The case would have gone on and on. In the end, because it began to cause such a stir in the general media, the injured party, the PM, withdrew the charge.'

'I do have a vague memory of something of the sort. He's not likely to take you on again,' Kevin observed. 'You sound like a good woman to have on one's side in a fight.'

'Too right,' she confirmed. 'Especially if one has got the truth on their side.'

The conversation shifted then, with Jerry asking about how Kevin and Laura had met. The newcomers thought it was just great, the way the two of them had combined and taken on such *crusade.*

At the use of the word, Kevin assumed a thoughtful visage, the expression not going unnoticed by their company. The pair exchanged conspiratorial looks—looks which Laura immediately picked up on.

'What are the pair of you up to?' she asked, but immediately it was said, a pair of waiters arrived with their meals, interrupting the conversation. A silence ensued as they set upon their meal, alleviated only in acknowledging the excellent quality of the fare.

Eventually, Christine set down her cutlery and took a sip of water. She studied Laura momentarily before saying,'I was forgetting your finely tuned sensibilities, Laura. Forgive me. Please do not take offence, dear. You know why we are here.' Laura did not respond verbally, only acknowledged the statement with a curt nod.

Kevin did respond verbally. 'Perhaps you would care to illuminate me as to the purpose of your visit? Laura has told me her version of the situation, but, if I were you two, I would also be interested in the veracity of my motives.'

'*Touche*, Kevin, Christine responded.

'If you are looking to prove me a fraud, and God only knows why anyone would think I had anything personal to gain from this mission impossible. . . it's always a tricky proposition, isn't it, the proving of a negative? So how do we play this game?' 'I'm not sure,' Christine replied. It's a conundrum, isn't it?' Kevin offered a wry smile, turned to Laura. 'How were you expecting this to play out?'

'I had no notion, dear. Only, we both know this has to be done. The acid test, right?'

Kevin nodded. 'Yep. Inevitable. I suggest we play it by ear and see what develops. One thing I can tell you to assist in passing judgement and in deciding whether or not you are willing to lend credence to my effort: My only platform, if it can be called that, is based entirely on logic, fact, scientific certainty, what history tells us and what lies within one's heart and in one's mind. I *do* have a vision, and everyone must decide its worth. Are we going to order desert before we finish, or perhaps we could take a short stroll before I'm due to go on? It's a lovely night out. It would be a shame to waste it, don't you think so?'

CHAPTER 10

The four of them walked in the direction of the Apex community hall. Directly across the road from it they found a well lit grassed area with bench seats and tables, an ideal spot to sit and talk. Kevin hauled himself up backwards to sit atop a bench facing the others. Laura and Christine made themselves comfortable sitting on the lawn while Jerry Bishop roamed, hands in pockets, slowly around the table while taking an interest in the night sky.

'Do you know anything about astronomy, Jerry?' Kevin asked. 'Some, I guess. No more than most, I suppose.' 'Yeah, me too. Big, ain't it?'

'Beggars the imagination,' Jerry replied. 'Staggering.'

'Yes it is,' Kevin agreed, finding a starting point for a real conversation.

'There's almost an unimaginable distance just between us and the next star. Mankind, out here on our precious piece of ground at the edge of our galaxy. . . and look what we're doing with it, and to ourselves.'

Jerry stopped walking and came over to sit at the bench table. 'Most are too preoccupied with survival to step back and really take a look at the big picture.'

'Agreed. But surely, someone needs to do it.'

'You?' Jerry asked poignantly.

'Me, you, someone else. What does it matter? But why not me?'

'And in doing so, what do you see?'

'I see exactly what you see, Jerry. Only, maybe I put a different interpretation on it all.'

'Tell us how *you* see it,' Christine chimed in conversationally. Kevin exhaled heavily, allowed himself to recline until he was lying flat on the benchtop, looking directly up into the sky. 'It's all about evolution, I think. Is it not? We evolved from the most basic of life forms, to this burgeoning state of being, on the precipice, perhaps, of becoming something truly marvellous. But. . .' he said, in sitting up again, 'take a good, hard, long, look at what we have done to ourselves. . . what we have surrounded ourselves with. . . the systems of control, the delineating lines separating between one thing and another. . . one person and another. . . race. . . religion. . . mere physical attributes. . . class structure allowing benefits to some, benefits withheld from many others. . . supposed superiority. . . tax bracket. . . country of origin. . . and I could go on all night long mentioning every needless and impeding fabrication we have invented to get in the way of a healthy culture.'

Christine Ghetti pulled a cigarette from her shoulder bag and lit it up while considering what was said. 'Systems of control are necessary, to a point.'

Kevin did not respond. He knew she was an intelligent woman and saw no need, waiting instead for her to think it through a little further. After taking a second draw on the cigarette, she stubbed it out and flicked it away. 'You think we're ready to stand on our own two feet, like adults?'

'We have to do so one day. Besides, these systems of control are antiquated and ill fitting. It's not unlike taking away the training wheels from a child's first bicycle. Until it is done, the child will never be confident and able to ride unaided.'

'It's something of a simple metaphor,' Jerry replied.

'It is,' Kevin conceded. 'There is no metaphor able to encompass the entirety of the problem. My main point is, we cripple ourselves with the unending management of everything. The real heart of our inhibition, suppressed advancement, if you like, is with our method of distribution—the distribution of everything, including trust, responsibility, education, access to health care, you name it.'

Christine and Jerry remained reticent for a long time; a hopeful indication, Kevin recognized. Each were thinking the proposition through. Christine was first to give voice to her thinking.

'All these things, I agree, are unfairly distributed or made available, and for exactly the reason you mention. The almost habitual action of drawing distinguishing lines between perceived differences.'

Her face almost reflected mischief, as if she may have discovered a thread leading to what Kevin was edging towards. Looking across to her companion, she cocked an eyebrow.

'What?' Jerry asked.

'Are you thinking what I'm thinking?' She chuckled derisively. 'No. Surely not. It too preposterous. I must be on the wrong track,' she remarked, returning her attention to Kevin who offered a little more in the way of bread crumbs.

'If everyone were given access to that which humanity has achieved; the combined effort of mankind made equally accessible and without discrimination between one delineated class and another, one person or another. No more haves and have nots. Do you realise the simplicity with which it could be achieved?'

'I think you may have to say it, Kevin,' Christine prodded. 'I cannot see simplicity here.'

'Okay,' he replied. 'What is the one thing runs this world? The one most prominent thing which divides into class structure?' 'Money,' Jerry answered, laughing, obviously meaning to be facetious, but Kevin's deadpan expression quietened him quickly. 'What, *money* is the answer? How is it?'

'It's totally outdated and should be made obsolete. Remove money from the equation of mankind's growth and you remove a vast impedance. How often are great ideas brushed aside on the excuse of it being unfordable? Right at the base of society, our ability to exist and the manner of our existence, is it not based on how much money we have? It's the great social divide. Christ, it even divides continents. It's why we talk of first and third world when it ought to be *one world!*'

Incredulity was plain to identify on Jerry's face. 'You want to do away with the one thing our world is ultimately reliant on? Its financial base?'

Even Laura looked taken aback by the suggestion, judging by her expression. She looked to each of her friends in trying to gage their response. With Jerry obviously dumbfounded, Christine remained impassive and fully engaged in thinking the scenario through.

Laura regarded Kevin with a look bespeaking total surprise.

One which caused him some amusement.

'Why are you, especially, looking so stunned?' he asked her. 'You've often heard me criticize the ridiculous importance placed on the accumulation of financial wealth. The imparity surrounding us is nearly all due to money, or lack thereof.'

'Yeah, but how does doing away with it solve anything? As if it's even possible.'

To all of them, who he assumed at this moment were totally incredulous, he said, 'I get that the notion borders on the bizarre, particularly to a mind conditioned through the generations by a status quo which says money is the most important thing. But I swear to you, upon thinking it through, there is absolutely no reason to continue with the concept of money. It is nothing but one colossal bad idea which has, in recent history, done nothing but stood in the way of our progress. It is the worst possible impedance, without which we could be light-years ahead of our present position, in every conceivable way.'

At that point he restrained his enthusiasm, knowing that becoming excited might make him appear a zealot. Instead, he remained quiet, waiting for further response.

Jerry spoke up once more. 'Man, that's some crazy quest.'

'I really do wish you would stop using words like, *quest* and *crusade*, Jerry. The connotations are kind of . . . I' don't know, ill fated, or beyond reach.'

'I'm sorry, Jerry replied, 'but you have to admit, Kevin. It's a bit out there, isn't it? I mean–'

'Forget the obvious difficulty of implementing the proposition, Jerry. A thing is either a good idea or it's not. I can explain how the change can be brought about another time. First, I need you to understand the incredible transformation an execution of such a basic foundational concept will make to—' he paused, searching for the right word— *'everything!*

'Look, it's impossible to appreciate everything involved in such a basic concept at first viewing. The ramifications are all encompassing. It will precipitate a total uplifting of human society. All I can say is, think it through for yourself. Give it some time to percolate through the old grey matter and we can talk it through at a later date. Is that a reasonable proposition?'

He looked at the three individuals who appeared, to him, to be regarding him somewhat oddly.

Laura stood up, brushed at the loose grass stuck to her dress.

Christine Ghetti followed suit, saying, 'That's one hell of an idea, Kevin. If it's of any value to you, I like it as an idea. I do. I happen to like crazy. But I have to tell you, I think it's madness even to think that anything approaching the template of such a design has better than zero chance of getting off the ground. But you're an intelligent man and I don't really need to tell you that, do I? Not even Jesus Christ in a second coming could stop the profit makers crushing you like a bug the very moment they think anyone is listening to you. And putting that aside, with the whole world geared to go one way, how is it possible to make it go the other? It can never be anything more than a pipe-dream, and, deep down, you must know that.' She shook her head ruefully. 'Not possible, Kevin. I'm sorry, I really am. People are going to think you mad.'

To this he replied, 'Then why am I about to go before a crowd of maybe a thousand people who have paid to listen to me speak tonight?'

The question caused Christine a moment's pause. 'Perhaps it's curiosity,' she replied. She looked thoughtful. 'That is a good question though. Maybe people are ready to listen to big ideas?' 'But, like you said,' Jerry spoke up, 'the profit makers. It's inconceivable. The big corporations rule this world. It's their world. Only the incredibly naive would not know that.'

'And that's exactly the kind of thinking which undermines any possibility that we might reshape our world into something better,' Kevin argued, 'something unimaginably sublime by today's standard. The statement is wrong on every possible level except one.' He smiled then. 'It's very nearly true,' but hell, to believe it ignores, completely, any notion of what is morally acceptable. It is without doubt a corruption of all that is right, good and true, just to accept that we have come to such an impasse to be able to say, *This world is a fucked up place, but that's just the way it is.*" Fact is, guys, we do not have the right to ignore it any longer.'

'Damn,' Christine was heard to mutter under her breath.

'What?' Laura asked.

'This is exactly what I was worried about.' Christine was looking down at the ground, shaking her head ruefully. 'Damned if what you say isn't correct. I really didn't want to get involved, and I was hoping that you would come off as half-baked.'

Laura stood beside Kevin, holding his arm close to her. 'What are you saying, Christine?'

'I'm saying, girl, that every goddamn thing your man is saying is absolutely true, whether we want it to be or not. And now I have to go and involve myself in a crazy crusade or come off looking like a coward, myself. That, Laura Maggs my old friend, is what I'm saying. Are you bloody happy now?'

Kevin smiled knowingly, placed a comforting hand on Christine's shoulder. 'I understand perfectly,' he told her. But, please, I do wish you wouldn't use the word *crusade*. It worries me terribly.'

With almost no time left before Kevin was due at the public assembly, the four of them made hasty arrangements to get together again for a kind of committee meeting, for the purpose of planning what Kevin's next move should be. Even though Jerry didn't quite understand his colleague's motives, he figured he would trust her integrity and follow her *into the fray*, as she had quipped before her departing.

The event at Apex hall lasted two hours and would have lasted longer but for Kevin experiencing sudden fatigue which brought the discourse to an abrupt end. In all, the night turned out to be an unadulterated success, with everyone departing the venue full of energy, feeling uplifted by Kevin's vision of a future surpassing all expectations.

The following day began with considerable mention of Kevin. His views and his ideas were being discussed on a morning radio talk-back show, which had rapidly overflowed into the general community, discussed in the street and in cafes or wherever people gathered in topical conversation. Jerry telephoned at nine o'clock in the morning to tell Laura of it, and proposed that he and Christine accompany them to their next destination, an acceptable offer according to Laura who had answered the call, but there was, unfortunately, no further destination planned. Not unless home was included. The plan for the moment was to pack up and call a taxi to drive them out to the airport, but with Jerry and Christine now asking to join *'the crusade'*, plans were temporarily forestalled.

In aid of contributing to something resembling a plan of action, Jerry and Christine agreed to meet them at the airport an hour before departure, there to sketch something out, but just as Jerry was about to end the call Christine could be heard calling out in the background: 'Wait! Do not hang up that phone.'

'What is it?' Laura asked, and in a moment Christine was heard, in an excited state, to take possession from Jerry.

'Hey, girl. I'm so glad I caught you before you left town. Have I got some news. You wouldn't believe it. Guess what has happened.'

Laura laughed with great amusement to hear her friend so excited. 'I cannot possibly imagine, Chris. Why don't you tell me?'

Kevin had awoken with a headache. Laura went down to the street to find a chemist or somewhere to purchase paracetamol while he showered and shaved. Apart from waking with the niggle of a headache, he was in good spirits. The evening had gone exceptionally well. All available tickets had sold out and all present had been enthusiastic; well versed with Kevin's campaign through the attention various media services had paid via regional newspapers, radio public events programs and internet discussions through the social media network, all due, in no small part, to Laura's relentless efforts and attention to detail in her capacity as publicity agent. For the first time since they had embarked on the idea of promoting serious attention into radical social change, Kevin was at last seeing the first signs of the populace being interested in exploring the possibility of revolutionary thought for the future. It pleased him immensely to see that the public at large were accepting of such ideas, in looking closely at society and the interlaced systems that controlled so many facets of everyday life, so much of which appeared in the light of day to be superfluous and restrictive to the point of doing no more than stifling an otherwise healthy, forward thinking population. Being freed of such a tangle of codified law, of the top-heavy nature of public service infrastructure and the obvious unchallenged manipulation and controlling influences by multinational companies' monopoly had hit a nerve with everyone who had learned of Kevin's efforts to draw attention to these things. His focus on the role of politicians, their self-applied special treatment and ability to pay themselves, almost without challenge, whatever salary they wanted, had drawn especial applause. His comments regarding a society's ability to function without citizens being treated like children by the powers that be, simply by the application of logic and commonsense had likewise attracted a huge and positive response from all who paid attention.

He had proceeded in casting a vision toward the future and how it might unfold, free of red tape and the numerous other drawbacks embedded within antiquated public service systems. He went further in projecting a revolution of intelligence and of self-determinism, the erasure of boarders, the dismantling of armies and weapons of war, releasing all the potential human endeavour tied up in such negative pursuits to be unleashed in the direction of the common good, revitalizing the health of the biosphere, plotting a powerful and sparkling future among the stars—a future which all mankind might become enthusiastic and uplifted by in its pursuit.

In the final summing up he had stunned all by describing a planetary community where people were able to immerse themselves in whatever endeavour they excelled in individually, working in unison, pulling together for the common good, the obsolescence of wages where need alone replaced the existence of finance, where nobody was overlooked, every requirement attended to as a matter of course and including every contingency: sustenance, education, health care and all the free time a person might require, with nothing overlooked and quality of life being held in highest regard. His recollection of the night brought satisfaction and a glimmer of hope for success.

Laura returned with not only the paracetamol but a small bundle of regional newspapers and a couple of national publications in hand.

'Come and look at this,' she beckoned, tossing the newspapers on the bar. 'Scan through some of these while I get you something to wash down your tablet. You've made the headline in one of these,' she expressed, beaming.

'You're kidding.'

He moved to sit at the breakfast bar, pulled up a stool to begin flipping through the selection while she poured water into a tumbler and popped two tablets out of the bubble pack for him.

He swallowed the medicine without taking his eyes away from the print. Laura wrapped him in a hug from behind, grinning from ear to ear the whole time.

'*Prophet of Paradise,*' he read out, shaking his head. He reached for another. '*An End To Poverty.*' And the next: '*Visionary Of the Proletariat.*'

'It's all rather crass, don't you think?' he asked, disappointed.

Laura released her grip and sat down on a stool beside him.

'Ignore all that. That's not what's important. What *is* important is that you gained their attention. *This* is attention. Promotion of the first order. Now we take advantage and we build while we have their notice.'

'*Hmm,*' he replied, absorbed in a report he was reading. 'I'm being seen as nothing more than a dreamer and an attention seeker. There's still so far to go. I don't know how to do this, Laura. Am I wasting my time? Is this what everybody thinks it is, nothing more than a fantasy? A daydream?'

'Stop that right now.' Laura demanded. 'Keep your eyes firmly fixed on the future. What is wrong with you this morning?'

He shrugged. 'I'm a little low, I suppose. Don't worry.'

'It's my job to worry,' she told him. 'When we get back home I'm making sure you get all the rest you need. But I've got some news for you, dear. Christine called while you were doing your Rip Van Winkle impersonation and sleeping late this morning. You'll never guess. Not in your wildest dreams.'

CHAPTER 11

Christine made Laura keep their secret until they all had gathered at the air terminal. Jerry was with her, as always, and Kevin was beginning to think that perhaps there was more than a mere professional liaison between them. With their baggage checked in and tickets purchased, they discovered the pair waiting at a coffee shop, where they awaited their own flight out of town.

'Hello, guys. Sleep well?' Christine asked in greeting. Setting down her coffee and pulling out a stool to sit on, Laura responded wryly. 'One of us did, at least. Mr lazybones here slept very well, didn't you dear?'

'Wonderfully well, thanks' he gibed. 'Thank's for asking,' he directed back at Christine Ghetti.

'We've reviewed the morning papers,' Jerry told them, 'and the social media, too. You went down a treat last night, Kevin. Congratulations, man. You talked up a storm. You almost had me all starry eyed and calling for revolution.'

Kevin chuckled appreciatively. 'Careful of that word. There's many would be in fear of anything even coming close to such a thing.'

'You're right about that,' Christine agreed. 'Glad to hear you say it.'

'Don't worry, I've thought it through. I just hope I've thought it through sufficiently well. If things continue on in this way, and if you guys are still thinking of coming along for the ride,' he added, looking at each of them purposefully—'You do realise, we may be treading dangerous ground?'

Laura appeared taken aback by the statement. 'What do you mean, dangerous ground?'

Kevin held her gaze for a moment before saying, 'Change scares many people. Even the mention of change can make people nervous.'

'Especially people in power,' Jerry added. 'Those who think they have most to lose.'

'Like their power,' Christine uttered gravely. The more they have, the more desperate they become in preserving it.'

Laura appeared a little taken aback. 'Are you trying to scare me?'

'I shouldn't have to,' her friend replied. 'Don't tell me you haven't thought about that?'

Laura shrugged, turning sheepishly to Kevin. 'I hadn't actually thought that far ahead, but. . . Yes, you're right of course.'

'You guys are getting into deep water rather more quickly than expected, aren't you?' Christine observed.

'You mean *we,* don't you?' Kevin quipped. 'Or is that what you have to tell me this morning? Last night you two were all *gung-ho* and wanting to be a part of this.'

'Oh, we're in,' Jerry assured him. 'Wouldn't miss it.'

Kevin sipped at his coffee, looking around insouciantly while waiting to see if anyone was going to raise the subject of a surprise.

Christine extracted a cigarette from her handbag, noticed a *'No Smoking'* sign on the wall and returned it, cursing. 'Bugger.

How is anyone supposed to enjoy a coffee without a cigarette?

It's like bread without butter. A pea without a pod.' She began laughing at the absurdity of it. Then, addressing Laura:

'Do you want to tell him or shall I? I thought he would be much more impatient than this. His self-control is impressive,' she joked, flashing a wink across the table to Kevin . 'Or have you already let the cat out of the bag?'

'Of course I haven't,' Laura responded, annoyed at the suggestion. 'It's your news. You tell him.'

'*Ferchristsake*, Kevin interjected, rolling his eyes. 'Will one of you tell me what's going on? Unless it's bad news. In which case you can damned well keep it to yourselves.'

Christine squared off across the table, a sober expression now. 'I received word this morning. *Early* this morning,' she impressed upon him. 'Of course, in Al Jahra it was likely the middle of the day, yesterday. I haven't worked that out yet.

'His name is Jonathan Blackthorn, aka *Abu Pisci*. Translating, I think, to 'disciple of the fish', although that's another story right there. He is personal aide to Hakim Abudi. His *aide de camp*.'

Laura could not wait any longer for Christine's long winded account.

'Hakim Abudi,' she blurted out. 'He's very interested in what you have been doing and saying. An oil sheik, Kevin. Can you imagine?'

Christine looked in amazement at Laura. 'Really?'

'Come off it, guys. I don't believe it,' Kevin scoffed. 'No way possible. You really expect me to believe–'

'You had better believe it,' Christine retorted. 'It may be difficult, but I tell you it's no lie, Kevin, however bizarre. An old family friend. He is, as I say, *aide-de-camp* to sheik Hakim Abudi. He called at three this morning to tell me the sheik wants to meet with you and talk, with a view to furthering your effort.'

Kevin could only stare at her, still thinking it a silly joke. How could they expect him to swallow something this ludicrous?

'A Muslim oil sheik wants to help me out,' he stated flatly, so that all could hear just how absurd it sounded.

'*Yes,*' the three of them chorused in reply.

Laura looked him in the eye. 'Has it sunk in, *finally?*'

After a moment, studying her face, searching for any telltale sign of it being a gag, he began slowly to nod in affirmation.

'At last,' she said, displaying relief. 'I thought it would take forever.' Then giggling excitedly, 'How incredible is it?'

'Keep your feet on the ground,' Christine warned. 'These Arab sheiks are a wily lot and you had best tread carefully. Keep your wits about you, Kevin.'

'I think we had better find out as much as we can about this character,' he replied. 'But, right now, perhaps we had better get to the departure gate. Our flight will be leaving without us if we don't get a move on.'

The airline provided rental laptops with wi-fi internet connection aboard the aeroplane, allowing Kevin to search out the sheik.

'This guy is *loaded!*' Kevin expressed in a hoarse whisper, not wanting to attract attention from passengers.

'And that surprises you?' Laura replied peevishly. 'I'm trying to take a nap here.'

Thus admonished, he continued browsing the sheik's background, discovering that he was born into a wealthy family whose fortune derived from oil and natural gas. After completing his Oxford University education, Abudi branched out as an independent and enterprising young man, investing in cutting edge technology. He had head hunted the best scientists in their respective fields, convincing them to come and work for him in factories scattered right across the globe. The hub of the organisation was located in Abu Dhabi, capital of the United Arab Emirates. There was an image of his *All-tech* company headquarters on the web page, a six hundred ten metre, two hundred and thirteen floor skyscraper, appearing like a colossal inverted spike protruding from the earth, beside the sparking waters of the Persian Gulf.

Delving deeper he learned Abudi had lately been diversifying into such things as nano-technology, cutting edge bio-technology, space exploitation and research, as well as hefty funding in the direction of socio-political resource management and ergonomic analysis. . . whatever that entailed?

A flight attendant woke them both in time to fasten their seatbelts as the plane descended in approach to the city. From the airport they collected their baggage and caught a taxi to cover the remaining twenty miles of the home journey, returning to Kevin's house late in the afternoon.

Ignoring their lack of vitality and the accumulated mail which had continued to arrive during their absence, there was still the unpacking to be done, after which Laura dialed for a pizza delivery, the plan being a quiet, relaxing night while dozing in front of the television.

'What do you want to watch?' she asked, joining Kevin on the couch, pizza box in hand while Kevin dispensed the wine.

'You choose, but, please, find something without guns, car chases, gratuitous violence or sex scenes and a hopeless, two dimensional plot.'

'Oh. Well that leaves us a whole lot to choose from, doesn't it? That must account for ninety percent of all the movies these days.'

'True. I'm honestly too tired to care,' he replied, settling back into the couch with a large slice of pizza on his plate.

'I am so glad to be home agin,' Laura sighed, doing the same.

'You did a great job, Laura. A terrific job.'

'Well thank-you, boss. Does that mean I get a raise?' 'Ha. . . Yeah, I'll look into it.'

The night went as planned. Home telephones were disconnected and mobiles turned off. With the lights turned low the entire evening was enjoyed without interruption, allowing them both to finally switch off and relax for the first time in a very long while.

The following day began in much the same way, with breakfast being taken on the back verandah, overlooking the garden beneath the bright summer sky.

Kevin sipped his coffee, enjoying the birdsong while watching the finches, sparrows, starlings and other small birds splashing in the bird-bath at the corner of the yard. Laura enjoyed watching him enjoy the birds, a broad smile spreading across her face as she remarked, 'Simple things.'

'Yes,' he replied, and turned to her. 'Watching the natural world go about its business undeterred by our craziness.'

'We're not part of the natural world?'

'We are, of course, but it's difficult to reconcile much of what we do. At the rate we're impinging on *their* world'—he indicated the birds fluttering and splashing about in the birdbath—'something as simple and joyful may be destined for an abrupt end. Birds are especially vul-nerable to environmental fluctuations.'

'Plenty of cockroaches though.'

Her mobile phone chimed. Jerry had text her a message. 'Who's disturbing our calm?'

She took a moment to read the message through, consternation reflecting in her face.

'Was there any mail this morning?'

'I haven't noticed,' he replied. 'Why?'

'Jerry says there's a package arriving from our Arab friend, sheik Hakim Abudi.'

Kevin did not respond.

She set down the phone in exchange for her coffee and took a sip. After a short silence Kevin picked up the conversation.

'Do you suppose I'm doing the right thing, Laura?' 'About what exactly?'

'We've come a ways down this track now. After these last few days I see the reality of how much further there is to travel.'

'You're tired, is all. Are there doubts?'

There was a long silence as he pondered an answer. 'Not in my thinking. . . Not in how I view it all.

'This morning I woke up, yes, with doubts. I lay in the silence of a bright new day while you slept peacefully. I wondered how many billions of others would wake today into the same world they have had to endure all their lives, and how it all would turn out if change were not sought after and brought about. My reasoning, I still trust. It's perfectly clear that we must put an end to the craziness and start pulling together in the same direction. Stop the influence of hierarchy, greed, separatism, the idea that the force of violence is still an option for bending the world to someone's egomaniacal vision. Our world is an abomination compared to what is possible, how we might have shaped it if only we had held to our notion of right and wrong. All of that I am rock solid sure of. But who hasn't dreamt that dream? What does it say about me to think I can bring change?'

He had risen as he spoke. Gripping the wooden rail of the steps leading down to the garden, he turned to face Laura. 'I must be nuts. Stark raving!'

'Come, sit back down here,' she soothed.

He resisted for a moment, then seemed to relax a little, and with a faint smile obeyed.

'It's beginning to get to you, like it does to everyone. You're only human you know.'

'Only human,' he repeated. 'The refrain of the weak-willed and devious.'

'Oh, stop it Kevin.' There was an edge to her voice now he had not heard before. 'Stop over analyzing everything the way you do and answer me one question, okay?'

'Okay.'

'If you do not do this thing, who will step up in your place? Who else has the will, the guts to tell it like it is?'

His expression reflected discomfort as he seemed unable to answer the question aloud. She saw no reason to press her point further.

'You're tired, my love. The task seems suddenly so much larger and you have doubts about staying the course. No one is making you do any of this, Kevin. You could pull out anytime you want to, but I know you far too well for that. No one is going to stand up in your place if you pull out of this. We both know that for a fact. No one else, as far as I can see, has anywhere near your vision, conviction or your heart. And anyway, pull out and do what? You don't follow through with this, wherever it leads, and you will never again have a peaceful night's sleep. Tell me I'm wrong.'

He could only acknowledge the truth of it with a rueful smile. 'Christ,' he said. 'What would I do without you?'

At that moment there came a resounding knock at the front door. A text message on Laura's mobile alerted them to the fact that a special delivery parcel was being delivered, requiring a signature on the delivery docket.

Returning to the verandah Kevin placed it on the outdoor table. 'From our Arab sheik friend, Mr Abudi.'

Unwrapping it revealed a small cardboard box containing a credit card: gold inscribed on black background: *Bank of United Arab Republic. Prepaid credit*. A short handwritten note accompanied, which Laura read aloud:

'Sahib McKinney. A common friend has explained to me your very impressive crusade. I hope you will please to bring your friends with you and be my guest.'

Kevin looked from the message to Laura. 'God, I wish people would stop calling it a crusade.'

CHAPTER 12

The two weeks that followed became a period fluctuating wildly between frenzied activity separated by inert states of languor as all preparations were hastily attended to. Passports had necessarily been hurriedly procured, achieved by the application of cash incentives through certain people of Christine's acquaintance. First class air travel to Abu Dhabi, United Arab Emirates and hotel bookings were arranged, all expenses paid in advance by means of the credit card sheik Abudi had delivered to Kevin's door. At last, with everything in place and every detail taken care of, Kevin, Laura, Jerry and Christine made the flight, landing in Abu Dhabi at 6:15 a.m. on a bright, hot, Friday morning, twenty three hours and twenty minutes after departure from Australia.

A large and well tanned Englishman dressed in chauffeur's livery greeted them at the arrivals bay after taking possession of their luggage immediately after clearing customs.

'Denis,' the large, well tanned Englishman said in introducing himself. 'I will convey you to your hotel, where you can freshen up after your long journey.'

They were driven to their hotel in a white stretch limousine, where upon arrival their chauffeur signaled to the uniformed doorman that Sheik Hakim Abudi's friends from Australia had arrived. Inside the door they were greeted by a concierge who whisked them through the check-in process and accompanied them in the highspeed elevator to their fortieth storey room, wishing them a pleasant stay at *The Oasis* before departing.

After sleeping soundly that night, Denis appeared at the door to pick them up and deliver them to Sheik Hakim Abudi's mansion, situated on a hilltop near the outskirts of the city, overlooking the Arabian Sea.

Denis parked their limousine before a white stone wall with arched entranceway, and with minarets reaching upwards, standing like bookends at the corners of this massive building, all curves, domes and arches suspended atop slender pillars, giving the entire structure an inexplicable visual aspect of exquisite delicacy, almost as if it were about to lift off, cloud-like, and float away on the slightest breeze.

'Extraordinary,' Laura commented as they disembarked and stood viewing the vast premises.

'Fabulous,' Christine affirmed.'Must have cost a pretty penny.' Denis rounded the car, ready to lead them inside as servants emerged from within to offer chilled cans of soft drink or fresh orange juice proffered on silver trays.

A central corridor led them inward, past a central colonnade and a grassed area at the centre of which grew lush, exotic vegetation. Interior walls were of marble, standing on grey slate floors and lit by the sunlight streaming in under the floating domes, allowing light and air deep into the heart of the building.

Denis led them up to a pair of large, mahogany, double doors on their left and near to the end of the passageway, where he halted, knocking twice. In a moment the doors swung silently inward on their hinges, exposing a large room ornately furnished with early French period chairs, tables and bookshelves. Against the back wall sat a man at an enormously large desk, behind him hanging a rich tapestry depicting a stylistic representation of a jungle scene, opening onto a glade and watering hole where lions, tigers, elephants, apes, ostrich and an eclectic collection of animals from differing continents vied for space to drink.

Sheik Hakim Abudi rose and rounded his desk, dressed in traditional Saudi red and white checkered ghuthra headwear and wearing the typical, white, flowing cotton thawb of male Saudi dress. Deeply tanned, exposing a white smile and with blue eyes shining, he approached swiftly in greeting.

'*Ahlan wa sahlan*, Mr McKinney. He turned to the others. '*Allah maeak*. Welcome to my home. You are most welcome.' Everyone exchanged greetings and introduced themselves.

Denis was dismissed with a nod and a thank-you.

'Come in. . . be seated, please.' Abudi invited, leading them to the far corner where a richly upholstered, comfortable looking lounge suite had been arranged around a wide, low table.

'How wonderful that you all could come. I hope you are well rested after your long flight?'

All replied in the positive, nodding, smiling, and their host allowed a minute to pass while everyone seated and composed themselves.

Laura was the first of the group to speak.

'Mr Abudi, this is somewhat of a mystery. We have come a long way without a great deal of understanding about what to expect. Except that you say that you wish to support Kevin in his—' she glanced toward Kevin before saying, with a smile on her face, *'campaign.'*

Abudi caught the secret between them, and smiling, asked, 'You have a joke between you?'

Kevin answered, 'Yes we do. Everyone keeps calling it a crusade. A word I do not favour. I thought Laura was going to call it exactly that.'

Abudi understood immediately, laughing amusedly. 'Yes, I see the problem. Crusades, historically they have not always gone very well for the crusader. We will then call it the *campaign*?' 'I can live with that,' Kevin agreed, and wanting to get to the reason for their coming all this way: 'Mr Abudi, what do you have in mind? Why have you decided to throw in with us, in this campaign? I am very curious to know why a wealthy Saudi Arabian Sheik would contemplate such a thing.'

'Yes, Mr McKinney, thank-you for coming to the point. Allow me to tell you about myself. Why I have such an interest in what you have committed your energies to.

'I think that we see the world in a very similar light, you and I. I too have often wondered about this world and the direction we are travelling. The waste, the needless afflictions and the so obvious mistakes. The fault lies in our foundations, and you also have recognised that fact.'

Kevin listened to the words without reaction, allowing him to continue for a long time.

'If you have looked at my background, Kevin, you have no doubt noticed my humanitarian credentials. I understand the nature of people and what it is you wish to do. You want to fundamentally revolutionize human society, and to streamline the culture so that we can achieve so much more. And I get that.' He looked around at their faces.

'Revolutionary thinkers. There is so much promise and I would love to be a part of it. Who knows what we might achieve together? Your great vision and ideas combined with my connections. . . My financial resources. We could achieve so much, do you not think so?'

'You do understand that part of my *vision*, as you call it, is to make redundant the notion of monetary reward? The gaining of financial influence? To develop a culture where everyone contributes, not for financial reward but simply to achieve and to contribute for its own sake?'

'It's a marvelous concept, Kevin,' Abudi responded. 'Truly revolutionary. I see the opening up of a whole new era of human achievement and endeavour.'

Kevin could not shake a niggling feeling of doubt. The man's words lacked something—something important—and he didn't know quite what it was. 'Personally, I see *evolution* rather than revolution,' he clarified.

Catherine now spoke for the first time. 'How do you see your contribution, Mr Abudi?'

'Ah, Catherine.' He straightened himself in his chair and leaned forward. 'I have such connections, particularly within the media. There is not a corner of the planet where I do not have at least some small influence. The resources I have at my fingertips,' he said, regarding them all now, 'Planet wide coverage. Influence within certain quarters. Spheres of influence including governments. Did you know that we are on the very cusp of colonizing the moons and planets of our solar system? Imagine a burgeoning society of a new world where man can erase all the mistakes we made here, by growing in the manner you proscribe, Kevin. It is the perfect chance to do it right from the very beginning.'

'But that's a long way off,' Jerry put in. 'What about in the short term?'

'Not so far off as you might imagine, my friend,' he replied, affecting a conspiratorial wink. 'In the short term, Jerry, we will begin at the grass root. Is that the right term? *Grass root?* To reform society one must begin in the classrooms of children. One must plant the seed of ideas in fertile ground and let it grow. This is how to change the world.'

After forty minutes Abudi made a display of noticing the time and made his excuses. Denis was summoned to ferry the group back to their hotel. The return trip was made for the most part in silence, for fear that

Denis might report back to his employer anything discussed during the journey. Before returning to their separate rooms it was decided they should regroup beside the pool later that afternoon.

Upon returning to the privacy of their room, Laura turned questioningly to Kevin. 'What do you make of it?' she asked.

He shrugged. 'I'm not sure. It's a bit soon to tell, isn't it? How do you judge a man you have only known for a little over an hour? What do *you* make of him?'

'He's impressive,' she stated flatly, 'and he is offering a hell of a lot. He could provide everything we need. The man is lightning in a bottle.'

'Better than a fart in a bottle,' Kevin replied, lightening the mood. 'I think I could use a drink. What about you?' He produced the black and gold credit card. 'Let's make use of this thing, shall we? Room service?'

'Room service,' Laura immediately agreed, a smile appearing. 'We may never have the chance again.'

Room service provided a cocktail waiter pushing a trolley replete with all the beverages, mixers and spirits. The waiter demonstrated to them how to mix their desired cocktails and departed, leaving them to their own devices.

Comfortably reclined across the couch while Kevin occupied a nearby armchair, Laura raised her cocktail glass in making a toast. *'The new world order!'* she announced, grandly, and sipping her rather large vodka martini, smacked her lips together in appreciation. *'Mmm,* I wonder what the poor people are doing today?'

Kevin responded to the comment in the appropriate manner.

He saw that Laura was attempting to extract a measure of enjoyment out of the situation; no doubt in order to keep him at ease, but ever since meeting the sheik he had instinctively come to be on his guard, though he could not fathom why that was.

Abudi was much as he had expected: self-assured, well educated, with a take charge manner about him. Men like him were well practiced in handling people and situations, but there had been something about the way Abudi had tried to perfectly align his motives with his own. His explanation had been entirely sound and reasonable, but, still Kevin had felt he detected something unsettling, as if he were trying to manufacture the perfect response. But, *'No',* he thought. I am over thinking things again, just as Laura says I always tend to do. This is too important an opportunity to go getting paranoid and doubting everything.

'A penny for them, mister?'

'Oh, I was just thinking,' he replied. 'This is a big step we're taking.'

'We haven't taken it yet,' she pointed out. 'Still, I have to admit, it does sound promising, doesn't it?'

'Perhaps we ought to take it slow. One step at a time,' Kevin replied.

'Slow? Do you think so? With this guy behind us we could be moving forward in leaps and bounds. What's the point in *'slow'* when there's so far yet to travel? I'm thinking we would be wise to engage with him. You're not getting cold feet again, I hope.'

He stood, walked to the drinks trolley to pour himself another martini from the shaker. 'Can you say that you trust his motives? He says he's willing to pour his time and his resources into promoting the notion of a finance free society, endorsing my concept of revolutionizing structured society. This from a man whose enormous wealth was created by the status quo. Doesn't that strike you as stretching the realm of possibility a mite far?' 'It is unusual,' she conceded, 'but maybe the man is simply altruistic, as are you. Perhaps we just got lucky and found a very wealthy, like-minded benefactor. Is that so difficult? I mean, such people are bound to exist. Why shouldn't he be one of them?'

Lowering himself into his lounge chair, Kevin thought on it momentarily. If he were honest with himself he would recognize there was no point at all in taking the time to dwell in consideration. The sheik was their only option. To turn the man's offer down would be tantamount to admitting they had come to the end of the road, that they had come as far as they were ever likely to, and that it had all been for nothing. *That's all I need,* he thought to himself. In a life already littered with incomplete and failed attempts, or, what was infinitely worse, a total lack of ambition, he could not countenance adding yet another defeat to the tally.

He shook his head, affecting a smile of contrition. 'Onward and upward,' he said, determined now, and draining the contents of the glass, 'Why don't we make our way down to the pool?'

Christine Ghetti and Jerry Bishop were already poolside, occupying a table beneath a brightly coloured umbrella. The group enjoyed a plunge and spent time frolicking at the deep end of the pool, wondering at the coolness and wonderful quality of the water in a land that was mostly desert. After the swim they toweled off to order drinks and to sit in the shade beneath a great blue and white awning attached to the hotel wall, where the bar opened up onto a grass covered terrace.

'How do you like it here?' Kevin asked them.

Christine lit a cigarette, took a deep draw. 'Are you kidding me? Talk about living the life of Reilly. I love it here.'

Kevin was pleased. 'You wouldn't like to pack up and go home then?'

'You go home if you want to. I'm staying here,' she joked.

'How about you?' she asked, turning to Jerry.

'Oh, I'm definitely with you. I'm staying put. Why do you ask?' he said to Kevin. Nothing's wrong, I hope?'

Laura answered in his stead. 'You know how he is. He was having doubts again.'

'What's the problem, Kevin?' Jerry asked, but Kevin only shrugged, responding:

'Don't concern yourself. There's no problem.'

Christine wasn't having it. She looked to Laura, quizzically. 'Come on. If you have doubts, I think it's best you share them. We are all in this together, are we not?'

Kevin relented, sighing wearily. 'I guess so.'

'You should know so,' Christine rejoined. 'I recognise that this is a big decision for you, and I am not at all surprised you have doubts. If you think you're biting off more than you can chew–?'

'No. That's not it,' he responded sharply.'

They sat, mute and attentive, allowing Kevin time to sip his iced tea and gather himself.

'Sorry. I didn't mean to snap.'

'If you're worried about offending me,' Christine answered, 'don't be. My hide is way too tough.' She laughed quietly, regarded Kevin briefly. 'We're all friends here. If you sense a problem, maybe it'll help to air it out?'

'Not this time,' he replied, moderately. 'Actually, I could use some exercise. The flight and the being couped up in a hotel room. If you guys will excuse me, I think I might just see if I can discover where they've hidden the gymnasium.'

They allowed him to depart without further questioning, and sat quietly until he was out of hearing range. Jerry, it was, who spoke first.

'What's going on with him, Laura? He seems a little out of sorts.'

'I'm not sure. I've not ever seen him like this before, Jerry. If I had to guess, I'd say he's feeling the pressure.' She gestured to the surroundings in saying, 'All this is. . . It's not what he's used to. When I met him he lived a quiet, secluded life.'

'Perhaps that's it then.'

'Don't be so sure,' Christine cautioned. 'What you say is entirely plausible, and likely the truth. Still, I think we should keep an eye on him, don't you? That man has been extending himself and it must be terribly taxing. This trip came suddenly, and tacked on at the end of your road trip, Laura. I would make sure he gets as much down time as he needs, hon.'

Instead of searching out the gym, Kevin walked out to the hotel's main entrance. He had been experiencing a growing feeling of claustrophobia since arriving here; nothing serious, but it had persisted long enough that he was beginning to feel trapped. Without really having anything in mind he allowed the doorman to signal for a cab from the waiting rank. He climbed in, asking the driver to take him down towards the coast; somewhere he could look out over the blue ocean and breathe the salt air, thinking it might alleviate the vague uneasiness he felt.

As he sat quietly in the back seat of the cab he wondered at his own behaviour. Lately there had been a kind of mounting urgency which had begun driving his actions. It had forced his decision to make something valuable and worthwhile of his life and to follow his heart—whatever it was that guided a man through life—and to influence the world in which he lived by applying as much positive energy and calculated reasoning to making everything right; some grand dream as was able to be mustered in hope of affecting change in that world—change for the better, where nothing short of change was exactly what was needed if great potential in life was to be realised, and great tragedy avoided.

He wondered about the meaning of the word *delusion* and risked to reason whether or not the word was something applying to him, his way of seeing and understanding the world. With considerable relief he did not see that it applied. Besides, the way in which he viewed the world was nothing new. His understanding of it, as would be the case with anyone, was something which had grown along with himself, with pieces of the whole gathered and assembling throughout the many years of his life, until it was a picture, clear, complete, without ambiguity.

He reasoned that his later life epiphany had resulted in his recognition that the greater part of humanity doubtless assembled those very same puzzle pieces to view an exact same picture; but, alternatively, they had decided for whatever reason to do their best in ignoring what they saw the complete picture to be. The common and pervasive condition of the abdication of responsibility. No one dared call out, *The emperor has no clothes!* The act of doing so after so long a time being wasted travelling in the wrong direction on the path to a promised *Shangrila*, was liable to cause the observer to be labelled antisocial, even crazy. The risks and the enormous effort required in effecting change of this magnitude was, understandably, mostly considered too great. Even in attempting such a thing as this might be to sacrifice one's entire lifespan to the task. And for what?

Well, that was the crux of the argument, he figured. For the instigator there was no reward; no prize to be claimed in this crazy life, except perhaps, in the satisfaction of knowing one tried to do what was right and necessary. The beneficiaries, if the attempt be successful, would be those future generations whose lives are freed of the dehumanizing absurdity. Development of humanity's evolving societal structure would be set right. At long last all would be liberated from the bonds they had unwittingly created for themselves, having been deceived so very long ago into thinking that an endless proliferation of laws, the endless systems of control, the complexity of a financial framework and with convoluted, inequitable taxation laws might lead to some kind of glorious existence in the future. How could they have not recognised the folly of it, the web of confinement being woven about us, generation after generation, which would inevitably and forever restrict and make a mockery the human ideal of freedom of spirit, fulfillment of god given potential and limitless, unfettered progress?

His thought processes raced uncontrollably until everything ceased to correspond, rapidly clouding and obscuring, beginning to compress until what remained transmuted into pressure, immense pain and intense white light flashing behind his eyes.

CHAPTER 13

The question of accepting Abudi's offer prompted a long discussion before finally being voted upon by the four of them. None voted to the contrary, despite some suspicion being voiced regarding the man's motives.

The decision to join forces was conveyed via the telephone and received very enthusiastically by Abudi. The sheik informed Kevin that Denis would immediately be dispatched to take him, and whoever wished to accompany him, to a recording studio where they could begin work on a promotional interview and video statement to be broadcast with the assistance of the sheik's media network friends and associates.

Laura elected to accompany him while Kevin asked if Jerry and Christine wouldn't mind remaining at the hotel, this time.

'It will be terribly boring,' he told them. 'It's going to take quite some time to formulate a script. You two will much better enjoy lolling around beside the pool than having to witness me making endless mistakes during the recording session.'

Denis introduced them both to a man known only as Aziz, a short, balding, middle aged man who presented as having many years of experience.

The studio occupied a downstairs space beneath a disused, five storey apartment building in a less prosperous section of the city.

Amply stocked with equipment; cameras, sound recorders, a mixing desk, compound microphones and with coaxial cables running everywhere throughout the room, it was illuminated within by whatever sunlight streamed in from street level outside, via long, narrow rectangular windows.

While Denis kept himself inconspicuously out of the way, Laura looked to be less than impressed with the arrangement as she stood, looking over the interior which, it was obvious, had not been cleaned in far too long.

'Welcome to radio free Islam,' Kevin joked in response to Laura's dour disposition.

Aziz, an animated man, waved his hands about in extolling the virtues of his domain. 'Everything we will need is right here, Mr Kevin. Come, come,' he beckoned in guiding them both towards a long table where chairs had been placed. As they sat, he went quickly to a very old refrigerator against the wall, flinging open the door. 'Refreshments!' He pointed out the coffee maker, moved rapidly across the intervening distance and switched it on at the wall socket.

He looked at his watch with considerable annoyance and uttered something in his native tongue needing no translation. At that exact moment another individual pushed open the door from the street above.

'Aha, you're here!' he called out in a distinctly Australian accent. Tall, of medium build, with long, dark hair tied back and a pork-pie hat sitting on top. Shorts, blue singlet, thongs on his feet and a canvas bag slung over one shoulder.

'Sorry I'm a bit late, folks. I'm Garry, your tech guy. Advisor or whatever. You've met Aziz, I see. He looks after the place when it's not in service.'

Coming to the table he offered greeting, shaking the hand of each in turn. 'Are we ready to get stuck in?'

Laura was hesitant. Kevin was ready to give it a try, however. 'I am ill prepared, I'm afraid, Garry. No script. I'm not sure *how* to start.'

'No worries,' Garry told him. 'No script is better. 'The boss has filled me in on what we're trying to do here.'

Divesting himself of the canvas knapsack and placing it on the table, he flipped it open to drag out a bundle of notes and blank note-pads. 'I made some notes.

Aziz! Why are you standing around? I want everything switched on and operational. When you've done that. . .' He paused. 'What do you guys drink? Beer, coffee, tea? Anything you like.'

Gary instructed Aziz to begin brewing fresh coffee for Laura, after which he was sent out to get a carton of Australian beer for anyone who wanted one. In order to get Kevin loosened up, he asked him to stand in front of the microphone and to begin talking about what it was he wanted to do, while Gary made certain the equipment functioned and that his voice level was set correctly.

That done, he set about rigging and adjusting a video camera on a tripod. A backdrop was unfurled against the wall behind where Kevin stood, depicting the skyline of a large city, the name of which was never discovered.

While Kevin practised his spiel, Kevin recorded video and made notes in the notepads he had brought along, at the end of each session they went over Gary's notes; suggestions of how his dissertation might be improved.

It continued this way for a day and a half, with Denis picking him up from the hotel early the following morning, Laura opting to remain at the hotel to relax with the others.

By mid afternoon on the second day, the relentless repetition of the exercise in addition to Kevin's newly learned ability to make concise the message and expand on the notes Gary made as he observed Kevin's progress in delivery of the oratory, a halt was at last called.

'That will do,' he told Kevin, giving applause. 'You've got it almost sewn up, buddy. Tell you what: Let's take a well deserved break. There's enough usable footage here. I can edit two, maybe three twenty minute addresses. They'll be perfect for what the boss wants. Let's chill for an hour. After that, I would like for you to deliver one, *extempore*. . . off the cuff and from the heart. Are you cool with that?'

'I guess, but why?' he asked, obviously tired. 'What's the point?There's nothing I missed, is there?'

'Not at all, but I know how you feel about this, and honestly, having listened to everything you've been saying these past couple of days, I'm blown away. I mean I was concentrating on my job at first. I wasn't paying attention to all you were saying, but man. . .' he placed a hand on his heart. 'I've been listening now. A world where everybody contributes according to their nature? The abolition of money and systems of finance? A world without borders, without wars, greed, poverty? A world where no one goes without, regardless of circumstances? I'm a definite believer in that. It's golden. If only, man. If only.

'I think you got it down pat, but if you say it without the prompts and just say it however it comes out. You know, from the heart. I been doing this sort of thing for a log time, my man. If you say it from way deep inside, looking right into the lens here, people will feel you, man. And they'll see it and hear the words and believe it's possible, that it can happen just like you say. I want you to succeed with this, and I'm tellin' you: Do it just like that and you're really going to reach them. Make 'em think about it.'

Absorbing all that was being said to him, he at last nodded.

'Maybe you're right. You *are* right, I think. Easier said than done though, Gary. But I've really got to take a break. This is more exhausting than it looks.'

'I believe you.' Gary replied. 'Let's sit awhile,' he said, moving towards the table and pulling out a chair for each of them.

Gary poured the coffees, placing one before Kevin. 'Thanks.' After taking a sip he set the cup back down and asked, 'How did you come to be working for Hakim Abudi?'

'He used to do business with Wasp Media. They're a big media company here. I used to work at Wasp but I got tired of takin' orders. I left to set up my own shop,' he said, spreading his arms to indicate what surrounded them. 'Hakim learned of my venture and has been diverting work my way for a couple of years now.'

'That's handy,' Kevin replied. 'Are you doing okay?' 'Making ends meet.' He nodded,'Yeah, I'm doin' okay.' 'What can you tell me about the man, Gary?'

'Hakim?' He shrugged. 'I don't know him that well. The man has an ego. He's a busy fellah and has a finger in every pie. Why he is financing this little endeavor, I couldn't say.'

Kevin nodded at that. 'That's what I'm wondering. I can't quite see what he has to gain from financing me.'

'Maybe he's just a fan and supporter? With his wealth he can certainly afford to be generous. He must have told you something about his motives?'

'He told me that he had a similar views regarding *so-called* human progress. I was thinking about that the other night. I did ask him, point blank, why he wanted to help, but he never really answered the question. He started to but got sidetracked. The real answer still eludes me.'

'The *real answer?*'Gary questioned.

'He may have an interest in what I'm doing, and he certainly is contributing. The thing is, if the basic changes to our systems are realized, his huge financial advantage and superior controlling position will evaporate.'

'Not a exactly a self-serving venture for him,' Gary agreed. 'I guess there's more to him than you first thought? Maybe he's the selfless type?'

'Maybe he is?'

They were both were keen to finish what they had set out to achieve and to call it a day. The coffees were consumed without much more conversation. As they returned to their previous positions Gary resumed his technician role, giving Kevin a last encouragement.

'Okay, you've got this. Just tell it like it is. We've already got some pretty good footage. This is just the broad strokes, remember. Tell it like you're talkin' to your friends and I'll stitch it all together over the next couple of days. In your own time, man. Okay. You ready?'

Kevin took a breath, straightened himself to stand tall in front of the microphone, and nodded.

'We're rolling,' Gary told him.

'Hello. . . My name Is Kevin McKinney, and I have something I would like for you all to consider.' He glanced across nervously to Gary, who signalled all was good.

'I want you to consider the way in which we live life, why we live the way we do and to consider making fundamental changes, setting ourselves free from those invisible chains that bind you, me, our children, and will go on to bind emerging generations of human kind for possibly thousands of years to follow.

'What does it take for us to survive? The basics are food, water, shelter, and community. Community because no one is an island, as we say. Most of us thrive and do much better when we live among friends, family and a broader community. I doubt many would argue that. A sense of belonging. These then, for human beings, are the basic needs for us to live happily.

'Think about what is involved in your life today. How needlessly complex our lives are. It mostly began, I believe, with the advent of the industrial revolution and, following that, the technological revolution. Our world is becoming more complex almost daily, and how difficult has it become just to keep up?

'We humans started out as hunter gatherers, and I say we were, in ourselves, so much better off then. For instance, when we aged the younger members of the tribe provided what was necessary in the way of food and shelter while the rightly venerated elders provided wisdom, knowhow, judgement, the benefit of all they had learned throughout their years. So simple, so well balanced and rewarding. Of course I'm not about to recommend we live that way again, hunting and gathering.'

He looked over to Gary. 'Sorry, it's getting a bit loose.' 'Don't sweat it. You're doing fine, keep going. I'll clean it up, don't worry.'

Kevin composed himself and continued.

'Today, now, we live in a world with the wage packet: structured finance, an income earned punching a time clock, living under the constant pressure of providing the necessities of life for ourselves and our loved ones. We pay the water rates, we buy food at the supermarket. We pay the electricity account, the rates and taxes which allow us to live in our homes on our little piece of ground. We pay health insurance, car insurance, ambulance cover, and if we're lucky we can put a bit aside. We pay so that our children, and ourselves, can be educated within an education system which, itself, is very questionable. We pay taxes every time we purchase something, in the form of sales tax. We earn a wage and we pay tax on it. We invest our savings and we pay tax on *that* when it earns interest, and so now we have paid tax twice on the same income.

'We work specialized jobs which service the system we have created. Instead of being competent in many activities we are expert at only one thing and we rely on those who are trained in their field of expertise to do for us that which we cannot do for ourselves. Our lives are, *have become*, compartmentalized. It's the way we have developed and it is fair to say that it has served us well enough. Just look around at all we have done. The trouble is, in doing all of this we have habituated ourselves to the almighty dollar, and in doing that we have fallen into a terrible trap. The worst imaginable trap.

'Without sufficient funds, any one of us are immediately separated from the things we depend on, like food, water, shelter, medical care, transport, access to countless necessities in life. We are even separated from enjoying life with others when our pockets are empty. In this world everything is dependent on money, and if you don't have enough of it, or, God forbid, none, you quickly find yourself in danger of becoming invisible, being without worth in this consumer society. Poverty in today's world is life threatening.

'The condition is inveterate and inescapable now, with millions upon millions being separated from the lifeline of financial security. Because of the way the world in which we live is structured, we find millions working positions they are ill suited for and cannot stand, making their lives miserable. A large percentage of us cannot even *find* employment and may never find employment. So many are destined to live unrewarding, difficult, unhappy lives, cut off from the system upon which we all have become so dependent. This is our society, a thumb-nail sketch of the way we have built it, and it becomes worse almost every day, as evermore layers of complexity are included. There is no doubting the fact.

'And our laws. We call them *our laws,* even though the vast majority of us do not have a say in their creation. Laws that prohibit this and outlaw that, permit and approve another thing and intruding into every corner of our lives. So many laws that it's becoming almost impossible not to transgress a single one in the course of our daily lives. Laws that politicians are able to create and vested interest groups through our police force are able to wield as weapons against anybody or group they choose. Indeed, one can be fined or imprisoned simply for having no money, nowhere safe to lay one's head at the end of a long, hard day, for want of nothing more than legal tender.

'We are living within a system so complex and binding so that we at last find ourselves not living and working for the enjoyment or the purpose of it, the betterment of ourselves and our families, but simply to keep up the payments, the never ending arrival of the bills which enable us to keep our shelter, our food, drink our water, run a vehicle to ensure our mobility.

'We have become slaves to our system – the system *we* constructed, thinking it would serve us, lead us to a better, easier or more comfortable existence where we can live in a world with all the trimmings, the technological gadgets, the smart phones without which we, again, find ourselves cut off from interacting with the greater part of society. How important has become the smart-phone in our ability to live our lives, work and survive?

'With the advent of cash currency and an over-reliance upon a system which is growing evermore complex, we have, in my view, inadvertently imprisoned and made slaves of ourselves. The system has become *master*. Who can deny it? And if we do not obey it. . . if we fail to pay a electric, the water bill, a traffic ticket, our rent, what happens? If we do not have enough money we end up on the street or perhaps in gaol.

'A computer code decides we have or have not paid an account and it issues a warning. If the warning is not responded to or if an error occurs, an automatic directive is issued, an arrest warrant issued. Avoidance is unlikely if you do not have the financial wherewithal. Without the even participation of a human being, except to carry out the directive as a mere functionary, we can be evicted, arrested, have our lives turned upside down simply for lack of sufficient funds. *Insufficient funds* . The unyielding, unreasoning system deems insufficient funds to be a transgression and *punishes us!* But the cure is so simple.

'We can return to the value of a human person. Take money out of the equation and life changes instantly for the better. It is the cure for a disease which has, for far too long, *aff*ected and *in*fected us, terribly. And there is another step we must take. One last measure to be taken that will reinstate the promise which once existed in life but was usurped by the intervention of the endless accumulation of monetary wealth earned by the sweat of others. We can *eliminate money.*

'In order to eliminate money, another currency must be employed, else everything we have built upon the foundation of monetary wealth will crumble. Money took the place of something so much more important. In a word, *trust.*

'We climb out of bed each morning and go to work to earn money in order to sustain the fabric of their lives, and in so doing maintain the broader fabric of society, and on the largest scale, our whole, complex, interrelated world. Would everyone climb out of bed in the morning if there was no rent, no bills to be paid? Think about a world without a financial base. What then will coax, impel or induce us to climb out of bed each morning, go to work and keep the wheels of civilization turning?

'Imagine a world where people are free to pursue the vocation of their own choosing and to perform tasks they are good at because they have a natural aptitude for it, or a job which best suits their habits, attributes and natural proclivities. There are plenty of us who will work a distasteful or unattractive job, if the hours are short, providing enough downtime so that we could enjoy the more pleasurable things in life during the greater portion of a working week.

'People will train, just as they do now, to be able to fly aircraft, to become doctors, lawyers, technicians. Trades can be pursued father to son, as is already often the case. Mother to daughter, mother to son and so on. In the absence of money there will be no jobs vacuum. Every job will have participants, even if we had to insist that everyone spend a month out of their lives to fill a position commonly avoided. Fair division of labour. One only needs to think through a blueprint for a better world to know that folks will take on the more distasteful occupations for the sake of upholding what is most beneficial for themselves and for society as a whole, especially if suitable concessions are made. And, of course, in considering the speed with which technology and knowhow are advancing, it can only be a relatively short time before machines and technology come to fill the gaps.

'The big picture is that an individual's natural talents should, can and will inevitably decide the work we perform. A society where people go to their occupations feeling greatly fulfilled and uplifted because it's what they are good at and what they want to do. No one misplaced and put in an ill-suited career. A working shift can be reduced to only a few hours a week if needs be, allowing a position for every human being on the planet. In all, everyone provides a service, having as much spare time as they want or need, and nobody goes without.

'In the area of the arts, every artisan and performer will be freed of the burden of affording the cost of survival. Never again would a project be rejected on the grounds of it being too expensive. Imagine that! Human endeavour can be set free of financial shortfall, leaving only the distance between the stars as any barrier to achievement.

'I cannot possibly enumerate the advantages gained by reshaping human society in this manner. Think it through and discuss it. We have the opportunity to construct a perfectly harmonious existence for humanity, one which transcends anything capable of being pursued within the confines of the system we currently suffer under. Such a paradigm shift will be tantamount to unleashing the unrealized potential of the human imagination. All that is good, noble and laudable at our heart and what within the human genome can be finally set free to reshape our future.

'It can be made real, I assure you. It *must* be made real. I say we can and must dismantle this unwholesome, crippling system we have built. All we need do is to start thinking on it, planing how we might initiate the great change. In time, and with the careful forethought of planning, we have it within our grasp to create something so far exceeding anything ever before dared or even considered possible for ourselves. This can mark the turning point, the pivot upon which a truly great future is unleashed for the species of homo sapiens.'

Kevin's demeanour changed at this juncture, becoming intense and acutely focussed as he stared down the lens of the video camera, and placing his hand over his heart, he continued.

'The thing is, if we cannot. . . If we will not or do not divert from the course we presently find ourselves blindly following for no better reason than because it is the way we have always done things and the way we have become conditioned, with our all-pervasive system eating into our everyday lives, overseen by a lust for control and the accumulation of financial wealth, we will become the exact antithesis of mankind's dream. By following our current course I can only see that we will, in all likelihood, become little more than simulacrum: Dull witted, obedient drones who have foolishly swapped their glorious future only to be subjugated and left to the whims of a vastly complex system of control—the monster of our own devising—which will ultimately come to rule our lives.'

He lowered his hand, and thinking he had finished looked over to Gary who was bent assiduously to his control desk. Then, as an afterthought he took it up again.

'I know only too well the consequences of saying these things. I will, undoubtedly, be held up to public ridicule and endure many derogatory things said about me, primarily by those who have the most to lose. But I cannot ignore what I know for a certainty will come to pass. We will have only one chance of turning our future around, and I have no other choice but to propose the one course of action which can save us from so deplorable a future. Do we fight for the future we always hoped for? One thing is certain, we will inherit the future we deserve, accord-

ing to our intelligence and how highly we regard the notion of an unen-
cumbered existence, free from the restrictive bindings we have created
in our ignorance, and which will ever stifle human endeavour unless we
fight to free ourselves of it. The future is still within our grasp if we but
find courage enough to reach out and claim it.'

CHAPTER 14

T he sheik's borrowed Fokker jet touched down in Stuttgart, Germany, the day following Kevin's speaking engagement in London. In the three months following the decision to accept Abudi's offer of financial assistance, combined with the wealth of resources including the world media connections that this association afforded, Kevin's cause quickly generated wide interest across the planet.

The cause, having been dubbed *The Movement for Human Investment* by international media, had rapidly gained huge support, being adopted by a rapidly swelling army of advocates across the globe. The idea of dismantling the worldwide financial construct took off quickly, rapidly reaching numbers counted in the hundreds of millions. Big business were not enthusiastic and spared no expense in campaigning, mocking the idea, but the general groundswell of support continued to rise among average people. So rapid a rise in numbers was fueled when the movement reached the less affluent countries via the information superhighway of the internet, becoming bolstered by the great numbers of well educated young people, those of the first world who exited universities and other places of higher education to find a job market entirely unable to cope with career placement for the most of them.

Like the revolution of thought and ideas in the sixties and seventies, the movement crossed social and cultural divides to encircle the globe, and in the parlance of world media, to ignite the biggest clash of ideas seen since early Christianity meet the Roman Empire.

Factions arose within the ranks of supporters, the largest and most dominant taking to quoting Nostradamus' prediction of the Antichrist, adopting the position that those supporting the continuance of financial wealth were aligning themselves with *the beast*. The insignia of a six within a six within a six had been adopted in condemnation and waved enthusiastically by supporters of the Movement for Human Investment in major cites everywhere.

The four core members of *'the movement'* alighted from the aircraft, quickly transferring to the waiting limousine, hoping to evade detection by the group of supporters who had gathered at the flight terminal.

Christine pulled the door to with an angry *thump*. 'How in hell did they find out we were arriving? Somebody around here has a big mouth.'

'Beats me,' Jerry replied, shrugging. 'Hell, I didn't know we were coming until I woke up this morning.'

Christine regarded him with disgust. 'Why would I find that surprising? The amount you've been drinking lately. . .'

'Give it a rest,' he returned meekly, and turned to Laura and Kevin, sitting opposite. 'Why was it necessary to arrive in Stuttgart a day early anyway? I was enjoying London.'

'So was I,' Kevin agreed.

'Interview,' Laura answered. 'Kevin has an interview with a German current affairs channel broadcasting across Europe. Not the sort of opportunity we can afford to miss. Nor with the current amount of misrepresentation going on. Or haven't you noticed, Jerry?'

'Someone somewhere is always spouting lies about the movement,' he countered. 'Like the reported massacre in that Swedish commune, a couple of weeks ago.'

Kevin looked up from his newspaper.'I don't remember hearing about that?'

'That's because it wasn't a commune and it wasn't in Sweden,' Christine replied, annoyed. A Norwegian community. A small town. They had successfully adopted the template for human investment. Doing very well, too, by all accounts. Burned down by the CNL.'

Jerry's face reflected bafflement.

'Capitalist Non-Conformist League, you dolt.'

'How am I supposed to keep up with all the crazy names? Christ, there's too many of them.'

'And that's a problem we have to tackle in the radio interview, Kevin,' Laura pointed out.

'I know,'he replied,' putting the newspaper aside. 'But what do you do with people like that?'

'It's a law and order issue,'Laura pointed out. 'Encourage the authorities to root out the troublemakers.'

'The authorities,' he answered wryly. 'The authorities there are likely the problem, with sheets pulled over their heads.'

'Brekstad,' Christine intervened, causing them all to wait for further clarification. 'Brekstad, Norway?'

'What about it,' Jerry responded.

'It's one of the success stories. The whole city functions entirely free of financial turpitude, and they're thriving by all accounts. Perhaps we would do better to focus on the places it's working and let the good people of smoldering Swedish villages deal with their own problems?'

'*Financial turpitude*. Can I use that?' Kevin asked. 'It's good.'

'It *is* good, isn't it?' Christine grinned. 'Be my guest.'

At the hotel everybody piled out, hoping to get to their rooms quickly. At the desk they discovered the four of them were booked in to one room, an error the booking clerk apologized for, but the hotel was already full and nothing could be done until morning, when guests would be departing.

No one was happy with the situation; in any event Kevin was already pressed for time, needing to depart for the radio station in less than forty five minutes. There was nothing for it but to make do, they decided, and so the four of them resignedly rode the elevator up to room 5013, to unpack and relax for a while.

After a short squabble over beds, with Jerry obstinately declaring he would only sleep in the bed nearest the window, they finally settled. Jerry and Christine reclined on their beds while Kevin took a shower and changed. Laura sat at the table reviewing their schedule for the next few days.

By the time Kevin emerged from the bathroom, Christine had dozed off. Jerry had found a few bottles of German beer in the refrigerator and seemed content, sipping from a beer stein while watching a morning entertainment show on television. Laura looked up to inspect his appearance: freshly scrubbed, shaved and wearing cotton trousers, white shirt open at the collar, casual sports jacket and a pair of white sneakers on his feet.

'Will I do?'

'No tie?' she observed.

'Radio. It's not necessary.'

She closed her laptop and rose to cross the room, grabbing a clothes brush from his suitcase in transit and proceeded to give his jacket a once over. 'There you go.'

'You sure you don't want to come along?' he asked. 'Do you want me to?'

'I'm a big boy. I think I can handle it, but I don't mind. Either way.'

'I have some work I would like to get out of the way,' she explained. 'Have you got your wallet? Security pass?'

He slapped his pockets in searching for the items, realized he didn't have them.

'Why are men always so disorganized,' she said, grinning. She pointed to the counter top in the corner of the room. 'There.'

He pocketed both and moved to the door. 'I'll see you in a couple of hours.'

'Break a leg,' she called after.

Jerry was still watching television.

'Why don't you go out and check the sites?' she said to him. 'We're in Stuttgart. I'm sure they have places of cultural interest.'

Christine raised her head from the pillow. 'That sounds like a good idea. Why don't we go and leave the alcoholic here to watch that brain rot on his own?'

'I've got emails to answer. A pile of them, and there's still the arena arrangements for Rome. Maybe we can go out this evening and have a meal at a restaurant?'

'That would be nice.' She turned to Jerry. 'What about you?' 'What?' he replied.

'Come on. We're going out to stretch our legs. I'm not sitting around in a hotel room all day. And I'm not roaming the streets of a foreign city on my own. You can make yourself useful.'

He switched off the television. 'Okay. Sounds good.' Christine and Jerry departed in short time, deciding to visit the fine arts gallery they discovered in a brochure beside the telephone that the hotel had provided for its guests.

Laura was enjoying the peace and quiet while working her way through the list of things to do. After about forty five minutes she decided to turn on the radio, tuning into the talk back station on which Kevin was to interviewed. She needed to consult her notebook in order to find the frequency and station call sign. *'Meschen Radio, 1332Mhz,'* she read from the entry. She found the station and was relieved to find they were English speaking, and returned to her task while keeping an ear tuned to the radio.

Kevin arrived at the radio station shortly before his scheduled interview at one in the afternoon. A security guard inspected his pass closely before nodding ascent. He spoke into his intercom, arranging for someone come down and take him up to the studio.

A public relations girl in a navy dress, white blouse and navy cardigan appeared in the hallway after a few minutes wait, bidding him to accompany her in the elevator to the third level, from where she guided him to a comfortable waiting room where he made use of the coffee machine while, through the speakers in the ceiling, he was able to monitor the radio program currently in progress.

In a moment a short, casually dressed man wearing a soft cap entered the room. He had headphones clasped around his neck, seeming preoccupied with notes on a clipboard which he held in one hand, reading it while the other pulled the wire-rim spectacles from his face.

The spectacles he stuffed into his pocket before stretching his hand in Kevin's direction.

'Mr McKinney. It's an honour. We're on in five minutes. I was beginning to think you wouldn't make it. Are there any questions before we begin?'

'I'm sorry about that. I stopped for a snack before coming in and lost track of time. Questions? I don't think so. Is there anything I should know?'

'It's very straight forward,' the man replied.

'Are you the one interviewing?'

From the speakers overhead, the host could be heard winding up his program. The man in front of Kevin pointed through the glass panel to where another announcer was entering the studio.

'That's your interviewer,' the man informed him. 'Carl Kruger. If you would care to follow me, I will take you through.'

Kevin followed him through and introductions were made. His interviewer was around forty-*ish*, he guessed. Stocky and with piercing blue eyes and a long, shaggy beard. He wore a tan coloured tracksuit with a black stripe down the sleeves and legs. His broad, pale face was framed by wooly, brown hair, cropped at shoulder length. Kevin was given a seat at the panel, a large microphone suspended from the ceiling on a cantilever was immediately adjusted to his position, and a fresh cup of coffee placed on a small, portable table beside him.

'How are you?' Carl Kruger asked, while shuffling through a bundle of papers. 'You're not nervous are you? You must be an old hand at this.'

'I'm always a little nervous at first,' he replied.

'Two minutes,' a voice warned, while next door the producer waved two fingers in the air.

'Don't be,' Kruger replied with an easy smile. 'I'll walk you through it. If you get stuck, I'll go to a break while you gather your thoughts, okay?'

Kevin nodded. 'Thanks.' He took a sip of coffee and waited.

'One minute,' the producer warned.

Back at the hotel the voice on the radio advised of the impending interview with, *'Kevin McKinney, futurist, radical intellectual and revolutionary, whose outlandish plan to substitute the status quo of the global financial system with human integrity has been making international governments nervous as millions of supporters demand change.'*

Laura pushed the laptop away and tried to stretch the cramp from her muscles. As she stood, intending go and lay atop the bed listening to Kevin's interview, there came a heavy knock at the door.

'Blast,' she cursed, much annoyed. 'What now?' She swung open the door, completely unprepared for what happened next.

With barely time to gasp, a man dressed in black impelled her backwards, followed by another similarly dressed. The second man quickly closed and locked the door behind him while the first kept her off balance, propelling her all the way across the room until she was forced down, to sit on the bed.

'Make no sound unless you want to be gagged,' her attacker instructed.

Laura could not make sense of what was happening. Two men wearing balaclavas, average in stature and dressed in alike black pants and swearers loomed threateningly before her.

'What do you want?' she quailed fearfully. It was the second man who responded.

'Where is McKinney?

Laura only shook her head.

To his cohort he snapped, 'search!' and the man crossed quickly to the only other room, the bathroom, and looked inside, finding it empty.

'Laura took a chance. 'Who is McKinney? There's only my Aunt Tilly and myself. What's this all about?'

The man appeared momentarily uncertain, looking around the room searchingly. He pointed a threatening finger at her face. 'Do not move,' and he began checking under the beds and inside drawers and cupboards.

Going by the luggage and belongings he discovered, it didn't take long before he reasoned there were at least three people sharing the room. One of them a man.

'Who is the man here?' he barked while pulling items from the suitcase, but there was no reason for her to answer. Intruder number one had found Kevin's note books, his name clearly inscribed on at least one cover.

He returned to stand before her, and before she could react he had struck her a stinging blow across the face.

'Where is he?'

Terrified now and trying to think fast, she stalled, but only until he raised his hand a second time.

'He's doing an interview on a radio show and won't be back until tomorrow.' There's nothing here for you,' she replied, becoming defiant.

'There's you,' the second man replied in a gruff voice. Silence then pervaded the room. The men were obviously stymied and needed to readjust their plan.

To his colleague the first instructed, 'The phone. Disable it—' to which the hotel phone was torn from the wall, the cable pulled out and cut with a knife.

'Perhaps we will wait,' he said to Laura, no doubt sneering beneath the balaclava. 'That son of a bitch is lucky.'

In the background Laura caught the sound of a radio commentator mentioning Kevin's name, introducing him to the listeners. Thankfully, the men in the room had not caught it.

'You will deliver this message,' he growled. 'You will tell Kevin McKinney that next time he will not be so lucky. Tell him he has made many enemies, to stop now unless he wants to die. Tell him from me: 'Your ridiculous and absurd ideas can amount to nothing but much trouble, so why to risk your life? Go home or die."

Having delivered the heartfelt message, he made for the door, opened it and peaked into the corridor.

'We will go now.' And they left as abruptly as they had come.

~

'What was the catalyst for this so called movement, Mr McKinney? What gave you the idea?'

'Are you suggesting it *isn't* a movement, Carl?' He waited. He wasn't going to let this guy get away with that.

'What would you call it?' the interviewer responded. 'A great idea.'

Carl Kruger laughed in response, a little disingenuously, Kevin thought.

'Actually,' he continued, 'it's more than an idea. I say it's nothing short of a requirement. A requirement in the ongoing evolution of mankind, especially as regards our thinking and the way we function. Such a change is an absolute existential must. 'If we do not, or cannot, rise to this challenge, we will have, for all time, crippled our chances of ever reaching the pinnacle of our potential as intelligent beings. It will constitute a *"dead end"* in the evolutionary tree of our species.

'Have you ever seen a film, *Planet of the Apes*, Karl? If we do not evolve past this point. . . if we cannot dispense with our pathetic need for the accumulation of monetary wealth, which only creates further disparity and friction among the *haves* and *have nots*, we will never be united as a race, and we will never be able to achieve the promise that exists in a united world. The eradication of monetary wealth will, in a single stroke, cure an abundance of Earthly ills.'

'That's some statement,' Kevin.

'Yes it is,' he replied confidently. Fact also. As I say to anyone who scoffs: "One has only to think the concept through. In this world everything is connected to every other thing in some way. Eradicate the core component of what is holding us back, and you eradicate the problem."

'And so we eradicate money, Kevin?' Can that even be done? The world economy relies on finance. How do we continue?'

'In truth,' Kevin responded, 'the world relies on cooperation.

You have to take it down to the lowest common denominator, Carl. Everyone naturally thinks we rely utterly on money, and it has become so imbedded in our thinking and in our culture, no one sees past that misconception. It's fallacy.

'If money were to disappear this instant, with a snap of the fingers—' he snapped his fingers '—what has changed? It's just a concept. An illusion. People would no longer have to watch their bank balance, that's all. Services can still function. The workforce can be reorganised to work shorter shifts, all the unemployed can quickly fill the positions needed to work, say, six four–hour shifts, leaving twenty hours left in the day, completely free to do with as one wishes. The only thing that changes, Carl, is that the wealthy industrialists, the demagogues and fat cat ruling classes become redundant. If one thinks it all the way through, human conflict becomes redundant as the human race comes to work together without borders, sharing the resources, and sharing, equally, in the fruits of all our labour. What we have now is only an illusion, and the only reason we continue with this wasteful practise is because the rich and powerful are needlessly scared of losing something they think is important, when it isn't. The only important thing here is adopting a far superior means of existing as we travel into a new and enlightened era.'

'Many say this is science fiction, Kevin. What would you say to them?'

'I would say they misunderstand what science fiction is. It's philosophy to me. Social engineering to others, I suppose.'

'You know what I mean, Kevin. I am saying that many do not think this is possible, to change the world. You are, maybe, attempting to catch rainbows?'

Kevin smiled, feeling entirely comfortable, and even beginning to enjoy himself. 'Yes, chasing rainbows. And I knew what you meant. I was just playing.

'Let me be totally honest with you and your listeners, Carl. One day it occurred to me what this world is all about, and the way we human beings have attempted to bend it to our will, even when we bend it so far out of shape that we end up with a distorted mockery based on greed, the pursuit of personal power and influence arising out of overinflated egos. Not to mention the inability to clearly think a proposition through. I realised that the only thing delivering power and influence into a person's hands is when that person has ownership of whatever things people need, and they are able to extort as much money as greed will allow for those people to have this thing, product, natural resource or whatever. Whoever said that money is the base of all evil certainly knew what they were talking about.'

'I'm sure many people have had similar dreams, Kevin. What made you take the next step, devoting your life, making merely a dream a reality? What even makes you think you can?'

'That's *the* question, isn't it, Carl?' He paused for a brief moment in thought. 'I think there comes a time in everybody's life when they question their existence. . . their legitimacy, if you will. And likewise the validity of all human beings.'

'Allow me to pull you up on that point, Kevin. You really think that people think that way?'

'Sure. Yes, I do. We are all born with inquisitiveness, with enquiring minds. It's much of what makes us human. I suppose we live such busy lives, under constant pressure of chasing the all mighty dollar so we can survive and maybe retire one day, that we scarcely find the time to reflect. A comfortable retirement, isn't that a dream of people? To dream of a day we have the money to retire and relax at long last, and to take life easy? We live such busy lives, I guess a moment of peace where we can step back and view it all has become a very *rare* moment indeed, and that is such a terrible shame.

'But, yes, given the chance to view it all in a quiet moment of contemplation, I believe most of us consider our existence, hoping to justify it. In doing so we are forced to consider the worth of all of our kind. But we have digressed, Carl. You asked about my setting off on this, *journey*, shall we call it?'

'I did,' Carl agreed. 'So you came to be thinking about these things one day. . . ?'

'Yes, and for myself, I could not see that my life counted for so much at all. Before that, and for many years leading up to that point, I had always spent considerable time being critical of how the human race has conducted itself over these many millennia of existence. I concluded that when small numbers of individuals began to lord it over the many, by holding claim to a resource, perhaps, and extorting payment for access to it, or taking by force whatever they desired, that was a turning point. Things like ego, lust for wealth, power, land, natural resources and all those things. . . It really wasn't until we began accepting such behaviour, obviously backed up by force of violence, that the behaviour began to increase and spread throughout our world as a means of controlling our fate. In the end, Carl, it became just the way the world was. How it worked. It is exactly this sort of behaviour which first distorted our evolutionary path. Had we the courage to oppose what we instinctively understand as being wrong, we would—*and there's no doubt in my mind*—be living much freer, more productive, healthier and enjoyable lives today. We allowed ourselves to be tainted by something nasty, and now, here we are, paying for our lack of forethought and patent stupidity.

'In a rare moment I realised that, if money were to disappear, nothing would change but for an extraordinary liberation of spirit, of imagination and creativity. It opens the door to a future no one ever imagined or dared hope for because of our conditioning and imprisonment by the status quo!'

Carl's producer was waving behind the glass, signaling frantically that they were overdue for an advertising break. He ignored it, asking:

'And so –'

'Why me?' Kevin preempted. 'Because no one else in all this time has done anything to point out the one most important fact. We got it wrong. We have been following an entirely wrong and destructive path for all these thousands of years.

'Why me? Because I was halfway through my wasteful, irrelevant life and looked like spending the second half in exactly the same way.

Why *not* me? What harm could it do to try and wake people up to the fact that we got it all so terribly wrong and are on a dead end path?

'And so what if I am taken for a fool, or an agitator, an attention seeker or any damn thing at all? I told myself that I had to at least try. How could I pretend to myself that I did not see clearly for the first time in my life that the world in which I live was a total corruption, a waste of thousands of generations of human continuation, effort and promise? I could not. And whatever happens now, at least I can tell myself I tried.'

The interviewer looked pleased, toggled a switch on his control board. 'We are talking with my guest, Mr Kevin McKinney, futurist, revolutionary thinker. Thank-you very much, Kevin.' While the advertisements ran, Kevin's was asked if there was anything he needed and was given a can of soda. The host flicked through a couple of pages of questions. 'This is going very well,' he told Kevin. 'We will field questions from the audience, now.

Are you comfortable with that?'

'Sure,' he answered, and they waited in silence for the ads to finish.

'Ten seconds,' they were informed by the producer. 'Four, three, two. . .'

'We're back with my guest, Kevin McKinney, controversial philosopher, futurist and social activist. Kevin is the initiator and prime mover behind the *Human Investment Movement*, a concept which is currently whipping up debate around the world, dividing pundits and lay people alike, and it's time for your say. Call us, won't you?'

'While we're waiting for our first call, Kevin: I'm interested in your team. The people who travel with you and have been doing so almost from the beginning, I'm told. Who are they?'

'You put me in an awkward position, Carl.' 'Why's that?'

'Well, they value their anonymity. Anyone having a problem with what I am doing could easily decide to get at me through the people I value most. My friends.'

'Can you tell me the roll they play?'

'That I can do, I guess. There is a lady who plans and orchestrates nearly every move we make. She's a talented strategist and a valued friend. As are they all.

'The others I met through this same lady. They are all fellow jour-nalists. Colleagues whose expertise and friendship serves me greatly in negotiating the ups and downs of what has become a hectic existence.'

'I'm sure,' Carl replied. 'Alright! We have people standing by with some questions. Caller number one, Mary. You have a question for our guest. You are on the air, so go ahead.'

'Thank-you Carl,' the caller began. 'Mr McKinney, there's an old saying that goes, *If it isn't broken, don't fix it.* Why do you persist in agi-tating and causing so much unrest when everything was just fine before you came along with your crazy ideas? Every day now, on the news, in this city and that, troublemakers and protesters demonstrating for the abolition of a structured financial system. It's just absurd. How do you sleep at night?'

'I'm sorry you feel that way, Mary. But look, I believe this is a necessary change. Change, is by its very nature, upsetting. It concerns me that those who oppose this, many of them have not yet fully grasped the way it works. On the reverse side I think many who support the con-cept are not serving the cause by agitating and causing upset. I would much prefer concerted discussion and debate though the many forms of media, allowing everyone's arguments to be settled by the simple appli-cation of reason within the public arena.'

'Than-you Mary.' The host switched to the next caller. 'Franz, you are on the air. Go ahead.'

'Hello, Kevin?'

'I'm here, Franz.'

'I live in a small town called Neibitz, population 1300 people. We had a town meeting and decided to trial your idea. We thought it wouldn't work but thought it an interesting experiment. That was six months ago. This is now the most happy town where we have all come together as one. We all apply our skills wherever need. I am a plumber and I will do repairs for people as needed, only, I have stopped asking for payment. My roof needed repair last week and Otto from down the road did that for me and my family, no charge. And even the replaced tiles were donated by the Horowitz brothers. The idea has caught on and it is working very well. It has really brought the community together, but we still cannot do without money at the supermarket to buy food and other essentials. That is a big problem. What do we do for food we cannot grow for ourselves?'

The question made Kevin frown. 'Yes, I understand the frustration, Franz. It's the problem we have to face in the initial stages, and I have thought about it a great deal. Until a larger portion of our population come on board, it's going to be difficult, and we have to come together as a community, perhaps forming a cooperative, locally, and begin growing certain important food crops for ourselves until we get past these teething problems.

'It's an unfortunate part of getting the larger processes up and running. To the town of Neibitz, I say, Thank-you for your contribution, and I hope we get past this problem quickly. Thank-you Franz.'

'Thank-you Franz,' the host repeated. 'Henk, you're on the air.' 'Mr McKinney, I run a business which has been in our family for six generations, producing dried fruit to be exported world wide. How do you suppose we can exist without the transference of finance to pay for harvesting, storage, shipping, to purchase the items necessary in the production process? I am not even mentioning wages for our employees? It cannot work. This is madness.'

'Thank-you for the very important question, Henk. The necessities of production, electricity for your machines, mechanical repairs, export transportation and wages. When the system reaches critical mass. . . when enough ancillary companies and their workers, when shipping companies and their oversees partners have made the transition, it will all work just as it does presently. Better, in fact.

'It is in achieving that *critical mass* where we naturally will have teething problems. I understand the problem and, like with anything that is new, it will take time to get to where we want to be. I can only say, in the short term, to keep your eye on the prize. The prize being a brand new world where nobody has to do without. A world where our children can follow any career path, any dream they might have for themselves, without having to jump the financial hurdles which prohibit the vast majority of young people these days. Especially if they are born into poverty, as it is with third world countries.'

'I think you may be dreaming,' Henk replied. 'I understand that dream, Mr McKinney, but we live in the real world and in the real world are the real facts. People cannot accept so much change. They have worked very hard for what they have and they do not want to give it up. They do not want to struggle all over again for this new world you have dreamed up.'

'You have thought about it, Henk,' Kevin replied. 'And you are not wrong in your understanding of people. This is one of my own concerns. The world population consists of almost as many older folk as it does of youngsters who still have the energy and tenacity to invest in the future. Those who have worked for most of their lives, and who have attained a level of comfort and stability, they will be resistant to change far more than those who have nothing or very little, and everything to gain.

'It is in this area we must be adult about the big decisions. We are talking about humanity as a whole, and of future generations. We need to use our intellect and weigh the future good for thousands of generations in the future, against a period of discomfort, turmoil and the effort required to breathe life into this new way of being. In the changing ages of man, Henk, there have been pivot points where enormous changes took place, bringing us into a new age, like the technological age. I believe that this will mark the culmination of all we have wished for ourselves. If we can finally conquer the temptation of hoarding perceived wealth, thinking we are bettering ourselves by it. . . If we can eliminate our wastefulness, abandon an innately flawed and dangerous system which, right from the beginning, was always going to enslave and restrict our visions for the future, we will at last have set our feet on the road to real and everlasting progress, with nothing further to stand in our way.'

'And that is all we have time for,' said the host.

CHAPTER 15

Kevin stepped out of the hotel elevator at his level, surprised to see a policeman standing in front of his hotel room door. 'What's going on here?'

'Who are you,' the uniformed officer replied.

'Who are you? This is my room.'

'You had better go in,' he was told, the officer standing aside to allow him entry.

Laura was in the company of another man, presumably a detective, seeing as he was dressed in plain clothes. She sat at the end of the bed while the detective stood, talking to her. At the sight of Kevin entering the room she called out and ran to him, wrapping him in an embrace.

'I was accosted by two men,' she told him. 'Two men looking for you,' and she stepped back, giving herself sufficient room to punch him in the chest. 'Did it ever occur to you to protect me from these lunatics?'

To that he could find no response, only turning to the detective for clarification.

'Inspector Eric Marshal,' he said, introducing himself. 'Miss Maggs has been subjected to intimidation tactics by a pair of unidentified men who apparently have a grievance with you.' Kevin reached out and drew Laura close to embrace her anew.

'Did they hurt you? Are you alright? What happened?' Laura pulled herself free. 'I'm fine.'

'I have assigned two of my officers to keep a low profile while keeping an eye out around the hotel, Mr McKinney. I've done what I can for now. The description miss Maggs gave us will be processed immediately. I'll get back to the office and start reviewing the security footage supplied by the hotel manager. Are there any questions before I go?'

By the time Jerry and Christine returned, Kevin had been given a full account of events, and tale was then retold for their benefit. For the moment there seemed nothing more to be done.

'They must have been a couple of disgruntled nut jobs,' Jerry commented. 'They were disorganised to the point of not even knowing who was in the room.'

'I agree,' Christine seconded, 'but we're going to have to be more careful in future.'

Laura was at the mirror, inspecting her face where a bruise had appeared.

'Are you terribly shaken?' Kevin moved up behind her to better view the injury in the reflection.

'I'm angry,' she replied sharply. 'That bastard. I would love to repay him for this. If I ever get the chance–'

'I'm sorry,' Kevin intoned miserably, raising his hands to his head in frustration. 'What the hell was I thinking, leaving you alone that way? God, I would never forgive myself if something happened. I can't believe we never even thought about the possibility of something like this happening. I'll arrange for protection. I'll call Hakim and see if he knows an outfit here in the city.'

~

In the middle of the night Laura was woken by Kevin's tossing and turning. She switched on the bedside lamp, finding him with his face pushed deep into the pillow, wrapping both ends of it around his head in attempt to contain his moaning and groaning.

'Darling, what is it?'

'Headache,' he told her, his voice heavily muffled. 'My damned head is about to explode. Do we have any paracetamol?'

Judging by the way he was suffering, she decided on other action, going straight to the telephone and calling the night clerk and directing him to call immediately for a doctor.

By the time the doctor arrived Kevin was at the end of his rope, doing all he could just to keep from crying out from the pain, and shaking everyone up in the process.

The doctor recommended an ambulance, telling those present that in such cases it was best to err on the side of caution. 'Migraine headaches are nasty,' he said, 'and your friend will be afforded the best care at the hospital. He needs to be on a drip for extra hydration, at least.'

Laura was very upset and terribly worried. She had wanted to accompany Kevin in the ambulance but he had insisted that she did not.

'It's only a migraine. I've had 'em before,' he maintained. 'It hurts like a son-of-a-bitch but they pass, so don't worry. Get a night's sleep and I'll be back in the morning,' he told her, and while the others climbed back into bed and were asleep again within thirty minutes of the ambulance taking him off for treatment, for the remainder of the night sleep would not come to her as she lay staring up at the ceiling, trying to convince herself that all would be well.

By the time eight o'clock came around, exhaustion began to tell on her. Her mind simply would not rest, her eyes were sore and she felt terribly drained, yet sleep still refused to come.

When she attempted to rise and dress for the trip to hospital, Christine insisted she stay where she was, telling her that she and Jerry would go to check on Kevin, bringing him back with them if he had recovered sufficiently.

From her suitcase Christine rooted out a small glass bottle containing diazepam tablets, administered one with a sip of milk, and not before Laura began exhibiting the initial signs of slipping off to sleep did the pair depart.

At the hospital they found Kevin in a quiet ward, dozing in a hospital bed with a saline drip attached to his arm. Talking to the ward sister at the nurses' station they were informed that they would have done better to call ahead, and that Kevin would be undergoing a number of tests throughout the day. It was likely he would not be released until the following day.

For the rest of that day the trio mostly remained indoors. That this sudden event had left them sitting idle impressed upon each of them just how pivotal Kevin had become in all of their lives.

'I'm not so surprised he's feeling the pressure,' Christine commented. 'I didn't realize until now how reliant we've become on him.'

Jerry looked up from his notes. 'You think that's all it is, pressure? I hope that's it.'

'Of course that's it,' she replied, tilting her head and quickly glancing toward Laura, attempting to convey her meaning to Jerry. 'He's been overdoing it way too much. We should have expected something like this. We need to keep a closer eye on the man.'

Laura replied, 'I hope you're not saying I don't look after him well enough. Because–'

'No, dear. No, nothing of the sort,' she said defensively. 'I've seen how you dote on him, honey. He's lucky to have you.'

Laura's unhappiness was evident in her body language, as she sat, slumped sideways on the couch, elbow on armrest, head supported by one hand, and with legs drawn up sideways on the cushions. 'I should have seen this coming.'

'What could you have done?' Jerry observed. 'No one can slow the guy down when he has a job in front of him. We all know that. It's impossible.'

Christine agreed, adding, 'He said that he's suffered migraines before, and he seems to be taking this in his stride. So don't worry too much, dear. He'll be back on his feet in no time. Just wait and see. We might as well try to enjoy this unexpected respite. He'll be up and cracking the whip again, soon enough,' she said, trying to impart a little humour. 'What shall we do with ourselves? We can't just mope around here all day like a bunch of *sad sacks*.'

'I'm still very tired,' Laura replied sullenly. 'We have another engagement coming up soon. I should attend to the preparations.'

Back at the hospital Kevin had much recovered. Glucose and a cocktail of vitamins were being administered in effort to raise his energy level. Initial blood analyses had reflected he was suffering from mild exhaustion, poor nutrition as well as a measure of dehydration, but the tests had also revealed some anomalies.

After Kevin had rested for a few hours, the doctor treating him approached his bedside. 'How are you feeling, Mr McKinney? Are you feeling better?'

He nodded, 'Yes, way better. Good enough to drag my butt out of here anyway.'

'Don't be so hasty. I've put a *hurry-up* on the results of your last tests, but it will be a few hours still, before they're in. Why don't you try to relax in the meantime?'

'I've been relaxing for most of my life. I have things to do, doc —' affecting a grin. 'I can't be lying around here all day like some senior citizen.'

The doctor responded with a smile in appreciation of the sentiment. 'I think it's for the best if you give us a chance to sort this out. I was able to contact your doctor in Australia a moment ago. He remembers you quite well. You received a concussion some time ago, he tells me.'

'That was a long time ago. I was mugged. Ever been mugged, doc?'

'No I haven't. It must have been frightening?'

'Not really,' he replied, thinking back on it. 'More surprising than anything. It's an interesting experience, you should try it sometime. Something like that has a way of snapping a person out of their complacency. It did with me.'

'Really? How so?'

'People. We live in our own little world most of the time. You know that, I'm sure. When someone jumps out from your preconceived notion of your surroundings to bop you on the noggin, it's quite the wake-up call. Like, *Wake up, fool. You live in the real world, and the real world is a dangerous place!* Something like that can have positive effects. It sure did for me.'

The doctor nodded appreciatively. 'I'm sure you're right about that. But right now I'm going to have you taken down to radiology and have some new scans taken, Kevin. Are you up to it?'

'I'm fine,' he replied. 'How long will that take? I'd like to be out of here by this evening, if I can. I'm not enjoying this one little bit.'

'I can't tie you down,' the doctor conceded. I'll help you out best I can, Kevin, but let's get all of the results in first, okay? Let me get this done and I'll come back to you with the results, post haste. Promise me you'll wait around until then, will you? Do me that favour and I'll have you out of here, asap. Deal?'

~

It was the following morning before Kevin was discharged, but at least he felt fully rested and keen to get back to work. Laura insisted on coming to fetch him, arriving at the hospital's front entrance at almost nine o'clock, finding him standing with a cool drink in his hand and a broad smile plastered across his face.

She hadn't intended showing anything much in the way of emotion, but as the taxi pulled up at the curb she found herself rushing to climb out of the back seat, and before she knew it she had covered the intervening distance and was warmly embraced in his arms. With tears streaming down her cheeks, she asked. 'Is everything alright?'

Kevin was surprised at his own upsurge of emotion, holding her close. 'Everything is fine, baby,' he reassured. 'Headaches come and go. Really, there's nothing to worry about. Everything us just fine.'

Many scheduled media appearances were undertaken during the course of the following six months. The television interviews arranged by the sheik, when they took place, were highly stylized, concise, intensely formulated and informative, with Wasp Media Company paying great attention to the study of audience demographics and popular responses, continuing always to fine tune the broadcast message while targeting specific sections of the community, particularly those most resistant to the proposed new order. At the end of this period the study revealed two clearly defined and opposing camps, with very little grey area in between. People were either adamantly for or against. The polled population groups were rarely indecisive. Statistics were revealing the older generations, predictably, being the group most opposed to so radical a change to the so long established status quo.

Sheik Abudi had always been confident of a later, moderating swing; an appreciable decline in numbers of those opposed, and his prediction soon proved to be accurate. The latter middle aged to elderly population were coming around to the opinion that the world belonged to the young, and if this was the way they wanted their world to go, what right did they have to oppose?

The longer the campaign ran, the more accustomed people became to the idea, and therefore less resistant to the notion. *'A war of attrition,'* it was termed within the ranks of the media company employed by Hakim. Change, after all, was the way of all things, and the longer the idea stayed on the agenda within the public realm, endlessly promoted as any product would be by the giants of advertising, the more people came to be accepting of the idea; perhaps as much tiring of continuing a sustained opposition to the new wave of thought and opinion as they were becoming converted by the relentlessness of the campaign in favour of the proposition. The science of human psychology was employed to maximum effect, and utilized by those who fiercely believed in what they were doing. They were designing a better world—*a perfect world*—a world where want was to become obsolete and a thing of the past. Kevin's shining vision spread across the globe, gaining momentum as it went, giving everybody, from the well educated, affluent populace to those for whom a dream of plenty would, at any other time, have been deemed as being nothing more than pure delusion.

The dream of a prosperous, egalitarian, world community seized the human imagination. In turn it sparked the new conversation, one regarding the collective consciousness—the *Zeitgeist* of the human population—and as ever more time went by, almost the entire world seemed fueled by the great vision of the future: The perfect society with everyone pulling together in the one direction, perfecting human existence on Earth, making plans for the colonization of space, seeking to surpass all previous concepts for the future with idealized, inspired and exciting discussions fast becoming commonplace, reaching new and dizzying heights of euphoria until nothing any longer seemed beyond the reach of humankind or the realm of possibility.

CHAPTER 16

November found the four of them holed up in the Pyrmont Tenement Building, Chicago. A north wind blasted the city straight off of Lake Michigan, with snow and ice building up everywhere. The roads and freeways had become choked with stranded motorists caught out by the speed of an approaching storm. Power supply had already gone down in many areas north of the city, with the national guard having been enlisted in readiness to assist distressed inhabitants in outlying suburbs should survival become an issue.

The Pyrmont was a ten story brownstone tenement, made available through one of the sheik's business connections, along with two security guards who would make themselves inconspicuous for the duration of their stay. The converted mansion, for Laura, was of a charming old architectural that she much loved and had always wanted to see first hand. It was also the lodgings for elderly, independent family members living on old money; well established families of an earlier generation and with professional backgrounds such as lawyers, bankers and important city officials. More modern accommodation would have been made available to the foursome had time permitted, but a cancelled speaking engagement came with almost no warning and the offer of what immediately had been considered a pleasant diversion was hastily added to the itinerary for the opportunity to visit the famous city and to take some much needed time off. All agreed that Chicago be added as a port of call, but no one had expected the terrific weather and a city besieged by an early winter storm.

Their accommodation encompassed the fifth level. The interior was nothing short of lavish and well appointed, with the option of wood burning fireplaces if ever the power supply was to fail, which looked very likely in present circumstances. With all the modern conveniences installed, and including a well stocked larder, arranged in preparation for their arrival, they were all ecstatic to at last reach the destination after a hellish commute through the frozen and windswept city from O'Hare International Airport.

The resident caretaker, a cheerful, rotund and ruddy faced man of Jewish extraction named Abraham, led them upstairs to the fifth storey premises and relinquished the key. He informed them that his wife, Alia, had prepared nourishment in welcome as well as for their convenience at the end of their long journey, which would be found atop the kitchen stove, whereupon he bade them adieu, leaving the group to settle in and recover from the long journey which had originated in Belgrade, Serbia, some forty eight hours prior.

The girls were over the moon with the new surroundings as they explored, room to room, taking it all in. The men, meanwhile, adjourned to the parlour at the front of the house, where plushly upholstered armchairs and couches provided exactly the atmosphere required in order to stretch out and relax quietly for a time.

'I'm bushed,' Jerry Bishop pronounced wearily, dropping his travel bag beside an arm chair and letting himself fall into it.

Kevin did likewise, positioning a footstool on which to rest his legs. 'Not bad,' he commented, as he twisted around, surveying the room. 'So this is how the rich people live?'

'Apparently.' Jerry noticed the large oil painting hanging on the wall beside him, depicting an English foxhunt. He pointed to it. 'Not exactly what one might expect to discover in a chic Chicago tenement.'

'An English connection. The aristocracy, possibly.' Kevin imagined. 'Who knows, but I like it here. It has a nice, restful atmosphere. I'm just glad to have found time to unwind for a bit. I gotta tell you, buddy, I'm absolutely pooped.'

In a moment the girls entered to find both men dozing peacefully. Christine suggested they go to the kitchen and leave the guys to rest.

'I'm quite famished,' she declared. 'I wonder what Alia prepared for us? It was so thoughtful of her, wasn't it? I hope to get the opportunity to thank her personally.'

In the kitchen Laura lifted the lid of the large cast iron pot atop the stove to investigate. 'It smells exquisite,' she intoned blissfully. 'It's called cholent.'

'What's that when it's at home?'

'Stew. A traditional Jewish stew. Are you having some?' The girls sat at the kitchen table, tucking in to the stew, leaving Kevin and Jerry to catnap for as long as they wished to, pleased to have some girl time.

'If I'm not mistaken,' Christine began, 'resistance appears to be decreasing. That Enlightenment League that Abudi orchestrated online. I looked at the membership the other day. Two point eight billion. Not too shabby.'

Laura got up to attend to the boiling kettle, setting about making the hot drinks. 'We've achieved phenomenal growth in recent months. It's been amazing.'

'And how many of them are industrialists, do you suppose?' Christine asked, arching an eyebrow.

'I know. That's where we will always fall down. Especially with the multinationals. It's causing terrible unrest. All the protesting, not to mention the violence. It's causing Kevin terrible anxiety.'

'How is he holding up?'

Laura brought the teapot to the table and began pouring. 'You can see that for yourself. Does he look well to you?'

'Tired,' Christine replied, 'but we're all that. Has he mentioned anything?'

'Yeah, right,' she responded ironically, but then took on a more serious demeanour. 'I'm worried about him, Chris.'

It was Christine's turn to employ irony. 'What, more than usual? When are you not?'

Laura put down her fork, pushed the emptied bowl aside. 'No, I mean, *really* worried.'

Christine could tell when her friend was hurting, and this was one of those times. Laura burst quietly into tears, covering her face with her hands and then angrily wiping at the tears which had begun streaming down her cheeks.

'Damn it,' she cursed, angry to have allowed emotion to betray her. 'I don't know why I'm so upset. If he wants to work himself into the ground, he can go right ahead. Why should I care?'

To this Christine responded with a knowing smile, and reached across the table to take Laura's hand in her own. 'Who do you think you're fooling, girl? You're stuck on the guy. Of course you care. It's how it works, dear. Have you tried getting him to slow down? Personally,

I think he has done as much as can be done. This whole show has long since reached critical mass and will continue under the force of its own momentum.'

'I've said as much to him, Chris. He's obsessed. I don't think he knows how let go, and I'm afraid that if he keeps going the way he is, he could well come to harm. We've already seen evidence of that. This next rally in Washington DC. There's going to be maybe a million people. A million, can you imagine? How do they guarantee his safety in front of a crowd that size, in *this* country, when the issue has become so divisive? I deal with dozens of death threats every day, already.'

'I'm not surprised to hear that. Does he know?'

Laura shook her head. 'Doesn't want to, but he must realize. And what good would it do anyway? Do you think he would take any notice of threats?'

'No I don't,' Christine answered soberly, 'but what more does he think he can do? The whole thing has only to run its course now, and it will if I'm any judge. If it was his intention to change the world, or at least to change the way people think, I say he's already succeeded.'

'Even Abudi agrees with you,' Laura acknowledged. 'The money that man has made from investing in Kevin's dream. I don't understand where it's going anymore. Do you? Why are we even still doing this?'

Christine studied Laura closely, noticing the way she chewed her bottom lip, as if contemplating something even more worrisome to her. To her friend's close scrutiny she timidly shied away to avoid eye contact.

Christine released her friend's hands to sit back in her chair, her expression now one of curiosity. 'I know that look,' she told Laura, suspicious now. 'I haven't seen it since the one time you cheated, handing in that copied homework assignment.'

'What on Earth are you talking about? Look? What look?' 'A secret. I'm sure of it.' Christine accused. 'What is it you're not telling me? And don't even think about denying it. I know you too damn well, girl. Come on. Spit it out.'

Laura affected innocence, but Christine only persisted with the look of certainty in her eyes, and finally, not because she couldn't keep up the subterfuge but because she realised there was no point to it, and that right now she very much needed her old friend and confidant.

She bit her bottom lip and took a sobering breath. 'I missed my period.'

Christine remained silent for a while, then responded: 'Missing a period isn't such a big deal, Laura. You know yourself, stress alone is a likely suspect.'

'I've missed two, actually,' she replied.

Christine nodded, thoughtful. 'One, two cycles. It does happen—' but sounding less convincing this time. 'It doesn't necessarily mean-'

'I'm pregnant,' Laura stated adamantly, and the words had escaped her lips at the precise moment Kevin entered the kitchen, looking as if he had just woken from his nap.

The statement halted him in his tracks so that Jerry, who had been following close behind, stumbled into the back of him. He stood dumbfounded, eyes widening as the full implication of the utterance forced itself through the sleep-dulled layers of his mind. When clarity at last struck, he glanced at everyone in the room, then back again to Laura.

'You're what?' —but she had already stood and was fast retreating through the door.

He remained standing, staring at Christine who was responding to his stupid expression by turning her hands palm up in helplessness. She shrugged, shook her head woefully. 'Well? Are you going to just stand there? Go after her you fool.'

Without wasting another second he turned on his heels and took off in pursuit.

Jerry was still stunned by what had just occurred, so she pointed to the large pot on the stove.

'Grab yourself a bowl of cholent,' she invited him. 'It's very good. And don't worry about those two. They'll work it out just fine.'

Kevin caught up with Laura before she was able to turn the lock on the bedroom door, and pushed it open, thrusting her backwards in the bargain.

She turned to move towards the back of the room, and realizing there was nowhere further to go, turned to confront him.

She opened her mouth as if to speak and found no words would come to her aid.

'Why didn't you say something?' he asked, approaching slowly, cautiously, but she did not know how to answer.

He wasn't entirely sure she wasn't about to run again, but as he reached her, now with arms outstretched to draw her to him, she leaned into his chest and began to sob.

'*Shoosh* now,' he soothed. 'Why would you not tell me? Were you afraid of my reaction? We're gong to be parents. That's so wonderful. I couldn't be happier. Aren't you happy?'

He leaned her away from himself, enough so that he could gage her response.

'Yes,' she nodded, now wiping the tears away. 'But are you sure? Are you *really* sure you are? I've been so afraid that you wouldn't want this. You're so immersed in everything, I didn't think you would welcome the news at all. I didn't know what would happen.'

He laughed aloud as he embraced her afresh. 'I couldn't be more pleased. I can't believe it. I really can't. This is wonderful news. *Wonderful!*

'Come and sit down,' he prompted, guiding her to sit at the edge of the bed, himself beside her. 'I'm not sure I entirely understand your reluctance to tell me. Do you not want. . . ?'

Laura turned to face him, an earnest expression evident. 'You never even have time enough for *me*, Kevin. Are you ready for this? Being a father is a big deal. I don't think you realise just how committed you need to be.'

It was a valid point and he was forced to think hard before replying. 'I won't disagree with you on that score, Laura. I suppose I'm not an obvious candidate for being a father. I am going to have to reassess. . . *change* my priorities.'

'But *can* you?' she responded with gravity. 'When the reality of this sinks in? I'm worried that you won't be so enthusiastic. If you were to change your mind, what then?'

Now he understood. What if he remained on his current trajectory? There would be little chance of this working out. What if he got cold feet and rejected the normal course of action? It would change everything.

He nodded. 'I get it,' he told her, and took her hand, adopting a sober appearance. 'There was a time in my life I thought something as good as this could never happen. Not to me. I had accepted that, long ago.

'I'm a fool, but not a *damn fool*,' he told her, raising a smile. 'Let me start winding things down, and delegating, so that I can climb out from under all this. By the time the baby is due, I promise you I'll be in a position to walk away. Is that okay with you?'

'You will be able to do that?'

'Sure. Why not? I really can't keep this up for very much longer anyway. I'm so tired of it all, if truth be known.' About to mention something else, he baulked at the last moment.

'What?' she asked.

'Nothing. Nothing at all. Are you okay with giving me the time needed to get out? We should get married,' he blurted out, and realising then what he had just said, allowed a look of uncertainty to darken his countenance.

Laura looked at him closely. 'You don't really mean that. I can tell.'

Her disappointment registered heavily on him. He knew he had made a terrible mistake. 'I'm sorry, hon. That hesitation you just saw, I realised as I was saying it, as far as proposals go it was a pretty poor one, and not anywhere near as good as you deserve. I do know how distracted I've been, and for how long. I'm sorry for that, and I know this has all been little more than hard work for you. Now, suddenly. . . I just realised how much better you deserve. This pregnancy has woken me up with quite a jolt. I feel terrible about how preoccupied I've been. It's time for a change. A big change, and if you would do my the enormous honour of becoming my wife, I'll be only too happy to make amends for my inattentiveness. How about it? Would you marry a bum like me?'

CHAPTER 17

Laura and Kevin decided that the New York appearance would be his final engagement, promptly advising Abudi of the decision. His reaction over the telephone was difficult to gage, but he did insist on coming to Chicago to meet with them two days before their departure for New York.

During the morning of the day of the sheik's arrival, the security team which had been stealthily keeping the group safe from further intimidation made themselves visible while informing them of the planned procedure for Abudi's arrival.

At three in the afternoon a pair security guards positioned themselves near the building's main entrance. Moments later the sheik's limousine arrived at the curb, whereupon two heavy set men alighted, one attending to the sheik's disembarkation, while the other signaled for the pair at the main entrance to come forward and receive instructions.

Christine had been standing at a window, overlooking the street as the limousine pulled up, and stood watching in amusement.

'Hey, guys! Come and get a load of this.'

Laura joined her at the window while the men remained seated, and watched as Abudi appeared from the vehicle, dressed in his usual manner, wearing the traditional red and white checkered head-wear with the flowing white cotton *thawb*.

'I have to admit it,' Christine commented. 'The man has style. Quite the dasher. If we're really going to throw it in, I just might make myself available,' she said, laughing mischievously. 'I'm not getting any younger.'

Laura gave her a playful bump as she stood alongside, watching their approach. 'I'll ask Kevin to put in a good word for you, shall I?' She turned to Kevin. 'You could do that, couldn't you, dear? It's the least we can do.'

'Sure,' he grinned. 'I'll see what I can do. Of course, it would make you wife number six. That's perfectly okay with you, is it Christine?'

'Oh dear. I forgot all about that. Five wives you say? I'll have to give it some thought. Maybe it would be an advantage, being number six, do you think? The other girls can be responsible for keeping a smile on his face while I go shopping.'

In short time they were welcoming Abudi across the threshold, while his escorts were instructed to take up sentry positions in the passageway.

'*Ahlan wa sahlan,*' Kevin welcomed, remembering the Arabic greeting.

'*Allah maeak,* Kevin, and to you all,' Abudi replied. 'Are you well?'

'Yes, very well thank-you, Hakim.'

The sheik walked straight up to Laura to take her hand, pressed his lips to her fingers and smiled serenely. 'You will make a most beautiful bride,' he told her, and turned to Kevin.

'You are a fine judge of womanhood, my friend' and he laughed good naturedly. 'Congratulations to you both. May Allah smile upon you, and bless you with many healthy children.'

Blushing a little, Laura reintroduced their friends and invited the sheik make himself comfortable, offering a nearby armchair.

'What are you doing here in the US, Hakim?' she asked. 'Our emancipation of mankind from the financial burden is presently balanced on a knife's edge,' Abudi answered her.

He then regarded Kevin, saying, 'We require a final push. You may be aware that the world council has been elected and assembled. It is to be convened next week, and it also is in New York City. If we are able to convince these people of the value of our world functioning without a monetary foundation, we will then be at the tipping point, Kevin. And even if they see the conversion as no more than a means of quelling the global unrest, it will be a tremendous step forward.'

Kevin looked appalled by the notion. 'But that is a travesty. It's no more than a compromise, in other words. What the hell, Hakim? To adopt this reform in the light of being considered anything less than our deliverance from servility, which is exactly what it is. *Travesty.* It almost defeats the whole purpose. Do you not see that?'

Abudi shrugged. 'I understand, my friend, but we have struggled so long and hard to arrive at our present juncture. Does it really matter so much?'

Kevin was not entirely convinced, but was forced to reconsider. 'Maybe not,' he grumbled, less than pleased. 'Not in the long run, but for me it taints the essence of the act. If only everyone were able grasp the beauty of the concept. It's *nobility*, for lack of a better word. It will be such a momentous event. Mankind finally stepping forward, untethered, into the future. But of course it has to be made into something tawdry. A compromise,' and he inflected the word with scorn. 'A means of avoiding further violence.'

'But the vote may decisively go our way, Kevin. You realize that it is centuries of tradition we are fighting here, and change never comes easy. It will still represent a momentous victory. A decision of great magnitude. Your revolutionary vision for the future is now so close to coming to fruition now.'

'Winged words, Hakim?' Kevin accused, wryly. 'Flattery. It's not much of a consolation. Pearls before swine,' he grumbled under his breath.

The sheik looked puzzled by the bitter remark, until memory served. 'Ah, yes—' and he quoted: *"Give not that which is holy unto the dogs, neither cast ye your pearls before swine, lest they trample them under their feet and turn again and rend you."*

'Impressive,' Kevin told him.

'What? That I have read your King James bible?'

'It's not *mine,* Hakim. No. . . the fact that you are able to accurately quote the passage. But, still, the King James is a useful tome.'

'I am blessed with a near perfect memory. For your information, I find the book to be an enlightening rendering. Also an important historical account, as is the holy Koran. They are not, as some would have us believe, mutually exclusive. After all, in the historical sense they are derived from the same epoch.'

Kevin merely nodded, resisting comment.

Laura found the perfect moment to intervene. 'Oh, you're not going to engage this guy in a religious discussion, Hakim. It isn't exactly a subject dear to his heart.'

'No?' Hakim was obviously surprised by the comment. Kevin answered for himself: 'Let's just say the subject matter has a tendency to upset my calm, and we'll leave it at that, shall we?'

Hakim nodded his understanding. 'Then let's you and I discuss matters of a different nature. Is there somewhere we can walk, my friend? I would like to take a stroll while we talk of things at greater length. I have been too long sitting, and despite the unnatural weather, a stroll would be beneficial.'

The request caught everyone off-guard, but no one commented. Jerry mentioned that there was a sizeable community park just around the corner.

'Sounds perfect,' Kevin acceded, rising. 'Shall we then?' Suitably warm clothing had to be pulled on to fend off the cold.

Orders were issued to bodyguards who hustled in formulating a strategy for the unscheduled walk in the park.

Exiting the building, the sheik and Kevin were escorted along the footpath, across the street and up to the park entrance, from there to be followed at a safe, discreet distance as they ambled along the jogging track which circled the inner perimeter.

'Chilly,' Kevin commented needlessly, thrusting his hands deep into his overcoat pockets. 'What was so important that you had to drag us both out here?'

'Privacy,' Hakim replied. 'There is a matter of some urgency we must speak of, and I think I guess right to say that it is a subject you have kept entirely private. Not even your beautiful intended wife is aware of your health problem, is she?'

Kevin pulled up mid stride, his face darkening despite some redness brought on by the cold air.

'I'm sorry,' said Hakim, holding his gaze. 'I never leave to chance anything which may prove troublesome when forming important alliances. Inquiring after a colleague's health is one thing I do when forming a long term arrangement, such as we have. Such a thing is of primary importance'

'Really,' Kevin responded, the sheik still holding his gaze, and he sighed in acceptance of the fact. 'Okay, go on.'

'I arranged a comprehensive medical report and saw that you were once hospitalized with a serious head injury. Your attending physician was a Dr. Kelly. I learned that he insisted on extra scans being taken before he released you. You never saw this doctor again. Why not?'

'I was fine. Some desperadoes lured me into a trap and mugged me while I was out jogging one afternoon. I was knocked about a bit, but I was fine.'

'You have not seen any doctor in all this time?'

It appeared that the sheik was on to him, and he greatly resented that fact. He had been delving into things Kevin considered most private. How much did he know? Hakim's timing with this was altogether suspicious.

'What do you think you know?' Kevin asked.

'Nothing. I am not sure what you are saying. The doctor was very much relieved that I had contacted him, that's all. He had tried several times to locate you, without success. You failed to keep in touch after leaving his care.'

'You know yourself how busy I've been since then. I've been on the road all this time, but, go on.'

'I must tell you he was concerned about the results of the tests he had run. There was some danger of complications arising from your injuries and he wanted to see you again as soon as could be arranged. I assured him I would pass on this message.'

'And that's the reason for your visit?'

'Of course. It seemed important. I did not want to concern your betrothed. This is a delicate matter. It's why I have sought privacy to convey the doctor's wishes. And I, of course, am concerned. So now I have done as I promised and you will call your doctor. Yes?'

Kevin failed to respond, turning from the sheik to look over the surrounding green expanse.

'What troubles you? Hakim asked, sensing that something was awry. He waited, sensing Kevin's need for thought.

'Okay, Hakim,' he said after a moment's silence. 'I have been having a hell of a time trying to decide what I should do. I'm in a bit of a bind.'

'Tell me. Who better than me to assist you? What burden's you, my brother? Come, let us continue to walk before we freeze and are stuck here for eternity.'

The two men resumed walking the track while Kevin gathered his thoughts, wondering how to relate to Hakim what only he knew. He had hoped to have more time in which to decide a course of action, without causing distress, especially to Laura, but to the others as well. Discussing with anyone something like what he had to tell did not come easy, and finding a starting point was presenting a problem.

After having walked some distance in silence he realised he just had to spit it out, and go from there.

'It seems that the kick in the head I received from the attack knocked a screw loose,' he began uncomfortably.

Hakim laughed at this. 'How do you mean?' 'Do you know what a sarcoma is, Hakim?'

Hakim would have stopped walking but for Kevin coaxing him onward. 'I would not want to say what I think it is.'

'Then you do have an idea,' Kevin replied. 'A tumour. One which started to form between the cellular walls of my brain tissue after being concussed.

'I've been getting the occasional headache. Not often, but frequently enough to be a nuisance. I really didn't think much of it and figured it was the pressure of living like this. I finally found out after being hospitalised with a real head-banger the other night. I haven't told Laura.'

'What? You have to. You know you must,' Hakim rebuked. 'How do I do that? God, this could not have come at a worse time. I have the New York appearance coming up.'

'Forget the New York appearance, Kevin. Your well being is more important.'

'A couple of days isn't going to make a difference, Hakim. No difference at all.'

'And Laura?'

'That's my biggest concern. It's going to tear her up. I have no idea what to do about her. She's so happy right now. How can I do this to her?'

Hakim grabbed Kevin by the arm to halt him. 'Stop a moment.' He looked Kevin square in the eye. 'You know what must be done. Why do you pretend there is a choice?'

Kevin looked very uncomfortable, being forced to face the truth of it. 'I will wait until after New York. It's only a couple of days away. I will attend to the problem when our list of engagements is cleared. New York is my last. After that, I'm done, Hakim.'

'All right then. We will get you through this, my friend. You have done enough. Much more than enough. I will look after everything. Come on now. Everything will be alright.'

'If you say so,' Kevin replied without humour. 'So do you think we can get out of this weather now? I can't feel my legs.' The two of them retraced the route they had travelled, this time without a word being spoken. The limousine had returned to the exact spot where it had delivered the sheik on arrival, perfectly timed as they approached the building. Before departure the sheik gave Kevin a brotherly hug and wished him well.

'I'll see you again, soon,' Kevin told Hakim. 'At the New York rally in two days time.'

'Take good care of yourself,' Hakim farewelled through the window of the limousine. 'Make the call to your doctor, Kevin. I promised Dr Kelly that you would do so,' and with that, the car pulled away from the curb.

He watched the limousine until it disappeared around a corner at the end of the street, then looked up at the apartment where the others waited. He would have to concoct a story to explain why Hakim had coaxed him out of the apartment, but that could be handled at a later juncture. For the moment, he was not in the least inclined to return to the apartment, and all the waiting questions. What he needed was some time alone, to think things through, and he remembered a street café only a short walk from where he presently stood.

CHAPTER 18

The open air gathering in Central Park, New York, would likely be the prelude to the new world financial order. The task before the newly appointed World Council was to assess the latest formulated blueprint of the initiative, revise it if necessary, and to vote on it, proceeding as it stands or going through another round of fine tuning before finally adopting the plan. In preparation for the inauguration of the momentous event, a three stage program of careful implementation had been formulated, containing adequate measures of graduated control which were woven within the fabric of the program, allowing for, it was hoped, the full and seamless transition to the universally adopted *Human Investment Initiative.*

Kevin, Laura, Christine and Jerry arrived at the New York Pennington Hotel at around ten o'clock on the morning of the impending Central Park gathering, which was scheduled to start at eight o'clock that evening. The priority was to catch up on lost sleep, eat a meal and spend the remainder of the day as each of them wished. A quiet, relaxing day. This time, at least, they had been able to secure two rooms, allowing Laura and Kevin the privacy they had lately been deprived of, but because the day represented the culmination of so long and arduous a campaign for them all, a state of relaxation was not the easiest condition to be achieved.

Kevin was terribly at odds with himself, unable to resolve the ongoing quandary. He could see only that to tell Laura of the tumour residing in his scull was a cruel option, especially since she had been displaying so much relief to be nearing the end of the long campaign. The flip side of the coin was that to tell Laura was the right, the obvious, and when all was said and done, the only thing to do, and although he told himself this repeatedly, he could not find it in his heart to break the news to her. He knew only too well what misery the revelation would cause her. At the moment, waiting until after the big night seemed the more prudent option. With a little ordinary luck an appropriate moment might present itself meantime. It was a difficult decision and it tormented relentlessly, testing his courage and causing such distraction that he could not be entirely sure she hadn't already realised something was up.

The quiet downtime they had planned for the early part of the day had been interrupted by a number of phone calls coming in from sections of the media, all wanting comment from Kevin about how he was feeling and to congratulate him on what appeared to be certain, impending victory. There were, of course, those who were not so jubilant, who insisted on expressing their sense of betrayal after a lifetime of work, building wealth in sectors of industry where they had defeated competitors by wresting powerful market influence from their control. He well understood their position. To such people as this the transition away from a monetary based world rendered their lifetime of work redundant. The accumulation of wealth and influence was, for them, the most effective way they could gage whether or not their lives were a success.

He lifted the receiver to yet another call: 'One moment,' he uttered to the caller. Laura had caught his attention by waving from across the room.

'I'm going downstairs and tell them to block these calls. I've drawn up a list of names who we will accept calls from. This is too much.'

Kevin looked thoughtful for a moment before replying. 'In all fairness, I think these people have a right to comment. In a couple of days the decision will have been made for them.'

'Allow me to make this decision for you,' she replied, defiant. 'If you don't get some rest. . . You should see yourself. You're almost dead on your feet,' she told him, angry now. 'You really haven not been looking after yourself well enough and I'm not allowing this continue any longer. I'm going down stairs right now and tell them to refuse calls from anyone we don't know.'

He could only smile in admiration, and with great affection he watched her depart to do just that. He much enjoyed the way she had come to dote over him, and he knew, as was usual, she was right. There was no force on Earth could stop Laura acting in his best interest. Especially when her mind was made up. He turned his attention back to the caller.

'I'm sorry for the interruption,' he said. 'How can I help you?' 'Am I speaking with Kevin McKinney, the author of the Human Investment Initiative?' asked a calm and measured male voice. 'You are. And you are?'

'My name is of no importance, Mr McKinney. Let us just say that I represent one of millions whose lives are to be forever ruined if this insanity is permitted.'

Knowing that this could take some time, Kevin stretched out the coiled receiver cord in moving to sit on a stool at the breakfast bar.

'I'm sorry to hear you say that. I really am. You don't see the value in ridding ourselves of the most common and needless burden in life?'

'That is fanciful, irrational tripe. Financial reward, and all that comes with it, is simply the truest measure and most fitting recompense for hard work and dedication that there is,' the caller replied angrily. 'It appears that you want every lazy, good-for-nothing, sycophant to benefit from the hard work the rest of us put in every day of our lives?

'I have worked hard, every day of my life, to raise myself up from almost nothing, and in one fell swoop you seek to take that away from me? I taught my children the value of education, of hard work and perseverance. You are attempting to make everything in life available simply for the asking, to any worthless scumbag who wouldn't know the meaning of hard work, or sacrifice, or diligence. In forty years I have built up a global company and earned the respect of my peers. I have damned well worked hard for it and nobody is going to take my life's work away from me, you hear me? Nobody.'

'I'm sorry you see it that way.' He sighed, realising that to calm this guy down was going to be a tall order.

'Look, he said wearily, 'have you taken the time to think it through properly? You're obviously an intelligent man. A global company, you say? That is some achievement.'

'Do not patronize me.' the caller snapped angrily. 'I am not calling to engage you in debate. I am calling to tell you this. There will be no victory. Not for you. I am telling you that I, and like minded people, all similarly self-made people with influence and with a very long reach. . . We will put a stop to this odious plot, and most certainly to you. Did you think you were untouchable?'

'Untouchable?' Kevin repeated, failing to understand the meaning. 'What do you mean?'

'You are receiving this one warning as a final chance to come to your senses. If you get up on that stage tonight and do not reveal the truth, you will be carried off. To make it perfectly clear, I repeat: Stand on that stage tonight without disavowing this ridiculous lunacy, and you will pay with your life. We will not allow this travesty to continue a moment longer. You have been warned, Mr McKinney.'

The caller hung up, leaving Kevin feeling unusually shaken. He had received any number of threatening calls from irate critics much like this. Such calls were to be expected, he had always argued. This one though? This was somehow different, if only by the way it had caused a knot to tighten in his stomach.

Before he could dwell any longer on the incident, Laura entered the room, smiling and with a look of triumph on her face. One look at Kevin and the look vanished.

'What's wrong?'

He was sitting with the telephone receiver held away from his face. Knowing that any lie, however well executed, would be detected at once, he told her, 'Another crank call.'

'Oh? Well I handed them the list. You won't be getting any more.'

She went to the refrigerator, opened the door to retrieve a can of soft drink. 'What was it this time, another conspiracy theorist? Are you an anarchist? Maybe the Antichrist?' She laughed, popped the seal of the can and began pouring into a tumbler.

When he failed to join in the banter she quenched her thirst while making obvious her concern as she studied his odd expression.

He had played it all wrong, he realised immediately. He should not have told her his discomfiture was due to another crank call. She had lately become too expert at reading his every nuance. It occurred to him that *now* might be a perfect time to raise the topic he had been avoiding for so long.

'Would you grab me one of those? There's something I've been wanting to discuss, and now that we at last have the privacy of our own room?'

'Sure,' she replied. 'Here, have this one. I'll grab another.' She joined him at the bench to sit opposite. 'Now then, what is it requires our discussing it in private?'

He drank from the can, put it down and sought to engage her eyes. 'You remember back when I was mugged?'

'Ha, how could I forget? It was because of that we met.'

He smiled. 'Yeah, it was, wasn't it. I had a bunch of scans and things taken while I was in hospital afterwards. I was so keen to get out of that place, I never did remain long enough to get a look at all the results. The doctor talked me into staying long enough to have the extra examinations. He promised me I would be fine to leave after they were done. So, of course I agreed.'

'Could you make this a longer story?' she asked sarcastically. 'I never went back.' he told her, getting to the point. I didn't even bother to contact him for the results. I figured everything would be fine.'

Laura regarded him with greater concern now. 'And?' she prompted, refraining from allowing her alarm to get the better of her.

'Everything was entirely fine, as it turns out. Don't go getting excited. I'm fine, it's just. . .'

'It's just what?'

This was so much more difficult than he had imagined, despite the fact that he had not expected it to be at all easy. The words would not pass his lips.

Laura reached over to take his hands in hers. 'Go on, you've come this far. I can take it, whatever you have to tell me. I promise.'

'The results raised a possible concern.' He paused, expecting a response, but she remained perfectly impassive. 'A swelling. The doctor wanted to look closer at it, but we were already on the road by then. And remember the other night when I was admitted? They, um. . . discovered something.'

'What kind of *something*?' she urged, trying to keep her voice even.

'It's called a sarcoma. It started with the whack in the head I received, I suppose. At first it was little more than damaged tissue. A bruise and maybe a bit of swelling. Since then it has gradually been getting larger, and–'

'The reason for your headaches,' she interrupted.

He nodded. 'There's no need to worry. We'll get it sorted. In just two more days there's nothing to keep us from going home. I'll get whatever treatment the moment we finish what we started.'

'What did the doctors say when you went in with the migraine?' He shrugged. 'To go back to my first doctor. Doctor Kelly. They gave me some tablets.' He pushed a hand into his pocket, withdrew it grasping the small container. 'Four times a day, to slow it down.'

'And you thought you would keep this to yourself?' she asked, maintaining the even tone.

He was about to respond to that when she raised a restraining hand. 'I'm sorry. I didn't mean to say that. I understand why you didn't say anything to me.' But then her emotions gained the upper hand.

'You fool. Did you really think this was something to hide from your wife to be?'

'I was hoping to find the right time,' he responded.

'What makes you think there's ever a right time?'

This he could not answer. 'I know. I'm sorry. Just. . . I didn't want to worry you.'

She sat, staring at him for a long time, at a loss to know how to respond.

'You're not to worry about this, Laura.' he told her.

'You don't think it's serious then?' she replied.

The question was a trap and he knew it. To reply *No*, he would be cut down in an instant. Replying *Yes* would leave him contradicted and looking foolish.

'You're angry?' he asked.

For a moment she remained silent, attempting to take stock of herself. 'It's a shock. I don't know how I feel, but in light of this, it provides an answer to a lot of things which have been worrying me for some time now. It's almost a relief to have you tell me this. Frightening too. I've been worried for such a long time.'

Her reply stunned him. 'Really? Why?' 'Your behaviour.'

He could only remain silent, unable to fathom what was meant by that.

'When we first met,' she began cautiously, 'you were nothing like the person sitting here in front of me today. There has been such a transformation. You don't see it?'

'You're right,' he said, after a moment's contemplation. 'You think. . . ?'

'Don't you?' she said, regarding him earnestly. It seems to make perfect sense, don't you think?'

The notion raced through his being as if he were gripped by icy fingers, his mind repulsed by the implication.

'God,' he expressed, shaken. 'Is it possible?' She didn't respond, only sat watching him.

As he thought it over he began to nod his head, recognizing all the red flags as he reviewed the past.

'I never used to be the sort to give a damn about the wider world. Especially social order. Frankly, I could not have given a damn about the world beyond my front door. And to tell you the truth, I think I did start to wonder at my sudden ability to grasp complexities I never used to be able to understand. The tumour, do you think? His face reflected deep consternation. 'Has one bump on the head changed me so much?'

Laura's grip tightened about his hand. 'It sound crazy, I know. I guess it is possible,' she said. 'You are so far removed from that laconic, unconcerned-about-everything person I met on that summer afternoon. Seeing is believing,' she told him.

She glanced at her wristwatch, noting the time. 'Come on. Let's lay down for a nap while we can. I know you've not been sleeping well, and tonight is going to be especially demanding on you. Come to bed and we'll work this out later, after we've rested.'

'How am I supposed to rest? I have a tumour in my head that has totally altered who I am and you want to go and lie down? Don't you see what has happened. . . what I've done? God almighty, I've changed the world. . . the way it functions. In just a few hours the world council will be voting to do away with the thousands of years of depending on monetary structure, and superseding it with nothing more than faith in humanity's ability to embrace the common good. *Ha!* What the hell have I done? And I'm not even *me!* I'm a tumour affected organism gone mad.'

Laura watched as Kevin's self-belief began to crumble. His agitation increased rapidly as he looked fearfully about, seemingly unable to find any anchor as reality receded.

Laura herself became alarmed, but realised she had to convey an aura of calm.

'Kevin,' she said sharply. 'Kevin, get a grip on yourself. Everything is alright. Nothing has changed.'

He fought to calm himself, taking long, measured breaths and wrapping his arms about his torso. In a moment he appeared to be regaining composure.

'Are you okay?'

'Panic attack,' he expressed, unnerved and embarrassed. 'God, that was awful. I've never experienced anything like it before.'

'Come on.' Laura stood, offering her hand to Kevin. 'You're understandably overwrought, and you're exhausted. If you can't sleep you can at least lie down and rest. I've got some temazepam in my purse. Take a couple. We need to discuss what to do about all this.'

Kevin allowed himself to be guided to the bed. Laura dispensed two temazepam tablets which he swallowed with milk before they both lay on the bed to relax quietly.

'I don't believe how weird that felt,' he told her in a subdued voice. 'I've not ever been so frightened before. And disorientated. It was like, I don't know. . . suddenly being two people, and I was out–of–body, and seeing myself from like somewhere else. Disembodied and outside myself and I couldn't breathe.'

'It must have been awful,' she replied. 'A classic panic attack. They're nasty,'she sympathized. 'You'll be fine after a nap. Just rest now, darling.'

He took a large breath, exhaled with a long, drawn out sigh.'It's difficult to believe when viewed from where we are today. Everything that has transpired since we began. It's been such a crazy ride. So crazy.'

A minute passed. 'Man or tumour?' he said softly to himself.

'I cannot reconcile it. The effect. . . must have had on me. . . over time. So driven. Me or the tumour? Kevin the tumour,' he chuckled, and at last remained silent, his breathing beginning to find rhythm as several more minutes passed by.

'So crazy,' he said once more, and when Laura was sure he had at last dozed off, she gently and as carefully as she could manage, slid off of the bed, leaving him to sleep for as long as time would permit.

Trusting that he would be alright, she went next door where she found Christine and Jerry sitting at a small table outside on the balcony.

She informed them of Kevin's panic attack, withholding anything to do with the tumour. Telling them of it served no real purpose that she could see. In any case, it wasn't her decision. Kevin would tell them if he thought it necessary. As he had said, himself, the problem would be dealt with upon returning home in a few short days.

Christine ordered sandwiches and a pot of coffee from room service, which the trio consumed while sat in the warm, late morning sunshine which bathed New York city. From their lofty perch they identified the few iconic towers they recognised but had never before seen for themselves.

'Thank goodness we're nearing the end of this madness,' Jerry commented. 'It sounds like our boy is about done. We can be flying out of here tomorrow, and for myself, I couldn't be happier about that. Kevin's not the only one who is feeling knackered.' 'And me,' Christine agreed. 'I don't know why people go off, gallivanting around the planet, especially if they have perfectly good homes to go to.' She looked down to the crowded streets and out at the concrete towers. 'It's like a termite nest, isn't it? All these people living in each other's pockets? It would drive me crazy. I couldn't live here, could you?' she asked, turning to Laura.

'Sorry, what was that?' she replied distractedly.

'I was saying, I couldn't live in a big city like this, could you?' She shrugged. 'I suppose people get used to it.'

'Rat city,' Jerry put in. 'The crime rate. It's not hard to reason why. Can you imagine being down and out, trying to survive in a city like this? Smoke, noise, concrete, half starved and with nowhere to hang your hat. Not mentioning the swarm of humanity. Man, life can become very cheap very quickly under conditions like that.'

'And under the new order?' Christine asked.

'A whole new ball game, obviously.'

'I'm not so sure,' Christine mused. 'I wonder how it will affect a city like this one? Those at the bottom of the pecking order. One has to wonder how it will play out.'

'I can't see that things will change very rapidly for the destitute,' Jerry answered. 'It's still going to depend on job availability, but seeing as produce and services will no longer have a price attached, food and shelter should soon become attainable. That'll be a boon for the poor buggers.'

Christine took up the train of thought. 'It will, of course, depend on the availability of lodgings, although, with the problem of those primary concerns taken care of, the chance of a normal life is suddenly opened up to all and sundry. Education and training, and. . . *Ha*, I was going to say paid employment! Boy, this change is going to take some getting used to.'

'Yes,' Laura agreed, 'but what a marvellous change. No more poverty. Who could ever have imagined we would, or *could*, begin heading in the right direction after getting it so wrong for so long? With life's basics taken care of, things like education, training and employment *will* be accessible to anyone who wants it. It's extraordinary just to real-ise it's about to become a reality. And don't forget all those in need of rehabilitation from their addictions. Removing the price-tag from health care and medicines. Those things alone will make such a significant difference. The lives that will be salvaged!'

'It's mind-blowing, if you ask me,' Jerry commented. 'To tell you the truth, I never really took the time to identify all the ramifications. They're so far-reaching. It really is extraordinary.

From the absolute bottom level of the social strata, to the absolute top, it completely levels the playing field. It provides equal opportunity for us all, limited by nothing except the choices people make and what-ever god given talent one is born with. How can anyone object to such an unfettered world?'

'Don't open that can of worms, Jerry,' Christine told him. 'You're raising the subject of human beings, now. You ought to know better.'

'I should,' he replied, chuckling sardonically.

Christine brightened, asking: 'Do you suppose they'll erect a two hundred foot statue of Kevin, standing all regal and insightful looking in conjuring his great vision for the future?'

The suggestion made them all laugh, until Jerry suggested that it was, perhaps, likely. 'Why not?' he told them. 'Hell, they've built statues for racehorses, explorers, almost anything you care to mention. Why not for Kevin? He deserves it as much as anyone else who has ever been celebrated in concrete.'

The thought quietened the girls as they realised the suggestion was not so absurd after all.

'Why not indeed?' Christine seconded. 'Kevin the great. The saviour of mankind. Kevin the visionary?'

~

Laura awakened Kevin late in the afternoon. She would have allowed him to sleep on but for a telephone call from Hakim. The sheik had wanted to speak to Kevin, but she had convinced him to call back later, allowing Kevin to rest for as long as possible.

'Did he say what it was about.' Kevin asked, pushing himself up to sit with his back against the headboard.

'Transportation to the event tonight,' she answered. 'He says the icy weather the other day caused a bridge some structural concern. They closed it down for inspection before repairs commence. He says there's a huge turnout expected for tonight's gathering and the roads will be choked, making it terribly difficult for us to get to there. He is arranging for a helicopter to deliver us, if we want it. Do we want it?'

'That'll be fun. Where are we supposed to board this chopper, I wonder?'

'You can ask him when he calls back. How are you feeling?' 'Much better. Good, in fact.'

'Are you hungry? How about we call room service and have a meal sent up? We can have a bit of time to ourselves before the shindig commences. Christine and Jerry will be over at about seven.'

Kevin showered and shaved while the meal was being prepared; soup and a hotel hamburger with fries, which they ate while relaxing in front of the television.

'This is nice,' Laura commented, sitting up close beside him on the couch, watching an old black and white movie while working her way through the enormous burger.

'It sure is. Just think of it. In a couple more days we will be back home. We can get back to doing normal things like this again. Give me the boring old life, anytime. I have absolutely had my fill of dragging my arse around the planet, living in hotels.' Laura nodded in emphatic agreement, washed down a mouthful of burger and fries with a sip of milk. 'You can say that again. It's going to be heaven. I don't care if we never see the inside of a hotel again.'

'Airplanes too,' Kevin added. 'I'm beginning to develop back problems from those damn seats.'

'They're meant to be ergonomically designed or something,' she replied. 'You would think a seat you pay so much to sit in would at least *not* give you a sore backside.'

'Who's that guy?' he asked, pointing to the television screen. 'The guy behind the desk?'

'No, the old guy with the cane.'

'He's the crooked dealer of ancient antiquities.'

'I know that. I mean the actor. What's the actor's name who's playing the role?'

'Oh, *um*. . .That's, *um*. . . Sydney Greenstreet,' she recalled. Kevin's mobile began to chirp. 'Ah, that'll be Hakim,' he guessed, switching it to speaker. 'Hakim. Hello, how are you?'

'*Uhyi sadiqiun*,' Hakim greeted.

CHAPTER 19

The chartered helicopter landed close by, at the same park he and Hakim had previously taken their stroll. When the four of them had climbed aboard, Hakim briefed them on the use of the headsets, enabling easy conversation over the noise of the rotors while in transit.

'It's a fifteen minute flight, Hakim told them, 'but I thought you all might enjoy a short scenic flight around the city before we touch down in Central Park.'

'I would love it,' Christine replied with exuberance. She looked in turn at each of the others who had not been as quick to respond. 'Oh, come on, guys. How often do you get the chance?'

The motion was carried, and after Hakim had radioed for permission and gained clearance for a circuit over the city, the chopper lifted high into the air.

'I'll take you out around the harbour,' Hakim told them. 'It's quite a sight at nighttime.'

He took them around the harbour, giving them the tourist ride over the famous liberty statue, the bridges and across the city, pointing out and naming the boroughs as they went. After twenty minutes of flight they headed towards the park, and coming within a couple of miles of the venue it was clear that the gathering crowd was enormous.

Four towers had been erected on which spotlights, coloured lights and parabolic communication dishes were installed in facilitation of global television coverage. Many technical crews with their service vehicles and other ancillary teams gathered close behind the stage. The stage comprised a steel skeleton covered over with sheets of canvas, while from the framework vast arrays of projectors and atmospheric lights swiveled about in casting brilliant beams, prismatic colours and complex, projected images over the jubilant spectators and surrounds.

Holographic displays adorned the darkening sky above the milling hoard with images of the flags of all nations, cartoon characters, caricatures of well known international celebrities, world leaders and politicians. A starburst firework exploded high in the sky, casting a garish light over all, seeming to momentarily capture in still-frame the pandemonium at ground level as the helicopter began cautiously to descend toward one of several helicopter landing pads clearly identified by a large, white H.

Everyone except for Kevin and Hakim had disembarked when Hakim sought to gain Kevin's attention, telling him, 'Reach behind your seat and pull out the package you find there.'

He twisted around, probed the space blindly before locating a package, retrieved it after a bit of jostling around in the confined space. 'What have we here?'

'It's your outfit for tonight.'

He pulled a face, affecting mock outrage. 'You don't approve of what I'm wearing?'

'I had this especially made for you. Something befitting a man who has changed the way the world works. Tonight is a theatrical event. An occasion, and you will need to look the part. Why don't you open it?'

'And it's not even my birthday,' Kevin joked, pulling the lid from the box.

What he discovered within was a white cotton robe with a red belt to tie about the waist, along with a pair loose-fitting trousers, also of white cotton.

'It's called a *thoub*, and the pants are called *sirwal*,' Hakim informed him, looking pleased and wearing a wide smile. 'Exactly what is needed for the ceremony. There are rooms available beside the stage where you can change.'

'Are you two coming?' Christine was heard to call from outside. 'Let's get out of the parking lot and find something to drink.'

A V. I. P. lounge had been set up for important guests. Christine worked her way to the bar in order to purchase the drinks while Kevin went to try on the outfit Hakim had presented him with while the others searched for a vacant table.

A roar of applause erupted from the throng as a rock band was introduced, and soon park was alive with festivity, the added element of rock music delighting spectators and transforming the occasion into one of joyous revelry.

After fifteen minutes Kevin approached the table wearing the *thoub* and *sirwal*; wearing also a sheepish expression.

'My goodness! Laura exclaimed, drawing her friends' attention to the sight.

Kevin extended his arms, humorously performing a spin for them to inspect the new apparel. 'So what do you think? My new party dress.'

'What's with the costume?' Jerry asked, looking puzzled. 'Hakim brought it for me as part of tonight's theatre.' 'Very Lawrence of Arabia,' Laura commented. 'I like it.' 'So do I,' Christine agreed. 'Very sexy.'

Hakim looked pleased. 'I told you so. It gives flair. Perfect for the cameras, and exactly the look for the famous Kevin McKinney.'

Heads continued to nod approvingly as they regarded the new look.

'Did anyone buy me a drink? It's time I loosened up and got in the mood. This is some great party.'

With the ceremony part of the night's proceedings not scheduled until much later, the group were able to let their hair down and enjoy themselves. Laura was having a wonderful time. Not only was the entertainment and the festive atmosphere much to her liking, but by the conclusion of the night, the long road they had journeyed would be, at long last, at an end.

Jerry and Christine ventured off by themselves to mix with the crowd at the front of the stage. Hakim excused himself after a while, in order to catch up with business acquaintances whom he had caught sight of, and to talk with the organizers regarding the scheduled program of events, leaving Laura and Kevin at the table to talk between themselves.

'Some shindig,' Kevin observed, for some reason finding himself hard pressed to make conversation.

'Are you feeling alright?' Laura responded.

'Me? Yeah. Fine.'

She continued to study him as he scanned their surroundings. What she was looking for she wasn't quite sure; for signs of anything untoward? Anxiety or discomfort perhaps? Her vigil had become constant since learning the truth.

Kevin's gaze swept the area in search of any familiar faces, though in his periphery he was well aware of Laura's close interest in him.

Without turning to address her, he asked, 'Why are you watching me so intensely, dear?'

'Sorry,' she replied. 'I didn't realize I was.'

He turned to smile at her. 'I'm fine, really. Lighten up and enjoy yourself, why don't you? In twenty or thirty years time we'll be reminiscing over tonight, remembering our youth and getting all misty-eyed. Truthfully though? I'll be glad when this is over.' 'Really?' she replied, surprised, and then reaching across the table to lay her hand over his: 'This is your big night, you know? Tonight you will finally get the recognition you deserve as the architect of the new age. And I couldn't be more proud.'

'Nothing so grand, surely.' he replied. 'And I'm just as proud of you, wife,' he told her, patting her hand and smiling affectionately. 'I guess we've all earned a rest.'

He glanced at his watch. 'At least another hour. I hope they get started on time. I get the feeling this is going to be a long night.'

'I hope not. I'll be as glad as you to have this done and over with, but I'm glad you told me how you feel. I was worried about spoiling your big night.'

'We can get a taxicab out of here immediately after the ceremony, if we have to,' he suggested. What do you say? I get the impression Hakim is in his element here tonight, and will be here for the duration.' He grinned sardonically. 'No doubt right now he's wheeling and dealing with his jet-setting, billionaire pals. There's no point in spoiling his night just to have him drop us home early.'

'That would be fine with me,' Laura agreed. 'So then, what are we going to do in the meantime?'

He shrugged. 'We can go out front and join the revellers at the concert, if you want to?'

She shook her head, 'No. I'm happy enough here with you.' 'Me too. Why don't I go to the bar and get us another drink?'

'I'll go, hon,' she told him. What are you having? A light beer? I don't want you getting drunk and making a fool of yourself, *worldwide*.'

He laughed at that, imagining the fallout if he were to get sozzled and cause an incident, letting fly a few well chosen epithets in the direction of certain politicians, those who had criticized constantly over the years.

Laura gathered the glasses and headed off toward the bar, leaving Kevin to sit, observing the crowd. He noticed that there was quite a mixture of internationals here. Very wealthy and very connected, if their expensive clothes and mannerisms were any indication. He found himself wondering how many of these people were in favour of the impending New Word Order?

They had nothing to fear from the change. Nobody would be sliding backwards under the new system. Everyone kept what they had already earned for themselves; and the reality was, those who had been struggling to keep their heads above water would quickly find themselves much better off. That was, if the motion were passed, which he felt it surely would be. It was very much a forgone conclusion, else what was the big ceremony about? A tap on the shoulder interrupted his reverie.

'Mr McKinney? Kevin McKinney?' A tall, middle-aged man, greying at the temples, wearing an expensive, dark coloured suit stood a step away, leaning toward him, asking if he were Kevin McKinney.

'I am he,' Kevin answered, caught very much off-guard.

'I thought it was you. Please excuse the interruption but my wife insisted on my coming over and confirming her suspicion.' He pointed and waved to his wife who sat a few yards away at a table further along the row. 'It is an honour to meet the much renowned Kevin McKinney, father of the revolution.'

'Vladimir Lenin I am not,' Kevin responded good-naturedly. A compulsive meddler, more like.'

The man thought it very amusing, and laughed perfunctorily. 'I am James White. Professor James White, actually. I only mention the appellation in case you recognize the name. I am on the World Council panel of appointees. One of those who are to vote on your fantastic proposal.'

'Oh?' Kevin affected surprise. 'If only I had known you guys were here tonight. I might have thought to bring along a bag of lucre. I don't suppose you would accept a cheque?'

Again the man laughed. Less superficially this time. 'I appreciate a sense of humour, Mr McKinney. Very amusing. I must tell my colleagues. Although, strictly speaking I should not be talking to you like this. I just wanted to meet the man who spawned the idea.' He stood closely regarding Kevin for a brief moment. 'My god, man.

What made you think you could pull it off? Even with the weight of Sheik Hakim Abudi's considerable network of power and influence behind you?'

Kevin sat, staring up at the man, unsure of whether it had been a statement or an actual question. 'Are you asking? I mean, you sound as though the idea is nothing more than an affront. And an audacious affront at that!'

'I didn't mean to give that impression, young man,' White replied, undaunted. 'Simply stated,' he attempted again, 'it's the most fantastically courageous act. You must have a set as large as King Kong's.'

'He does,' Laura replied, having overheard while returning to her seat. 'I can vouch for it.' White looked embarrassed. 'Who's your friend,' she asked, feigning annoyance.

'My wife,' Kevin said in introduction. 'This is Mr... sorry, *Professor* James White, a member of the World Council panel of appointees, who will be voting on the resolution quite soon.'

'Well I mustn't leave the good lady wife unattended any longer than I have already,' White said, looking unsettled by Laura's sudden arrival. 'Very nice to have met you both,' he said in parting, and hurried back to his table where his wife waited for him.

Laura pushed Kevin's beer across the table to him, asking, 'What was that about?'

'Damned if I know.' He took a sip and returned the glass to the tabletop. 'I'm glad he's gone though.'

'I could tell he was pestering you as I approached. I was hoping my arrival might cause him to scuttle away, and it did.' She affected a smug smile, but then sensed something.

'What did he say to you?'

'The sod was winding me up, I think. Forget it.' He noticed Laura's glass. 'What is that you're drinking?'

'Squash,' she replied. 'Have you forgotten we're pregnant?' 'Good girl. I hadn't thought. In fact, I'll climb on the waggon with you. I have no desire for alcohol anymore.'

He caught sight of Hakim moving through the crowd towards their table. 'Ah, here comes the sheik, returning from hobnobbing it with the movers and shakers.'

'Are you enjoying yourselves?' he asked upon arrival. He pulled out a chair and seated himself. 'Everybody else seems to be enjoying themselves immensely.'

'Very festive,' Kevin responded. 'Truth be told, there's plenty of other places I would rather be right now.'

Hakim was surprised by the admission and turned to Laura. 'And are you of the same opinion as your taciturn partner?'

'I'm afraid so. In fact, we are going to withdraw the moment Kevin's address is over. We won't trouble you for a ride home.' 'But it's no trouble, I promise. Of course I will return you whenever you wish. What were you going to do, take the subway?'

'But you're having such a good time, Hakim. There's plenty of cabs in this city, I'm told.'

'This is nothing more than a business opportunity. *Schmoozing*, is that the word? Yes? But I thought you both would be wanting to celebrate.'

'Too tired to celebrate, my friend,' Kevin told him. 'Besides, Laura is sworn off of the demon drink during the pregnancy.'

Laura nodded in agreement. 'It appears we have outgrown that sort of thing, Hakim. You're looking at two, soon-to-be, boring, middle class home-bodies who want nothing more for the future than a nice, quiet existence.'

Hakim laughed good-naturedly. 'That will be the day. You two? I do not know exactly what the future holds in store for the two of you, but nice, quiet and boring? I will believe that when I see it.'

He became briefly thoughtful. 'You will come and holiday with my family. I too have little ones. We will sail to the Bahamas once a year and have a wonderful time.' He raise a finger in the air. 'Better than that. I have many wonderful houses. You will live in one until I build you a new one, anywhere in the world you would like. This will be my wedding present to you both.'

'That sounds wonderful, Hakim. You have been an absolute angel,' Laura told him, grabbing his arm. 'Without you, I can't imagine where we would be.'

'That's right,' Kevin agreed, facetiously. 'If it weren't for the little people like yourself, working behind the scenes. . .'

~

By ten forty five all of the dignitaries and special guests were summoned back stage in readiness for the speech and presentation segment of the evening. The number included among its rank the International Council of Nations president, Julia Da Salvia, officials of the Human Investment Movement, sundry world leaders, assorted luminaries and film stars whose faces it was hoped would be recognizable to the international audience. The gathered dignitaries were briefed on their order of stage appearance and reminded of the time restriction at the microphone. Preparations thus made, the order was given to intervene in the entertainment. The musicians were signalled to relinquish their instruments at the conclusion of their current musical offering. The audience, bemoaning the cessation of entertainment, and who were by this time fully immersed in the party atmosphere, became restless until the master of ceremonies, an international motion picture celebrity by the name of Dirk Cameron, took the microphone and attempted to call the crowd's attention to the reason for the night's celebration.

When a measure of calm had been instilled, dignitaries were invited to the stage, one at a time, each extolling the virtues of their organization, giving praise to colleagues and wrapping it up by introducing the person to follow. The process went on, all the while with helicopters circling and maneuvering in a coordinated pattern above, allowing each in turn to approach with television cameramen leaning out of the side door to capture, as best they could, every moment of the onstage proceedings.

Kevin stood in line with the remaining speakers at the rear of the stage, doing his best to ignore the fact that beside him stood professor James White, the man who had approached the table. The professor had answered a mobile phone call and was earnestly discussing Kevin knew not what, with the man taking pains to maintain privacy by turning away and keeping his voice low.

Kevin tried to occupy his mind with anything that might distract from the fast approaching moment when he would walk out to centre stage. He was appalled in realize his knees really *were* knocking in anticipation of addressing not only the hoard of people gathered over the landscape before him, but a world audience of who knew how many millions of people? He tried not to look at the vast crowd, diverting his gaze instead to look up at the crisscrossing steel framework, the many lights and laser projectors suspended above their heads.

His mind began to wonder then, and he found himself reviewing the journey which had brought him to his present position. It was so long ago, it seemed to him at the moment. That so much had come to pass fairly boggled the mind. Funny, he thought, that not until this very moment had he allowed himself to look back to the beginning. It had been all about keeping up momentum, moving forward at all cost and then only allowing himself to take it one day at a time. To attempt to look ahead would have been daunting to the point of almost certainly backing down from the challenge. If he had known all that was in store, the sacrifice and hard work, the endless travelling, the hotel rooms, the weariness and fatigue, not to mention the dealing with so many people, such a variety of professionals and points of view, the emotional and physical strain of keeping the show on the road? Whatever had possessed him to set his feet on such a path?

That damn mugging and the bang on the head which had put him in hospital. The evil lump that right now resided in his head; inexorable and implacable, it existed like some harbinger of impending doom. It was that which had triggered all of it. What a double edged sword it was. It had changed his life, he was forced to concede. It was that which had altered his life perception, changed everything about the way he viewed his own existence, forcing him to acknowledge the degree to which he had wasted his life up to that point, caring only about his own little world and personal comfort. Overnight, it seemed, his whole concept of what it meant to be alive and a part of a wider community had irrevocably been altered. And, too, the mind itself had suddenly become more alert than ever before, as if for years it had been functioning on only a small proportion of its actual capability. He recalled how, on the morning after coming home from the hospital, the brilliance and clarity, the way in which what had previously been the unsolvable puzzle of life had, quite suddenly and entirely without explanation, snapped into focus to reveal the glaring inconsistencies and contradictions. It had been, from that moment on, impossible to live in the manner he had always done, knowing that there was the likely simple solution to the dichotomy of conflicting opposites woven into the very fabric of mankind's convoluted system of survival, one which would continue ever to mar and deflect away from a much more wondrous future, one which should otherwise be entirely within the grasp of all.

As he stood reviewing all that had come to pass, his mind briefly touched on an, at first, seemingly insignificant event, but suddenly identified, the mind seized upon it, propelling it forward to be viewed under the full glare of consciousness.

A dream he had from long ago. A dream long since forgotten until this very moment, and it hit with an impact like nothing before experienced so that it made his mind begin to swim and reel with its remembrance.

When a hand firmly gripped his upper arm it startled him so much that he almost let out a cry of surprise.

'Christ, Hakim, you frightened me half to death.'

'Are you alright my brother?' his friend asked, obvious concern reflecting in his face. But there was no time to respond. The man at the microphone had spoken Kevin's name. . .

'The man whose immaculate vision for the new world order —' the president of the Human Investment Movement was saying to the audience—'the man whose energies, belief and singular determination have brought us to the threshold of a new beginning, a new frontier in the continuing history of the human universe. . .'

Beside him the professor ended the phone conversation he had been having, pocketed his phone and leaned over to speak into Kevin's ear.

'It's official, my dear mister McKinney. There is no longer the need for tomorrow's vote by the members. It has been decided. Unanimously so. Monetary transactions are to become obsolete in favour of your new system of Human Investment. The measure will be fully implemented by the end of the year. Congratulations,' he added, reaching to shake Kevin's hand.

At the same time, from the public address system a stentorian voice announced, 'I give you Kevin McKinney!'

The crowd erupted with a roar of approval loud enough to hit him as an enormous wave, striking and washing over him so that he was momentarily stunned. Beside him, Hakim grinned broadly as he also applauded his friend enthusiastically. The moment so overwhelmed that he seemed at a loss as to how to respond.

'Come,' Hakim said to him, grasping him by the arm and leading him slowly towards the microphone. 'Don't worry,' he told him over the roar of the crowd. 'I am here by your side. You need only smile and look grateful. Just stand for a moment and accept the gratitude of those whose respect you have earned.'

These words came to Kevin through a torrent of sensory information. It was not merely the immense aural response of the adoring crowd. Now something else had come into play, and as if under assault his mind recoiled in recognition of something experienced many months prior—experienced not in the normal sense of the word—it came to him out of that long ago dream. He remembered it perfectly now, and the memory of the dream perfectly matched, precisely overlaying the present. Two converging instances of a single moment upturned his sense of reality to the point that he needed to stop where he was, and in attempt to steady himself grab Hakim firmly by the shoulder.

To the left and behind the crowd stood the huge screen, on it an image of himself taken from one of the hovering network television helicopters. The man dressed all in white. The Arabian *thoub* and *sirwal* gifted to him by Hakim, the means of presenting a suitable image for the international audience. He was the man in the dream and this was both the reality and the dream; although, in the moment none of it felt in the slightest bit real.

'I am in a dream,' he said to Hakim. 'This is only a dream.' 'Never mind all that,' Hakim replied, not at all understanding.

'You can do this. Pull yourself together.'

With Hakim steadying him Kevin resumed cautiously moving toward the presenter who waited at the microphone. The crowd seemed not to notice that anything was amiss, continuing only to cheer and clap enthusiastically as the presenter deferred, giving Kevin precedence at the front of the stage.

The applause continued, which suited him just fine. He was happy to allow it to do so, bathing in a most unusual ambiance while firmly gripping the microphone stand for added support, wondering when, or perhaps *if*, everything around him would return to something more earthly and recognizable.

Turning to Hakim, beside him still, he said, 'This is very strange. I have been here before.' He turned back to the crowd, raising a hand in acknowledgment, then placed it over his heart in a sign of kinship and endearment.

'Thank-you,' he said at last, his voice carrying across the expanse and resound in the distance.

Helicopters edged ever closer, transgressing regulations in order to obtain the best possible coverage. With the crowd continuing their cacophonous expression of appreciation he saw no need to interrupt their jubilation, merely accepting the opportunity to absorb as much of the moment as possible while it persisted; a moment to be remembered and much savoured in days to come. A glorious and wonderful night.

In the sky above the lit arena he looked toward the moon, full round and shining down on the Earth as it had for so many millions of years. One of the choppers began edging quite close; perhaps dangerously so, and raising a din while the rotor wash began to upset and topple the props on the stage. He glimpsed a figure within the open door, leaning back with something other than a camera. A flash of light caught his eye; a reflection perhaps, but something had impacted, smashing into his body, accompanied by the unmistakable retort of a high powered rifle. A second impact sent him sprawling sideways as the world faded swiftly from view to be replaced by an all consuming, irresistible fall into darkness.

CHAPTER 20

For seventy two hours Kevin teetered on the brink of death at New York's Lenox Hill Hospital, where Hakim felt the best care would quickly be afforded him. The bullet wounds alone could easily have killed him, the surgeon informed them, but for a strong heart. Miraculously, the body had begun holding its own.

At nine o'clock on the morning of the fifth day it was decided that Kevin had recovering well enough to be woken from the coma doctor Quin had induced to facilitate his healing while attached to a ventilator, as well as allowing him to escape the worst of the pain. At nine fifteen Kevin's respiration and blood pressure began to increase gradually and steadied. A very good sign. The attending nurse came quietly into the room, being careful not to wake Laura who had fallen asleep after keeping vigil all through the night, and as she had done on all previous nights since his arrival. Blood-oxygen concentration rose as respiration strengthened, and in a while Kevin's eyes opened, attempting to find focus.

He noticed Laura beside him, asleep in the bedside chair, with her head resting against him while holding his hand. A slight squeeze was all it took before, murmuring, she raised her head dreamily.

'You're back,' she said, smiling, but not yet fully awake. She resisted the impulse to take hold of him for fear of the pain it might cause; instead, leaning across to tenderly kiss his face.

He responded with a wan smile, saying, 'I'm back, and you wouldn't believe where from.'

The next few days involved as much medical attention as he could endure, until, by the end of the first week, he was able to leave the confines of the bed to take his first tentative steps, aided only by a walking stick.

During the days that followed, however, his condition ceased improving as it initially had. Before long, taking only a few unaided steps within the confines of the ward were the best he could accomplish before fatigue claimed him and he was returned, either to the hospital bed or seated in the wheelchair that remained always at the ready.

The tumour had metastasized, becoming inoperable. A mild form of chemotherapy had been agreed to by Kevin and initiated in order to slow the spread. The prognosis forecast a few weeks of restricted movement at best, before things would begin to accelerate downhill quite rapidly. Morphine helped manage the ever-present pain, and would be increased as needed in the final term. Except for the intervention of a miracle, Kevin had *'Maybe a month or two. Such predictions are impossible to make accurately,* Dr Quin explained, sorrowfully. *'The human will is powerful and often a dominant factor in these cases.'*

Being suddenly confronted with impending death launched Kevin at first into a state of bitterness and of feeling cheated by a universe which had waited so late in his life to grant clarity and a measure of happiness, only to snatch these things from his grasp at the very moment of attainment. With the madness of the campaign behind him now, he realized he could, for the time remaining, experience the feeling coming from having served a real purpose; a meaningful one at that, he judged. Before having pursued this crazy course of action he had known, only too well, how his life had amounted to very little.

Remedying this situation had been as much his objective as it had been to put right an obvious flaw in human existence, he reminded himself. There was satisfaction in that, and in quiet moments filled with deep reflection he knew that he was comfortable with the outcome of events, regretting nothing but the fact that his time with Laura was to be cut short, and that he would not get to watch their son grow up.

Upon returning home palliative care had been arranged, to be provided as long as it was required. It was a time requiring rapid assimilation to an uncompromising reality, and the hours of a day soon became something to be cherished. Rising early of a morning became important to Kevin. Each morning he rose in the hours before dawn so that he could experience the microcosm of the natural world which existed in his garden and surrounding area, undisturbed and in relative silence. In the pale predawn light the birds of the area began their chirping, twittering and calling from all around. After a while he became familiar with the different voices, learning to relate them to this or that bird identified in full light later in the day. As the sky began gradually to lighten, the air felt to him to be charged with anticipation, as if every denizen were waiting for the starter to sound the signal in commencing activities for the day. A silly notion, he realised, but it had been so long a while since he had viewed the detail, noticed the many small things which happened in a day, and it gave him pause to wonder about the fact. How much of life did we blithely ignore or miss completely in pursuit of our self-serving endeavours; our human comings and goings? Of course, for many, he realised very well, that life was a thing to be endured rather than enjoyed and able to be lived to its fullest. So much a pity, and something another would have to attend to should his own efforts not bring about sufficient impetus to remedy the situation. He was out of time, but the solution was well enough within grasp and need only be applied.

If anyone were ever to ask him, he would certainly say that mornings were his favourite time of day. It was the time when musings would ramble of their own accord, seeking out all manner of pathways. There was for Kevin something magical in the beginning of a new day that he had never really noticed until now. He liked to brew coffee at the kitchen bench at around five, bring it here to the verandah, to sit for an hour or two, lost in thought, drawing immense pleasure from even the smallest things—the soft mews and sighs of existence which had, for all his previous life, somehow escaped his notice.

Sitting here on the verandah upon this morning he realised he had come fully to accept all that had come to pass. No longer was there a feeling of being cheated: the universe neither favoured nor disadvantaged a participant; it merely set the rules of the game and provided a means of advancement, and from there it was up to the player to do according to their nature, and their better selves. All quite simple enough; and naturally there were the unexpected things, those which one identified either as advantage or disadvantage, according to the perception of a thing. The conundrum of the tumour having altered his perceptions had not yet been entirely resolved. A wry smile curled his lips as he sat, overlooking the yard now bathed in the morning light, once again reviewing the facts while delighting in the puzzling of them all.

He saw that he had played an important, even a pivotal, role in the passage of events. On that, at least, he was clear; but had it not been for the decision on that fateful day to pull on his track pants and runners, to take up the moderate constitutional he had let slip for several months, he might yet be sitting on the couch, ruing, still, the fact of his sedentary and mundane existence.

It was impossible to take credit for all that had happened. There was no doubting that the blow to the head had resulted in the tumour, and had in turn altered his inner-self. It had changed the way he thought, the way he viewed his world and how he regarded his roll within it. Had the tumour altered who he was or had it rather exposed and given rise to a deeper, truer Kevin?

He reflected occasionally on the sudden urge to discard his old wardrobe in favour of more stylish garments. If he had been a little more observant, perhaps he would have realised then that something unusual was occurring and been able to prevent his current predicament. But then again, would he want to? he was forced to ask of himself. That was difficult, and a choice he was only too glad he was never in danger of having to consider. His views of the human animal and of its behaviour had always been so poor that it was likely, given the choice, he may well have chosen an extended lifespan over the adjustment in humanity's habit of ascribing monetary worth to all it saw. Clearly it was a madness which had to be remedied whatever the cost to himself, and so he was forced to concede that he had acted in the only manner open to him, especially in view of the fact that, performance wise, his brain function had incongruously been much improved by the blow. A providential encounter, he mused, and smiled to himself at the thought.

Without his being mugged—the bump on the head and the resulting tumour—his life would otherwise have continued being shallow and meaningless beyond endurance; replete in hiding away from the world, tinkering in a shed with one lame project or another, whiling away the nights, watching inane television and snacking on junk food. A small life going nowhere, serving nothing and no one. The very thought caused him to cringe ashamedly within. It also gave rise to something irresistible and at once confounding; the *old chestnut* which, he considered, must drive anyone who ever ponders the notion completely around the twist for lack of any substantial answer. The *what ifs* and *why fores* of life that cause such impossible meanderings of contemplation only to wind up back at the point of departure. There was no point in it, and yet the mind refused totally to leave it alone, ever searching for meaning where, demonstrably, there was none, and now he picked at it as his recalcitrant mind insisted on doing, like a sore that would never heal.

What in the name of all that we hold dear is the point of it all? Is there meaning in what we do? Is there value in who we are? Is there any point at all in our existence and our struggle when time will eventually have its way and return us all to the dust from whence we came? What possible response could be conjured?

He meditated on the idea of a higher truth, the possibility of elevated plains of existence where the self was contained entirely within an energetic spirit, freed of its corporeal form to serve some higher purpose for which we could have no inkling, here at the beginning of the journey. Perhaps it was the calling of this supposed higher purpose which had driven him on this seemingly impossible and often judged foolish quest to free the society of man of its attachment to things existing only as fabrications of the mind? Perhaps there was indeed some vast and intricate multidimensional web of a plan existing within the woven fabric of the cosmos, invisible to all but the most highly developed, sophisticated and enlightened minds whose ascension through multiple levels of existence enabled understanding far beyond the knowing of man?

These peaceful musings continued with the coming of dawn and on as the sun climbed higher into the sky. He imagined further adjustments to the society of modern man. International borders would have to come down. Only in this way could the world truly become united, able to tackle the next revelational step in the development of homo sapiens' journey, to reach beyond neighbouring stars and on, into the yet-to-be landscape of our future.

From the kitchen emanated the sounds of Laura shuffling through cupboards, boiling the kettle and preparing breakfast for them both, her belly already becoming round and plump, carrying the next generation of the McKinney bloodline.

How wonderful, he considered, that his offspring would be born into a world become able to leave behind the vestiges of infancy, to at last grasp the importance of commonality, not just what is unique and different about us, and the advantages of pulling together toward more rewarding goals than mere financial viability.

He knew that a couple of years ago, having to face this early demise would have utterly defeated his ability to accept the fact. He was thankful for the journey which had allowed him to grow in that regard, and in that thought he saw that there was no remaining bitterness over this sudden turn of events. If anything, he discovered that he was grateful for the tumour, and saw that it was a most curious, even amusing point of view to be having. All the things that had occurred; the accrued total of events and surrounding circumstances were the very things which had come to shape the person he was today, a person who was able to see in far greater detail the grandeur of a given moment of existence, while simultaneously glimpsing what lies beyond tomorrow's horizon. He would not want to change a single thing if it meant that he was other than who was sitting here, now, at this very moment. The notion caused him to reflect on his reason for feeling that way. Another curiosity of the human psyche, he supposed. The mind could not conceive of being other than what it was. That was a very interesting proposition, but perhaps he was wrong about that. It may well be that many would exchange, in the blink of an eye, what and who they were if it presented an escape of some kind, and he supposed that it was so, but certainly not for himself. Time was fleeting, he observed, particularly so from the vantage of the future.

A little while later Laura emerged from the kitchen onto the veranda, carrying their breakfast on a tray and a freshly prepared coffee for Kevin.

'Good morning,' she intoned sweetly, placing the breakfast tray gently atop the table. 'You've dozed off again, I see,' and she wondered briefly whether or not to rouse him.

'Another gorgeous start to the day,' she observed, deciding to make a game of it.

She sat, observing the peacefulness in the face she had come to adore. Smiling to herself she recalled the day it had all begun, the day Bill Brier had sent her to this address in order to elicit a story from the man who had been mugged while taking an innocent run through a neighbourhood park.

It was an amusing story and never failed to make them laugh. The annoying young reporter on her first assignment, who would not be deterred by the gruff exterior of the man who only wanted to be left alone.

'Don't let your breakfast get cold,' she told him. 'I might just eat it myself,' she teased. 'I'm eating for two now, and I'm quite ravenous this morning.'

A group of magpies swooped in over the fence and landed on the lawn. A family. Two adults and a pair of juveniles whose habit it had become each morning to scour the garden for insects, scratching in-between the vegetables and around the flowerbed in search of movement and a meal.

She watched them with interest, noting how the adolescents followed their parents and how they ran up whenever one found food, to plaintively beg for a morsel.

Birdwatching, she mused humorously. A pleasant pastime and something she had never done before coming here; her hurried, workaday existence never allowing the time for such a simple pleasure.

'Okay, mister. Wake up and eat your breakfast,' she said, turning now to Kevin with purpose. 'Hey. Wakey-wakey.'

She studied his face and the relaxed pose—perfectly at peace, as if deep in sleep and pleasantly dreaming. In that moment there was a perfect stillness; a serenity which, for the longest moment, cast a serene, almost eerie spell, and she knew for a certainty the reason for Kevin's unresponsiveness.

When the magpies began to choral she turned her attention to the simple beauty surrounding. The garden was in full bloom at this time of year. Kevin had installed a birdbath at her request, so that on the very hot days the local birds might gather and refresh themselves, providing extra joy and loveliness to the yard in the bargain.

A group of finches splashed and chirped merrily, making greater noise than one would think possible for so small a bird.

'I've always loved your garden,' she said to Kevin. 'I will always remember you in that old hammock, lazing in the shade and taking it easy while dreaming up some harebrained scheme or another. 'Ha—' she intoned in mock scorn, and the tears began to stream. 'Laying there dreaming of what big plans now? I would love to know. Did you really think you had any chance of changing the world?'

end